FRENCH QUARTER CLUES

CLUES

THE MYSTERY HOUSE SERIES, BOOK THREE

Eva Pohler

Eva Pohler Books
20011 Park Ranch
San Antonio, Texas 78259
www.evapohler.com

Publisher's Note: This is a work of fiction. Names, characters, places, and incidents are a product of the author's imagination. Locales and public names are sometimes used for atmospheric purposes. Any resemblance to actual people, living or dead, or to businesses, companies, events, institutions, or locales is completely coincidental.

Book Layout ©2017 BookDesignTemplates.com

Book Cover Design by Keri Knutson

French Quarter Clues/ Eva Pohler. -- 1st ed.
Paperback ISBN 978-1-958390-26-9

Contents

For the victims of Hurricane Katrina and their families.

CHAPTER ONE

Return to Tulsa

Tanya's long, thin form lay horizontally across the hotel bed. "Like *this?*"

"Hang your head over a bit more." Sue moved her short, round body closer to Tanya. "And keep it turned at a forty-five-degree angle."

Tanya followed Sue's instructions, her blonde hair nearly touching the carpet.

"What's this called again?" Ellen asked.

"The Epley Maneuver," Sue said.

Ellen's son, Nolan, who was in medical school, had suggested it at dinner earlier, explaining that the airplane ride that morning had likely dislodged a crystal in Tanya's inner ear, causing the vertigo.

"I really hope this helps," Tanya said.

Ellen hoped so, too. She'd been looking forward to this trip for months. She and her friends planned to drive their rental car from Oklahoma City to Tulsa the next day to lunch with Sue's daughter, Lexi. Sue's mother, Jan, had sent an anniversary gift with them for Lexi. They were all dying to see what was in the box that Sue had had to lug around two airports, two planes, and a shuttle. Jan had said it was a surprise and wouldn't budge, not even with a hint.

"A few more seconds," Sue said as she pushed her dark bangs from her eyes.

After their lunch with Lexi, Ellen and her friends were to attend a scholarship awards ceremony at the Greenwood Cultural Center, which was the main reason for their trip.

From Tulsa, they were going to drive up to Pawhuska, to lunch at the Pioneer Woman's Mercantile and to tour the lodge where her cooking show was recorded.

"Now what?" Tanya asked.

"Turn your head to the other side," Sue said. "For another forty seconds or so."

Ellen studied Tanya over Sue's shoulder. "I thought her eyes would be fluttering back and forth." That's what Nolan had said, anyway.

"They aren't?" Tanya asked.

Ellen bent over and looked more closely. "No."

"Let's just finish the maneuver and see if it helps," Sue suggested. "Now roll over on your side and hold that position for another forty seconds."

"If it doesn't help, you two go on without me," Tanya said as she rolled over.

"Let's not get ahead of ourselves just yet," Sue said.

Ellen said a silent prayer, asking for Tanya's healing. She'd hate for her to miss out on the fun.

"Okay, now sit up," Sue said, as she and Ellen helped Tanya to a sitting position.

"How do you feel?" Ellen asked.

"I don't know yet," Tanya said. "I think it may have helped. I'm not sure."

"Can you make it through a movie?" Sue asked.

Ellen slipped on her shoes. "It won't make much difference whether you rest here or in the theater, will it?"

"I guess you're right," Tanya said, though she didn't seem convinced. "I'll just use the restroom, and then I'll be ready to go."

Sue grabbed her purse. "As often as the two of you had to pee during the flight, I think we may have to hook you both up to catheters."

Tanya made a face at Sue before she disappeared behind the bathroom door.

Ellen laughed. "Why don't you ever have to go, Sue? What's your secret?"

Sue opened the hotel door and stepped into the hall. "I guess I don't have a bladder the size of a thimble."

Ellen laughed again, but, when Tanya rejoined them in the hallway, her friend seemed quiet. Ellen hoped she and Sue weren't pushing Tanya too hard by taking her to the movie. The Epley Maneuver hadn't seemed to be the miracle cure they'd been hoping for.

Once inside the darkened movie theater, where Sue had smuggled in a can of Cherry Coke and a chocolate muffin, Sue made them move twice. Although Ellen had preferred their original seats in back, she had to admit that she, too, had noticed the horrible smell that had prompted Sue to want to move. But, even now, as they settled into their seats closer to the screen, the odor lingered.

"Did you step in something, Tanya?" Sue, who preferred the aisle seat even though she had the better bladder, whispered to Tanya.

Tanya, in the middle seat, checked the bottom of her shoes. "I don't think so. Do I smell bad?"

Ellen didn't reply, because she'd come to suspect that Tanya had been the cause of the odor all along. Maybe she had a sour stomach and bad gas.

"They say your nose adjusts eventually," Sue commented as she cracked open her Cherry Coke.

"Is it really that bad?" Tanya asked, her cheeks turning red. "I don't smell anything."

"Evidently, your nose already adjusted," Sue added. "I guess your skills of adaptation are superior to ours."

"Oh, Sue," Ellen scolded.

That night, Ellen was awakened in the hotel room by a shriek. Tanya, sleeping in the bed opposite her, was crying out. Ellen flipped on the bedside lamp and sat up.

"Tanya?"

Tanya turned onto her side toward Ellen. "Huh?" She blinked several times.

Ellen was shocked by the very dark rings beneath her friend's eyes and by her pale, pasty complexion.

"Are you feeling okay?" Ellen asked.

"Just tired," Tanya said as she closed her eyes. "Bad dream."

But Ellen was worried and felt like Tanya might need medical attention. She wished Sue was there to give an opinion. Both Tanya and Ellen had told Sue that her snoring didn't bother them, but she had reserved her own room anyway.

Ellen crawled out of bed and inspected Tanya's face beneath the light of the lamp. Deciding not to waken Tanya a second time, Ellen climbed back beneath her covers and flipped off the light. She lay there, worrying, for many hours.

Tanya slept in the passenger seat for most of the trip to Tulsa, as Ellen drove, and Sue navigated from the back seat. Ellen had hoped her friends would trade places, so she and Sue could visit and make the drive go by faster, but they were afraid Tanya would get carsick in the back. Plus, Sue preferred the back seat because she didn't have to wear a seatbelt.

When they were still a half hour away from Tulsa, Sue leaned toward the front and said, "Tanya? You awake?"

Tanya didn't move.

Then, to Ellen, Sue said, "I've been Googling her symptoms."

"You don't think it's her inner ear?" Ellen asked.

"If it were, the Epley Maneuver would have worked."

"Maybe we didn't do it right."

Sue frowned. "I followed the video exactly."

"What does Dr. Google say then?" Ellen asked, secretly wishing Sue would sit back in her seat and wear her seatbelt.

"Well, we know she's not diabetic," Sue said. "Her doctor would have caught that last month when she had her annual checkup."

"True."

"And we know it's not her thyroid, because she just had that checked when they removed that tumor from her parathyroid in Houston a few months ago, right?"

"But it could be related to that, couldn't it?"

Sue lowered her voice. "Ellen, brace yourself."

Ellen glanced at Sue's reflection in the rearview mirror.

Sue whispered, "I think it's a demon attachment."

Ellen narrowed her eyes at Sue in the mirror. "Seriously? What makes you think that?"

"You didn't think something was strange about the nightmare she had last night?"

At breakfast, Tanya had told them about a horrible dream in which Tanya had murdered them in their sleep and had gorged on their blood. Tanya hadn't been able to eat breakfast because she had still felt nauseated from the experience, which she'd said had felt disturbingly real.

"It was just a bad dream," Ellen insisted.

"Here are some of the symptoms of demon attachment: Severe nightmares or night terrors, strange lingering odors, depression, fatigue, personality changes, blackouts in memory, and abusive behavior."

Ellen laughed. "Tanya is the last person on earth who'd be abusive. And those symptoms apply to at least a dozen health issues I can think of right off the top of my head."

"Maybe, but I think we should be on the lookout, just in case. I've been sensing something unusual lately. It went away when I was in my own hotel room, but it came back when we met for breakfast this morning. Also, my phone keeps dying when I'm around her. It's fine in my own room, but when I'm with you two, the battery drains."

Ellen had learned not to assume that every claim Sue made about her "gift" was based purely on her imagination. While Ellen tended to be a skeptic first and foremost, she'd seen enough to be a believer, too.

And Ellen had been having a problem with her phone battery, too.

She glanced at their friend sleeping in the passenger's seat beside her. Tanya's pale complexion and the dark circles beneath her eyes continued to worry Ellen.

"You have to admit we've been a little careless with our use of the Ouija Board and other occult practices," Sue added. "We may have invited something in."

Just then, Tanya opened her eyes and met Ellen's gaze.

"Why are you looking at me like that?" Tanya asked.

Ellen gasped, suddenly nervous. "I was just checking on you. How do you feel?"

"Does it really matter?" Tanya snapped, as she closed her eyes and turned to face the window.

Ellen glanced at Sue in the rearview mirror.

Sue's brows were lifted as she mouthed, "Demon attachment."

After Ellen had parked the rental in front of the Mayo Hotel in Tulsa, Tanya lifted her head and looked around.

"Are we here?" Tanya asked sleepily.

Ellen turned to her friend. "What did you mean when you asked if it really mattered how you felt? We care about your feelings and don't want to push you, if you can't handle the trip."

"What are you talking about?" Tanya asked.

Sue leaned forward. "I'm sure she didn't mean it, Ellen."

"Mean what?" Tanya asked.

"Ellen asked how you felt, and you said, 'Does it really matter?'"

"I didn't say that," Tanya insisted. "I would never say that."

"We both heard you, Tanya," Ellen pointed out.

Tanya's cheeks turned pink. "I must have been talking in my sleep."

Later, Ellen and Sue met Lexi for lunch at the Greek restaurant across from the Old Lady on Brady. Tanya had decided to stay behind at the hotel and rest.

As they waited for their food, Lexi opened her present from Jan.

"It's Grandma's cuckoo clock," Lexi said.

"Oh, how nice!" Sue's face lit up. "She must have had it repaired. It's been in the family for decades, you know. I always wished she'd given it to me, but I'm glad she's given it to you."

"It's beautiful," Ellen said, admiring the intricate details. "No wonder she didn't want to ship it. It's so delicate."

"This little bird will slide from the house and tweet on every hour," Sue said.

"*Every* hour?" Lexi asked. "All through the night?"

"You get used to it," Sue said dismissively, but Lexi looked concerned.

"It cost a fortune to fix, I'm sure," Sue added. "Be sure to write Grandma a thank you note."

"Mom," Lexi complained. "I'm not a kid anymore. I know I'm supposed to write thank you notes."

"Well, your lunch is on me," Ellen said, "and I'm expecting a thank you note, too." Ellen gave Lexi a wink, to show she was only teasing.

Sue laughed. "I'm still waiting on my thank you from Nolan for his high school graduation gift from, what, eight years ago?"

Ellen shook her head. "I have a feeling you'll be waiting a lot longer for that one."

"Do you have time to come see what we've done to our new house?" Lexi asked them.

Sue had bought Lexi and Stephen a new house with some of the oil money. It was the only extravagant thing any of them had done. They were hesitant to spend too much of it while they still weren't sure how long the well would produce. More importantly, they had agreed that Greenwood deserved more than ten percent of the oil money, since the ghosts of their past had been responsible for helping them to find it.

"I wish we could," Sue said. "But we're worried about Tanya. Maybe we can come by before we head back to San Antonio."

After lunch, Ellen and Sue said goodbye to Lexi and then walked across the street to the Brady Theater to check out its recent renovations. Jared was working the box office and seemed glad to see them again as he showed them the new flooring, seating, and repairs to some of the interior art deco architecture. Ellen took pictures with her phone to share with Tanya, but when they returned to the hotel, Ellen and Sue were shocked with what they found: Tanya was lying with her legs stretched up over the headboard, her hips on pillows, and her head hanging over the side of the bed, her eyes closed and ringed with black circles.

"Tanya!" Ellen cried as she rushed to her friend's side.

"Don't touch her," Sue warned. "You don't want the demon on your back, too."

Tanya opened her eyes and blinked several times before she swung her legs from the headboard and tried to sit up.

"Tanya?" Ellen said gently.

"What's wrong?" Tanya asked, disoriented.

"You were sleeping upside down," Sue explained.

"I, what?" Tanya blinked.

"We need to take you to a hospital," Ellen said. "Something's not right."

"I'm not sure a hospital will do her any good," Sue whispered.

"She's dehydrated and delirious," Ellen argued, but she, too, worried that a hospital might not be the solution they needed.

Although the scholarship ceremony at the Greenwood Cultural Center that evening had been rewarding, Ellen hadn't been able to enjoy herself, because she'd been worried about Tanya. Ellen could tell Sue was feeling the same way as they left the reception to return to the hospital.

Hooked up to an IV, Tanya was awake and watching television in a private room when they arrived. Her complexion was no longer pale, the dark circles were significantly reduced, and she was even smiling.

"You were right, Ellen. I was dehydrated," Tanya said cheerfully. "They couldn't find anything else wrong with me."

"And you feel better?" Ellen asked.

"You look better," Sue commented.

"I feel fine," Tanya said. "They're keeping me overnight for observation, but I should be ready to leave tomorrow. How was the scholarship ceremony?"

Ellen and Sue recounted how impressed they'd been with the six recipients. One would be attending Harvard, two Yale, and three OSU. Although Ellen and her friends had lost their case against the state of Oklahoma and against the city of Tulsa for reparations owed to the descendants of the 1921 Race Riot victims, the oil money was being put to good use in helping repair the damages done to Greenwood.

"Will you be up to touring the social club tomorrow, do you think?" Sue asked Tanya.

"Definitely," Tanya said. "I feel fine."

Ellen exchanged a worried glance with Sue, doubting their friend was out of the woods yet. If a demon *had* attached itself to Tanya, saline through an IV wouldn't be enough to get rid of it.

CHAPTER TWO

Tanya's Demon

As they stood in line outside of the Mercantile in Pawhuska in the blazing summer sun, Ellen said, not for the first time, "I'm so pleased for Simol."

The old Native American woman, who had lived for decades in the abandoned building across from Cain's Ballroom, had seemed happy and at peace with what had become of her home. She'd been allowed to keep her old room, its interior walls and furnishings new, and she seemed to enjoy being the caretaker and manager of the place. Since its grand opening, Monroe's Social Club had been booked every Saturday for wedding receptions, birthday parties, family reunions, and other celebrations, and its doors had been opened every Friday night for the public to skate, bowl, and dine.

When they reached the front of the line at the Mercantile, an old man with bright blue eyes stepped from the restaurant, and Ellen, eager to learn everything there was to know about the Pioneer Woman's menu, asked, "How was it? Was it good?"

"Always is," the old man replied in a gravelly voice.

"This is my first time," Ellen said. "What would you recommend?"

"The Marlborough Man Sandwich," the man replied. "It's the best thing on the menu. And get it rare."

"Mmm, that sounds delicious," Sue said. "Thanks for the tip."

"Can you believe they made me pay today?" the man asked.

Ellen gave her friends a look of confusion. Why *wouldn't* the man be made to pay?

Before they could ask, the hostess waved them inside for a table, and, as the young woman handed over the menus, she said, "I see you met Chuck, Ree's father-in-law."

Ellen's mouth dropped open as she took her seat. "That was *Chuck*?"

"As obsessed as you are with the show, I'm surprised you didn't recognize him," Tanya, taking the seat beside her, commented.

"He seemed shorter in real life," Ellen said. "On TV, he looks so much taller and bigger."

"Are you going to get the Marlborough Man Sandwich, like he suggested?" Sue asked, as she opened the menu.

"I can't believe I just talked to Chuck!" Ellen pulled out her phone to post about it on Facebook.

Once the surprise had worn off, Ellen returned to her senses and decided to try the French Onion Soup and Olive Cheese Bread. Sue stuck with Chuck's recommendation, and Tanya chose a salad. For dessert, the three friends shared a bowl of Tres Leches before heading over to the shopping side of the Mercantile, where Ellen bought a set of nesting bird measuring cups and an apron.

Afterward, Ellen drove the rental past the Drummond Ranch to the lodge, where *The Pioneer Woman* was filmed. If it hadn't been for the wind, the summer heat would have exhausted them as they walked across the parking lot, past a few other cars already there. The view out to the ranch from the hillside lodge was breathtaking, so they snapped a few photos before entering the building.

Ellen rushed behind the kitchen bar, where Ree always stood during her show. "Take my picture!"

Sue took one and then asked another woman if she would mind taking one of the three of them. Sue and Tanya joined Ellen behind the kitchen bar, where they pretended to be cooking together with the props on the counter. Ellen quickly posted the photo to Facebook but was disappointed by the shadow on Tanya. Otherwise, the photo was a hoot.

From the kitchen, they walked past the farmhouse table and the chunky fireplace, to the living area, where the television was playing one of Ree's shows.

"I have to use the restroom," Tanya muttered as she went on ahead of them down the hall.

"Didn't she just go before we left the Mercantile?" Sue said with a laugh.

Ellen shrugged. "You know how it is for us of the thimble-sized bladders."

Ellen watched the show on the television for a few more minutes before she followed Sue to the first bedroom. They passed a pair of sliding barn doors leading to the restroom, and inside, as clear as day, was Tanya sitting on the commode behind a beveled glass door.

Ellen grabbed the barn doors and cried, "Oh, my gosh, Tanya!" as she pulled them closed, noticing two women, who'd gone ahead of them, giggling.

"You can see me?" Tanya shouted from the commode.

"Can *you* see *us*?" Sue asked.

"Yes, but…" Tanya leaned over her lap, trying to hide.

As Ellen pulled the barn doors closed, she thought she saw something else, too: a dark, menacing face just behind Tanya.

Sue shook her head. "If you can see us, we can see you. Or did you think it was like a one-way mirror inside an interrogation room?"

"Oh, hush!" Tanya complained.

Ellen turned to Sue, who stood beside her laughing. "Did you see that?"

"Apparently everyone did," Sue said.

The women ahead of them broke into laughter.

"Guys, I can hear you!" Tanya called out.

Ellen lowered her voice. "Not Tanya. Look again."

Ellen pulled the barn doors apart, just a crack, so Sue could take another look. Crouched in the corner, behind Tanya, was a dark shadowy figure with bright, red eyes.

"Guys!" Tanya shouted. "Close the doors!"

Ellen closed the doors, but not before a chill crept down her spine and every hair on the back of her neck stood to attention.

"We need help," Sue whispered. "And we need it now."

Sue and Ellen didn't mention what they'd seen to Tanya as they made the return trip to Tulsa, because they didn't think it would do her any good. Moreover, Tanya had been feeling dizzy and carsick, and the terror of knowing she had a demon on her back wouldn't help her condition. It was hard enough on Ellen and Sue knowing it was in the car with them. Ellen felt her hands shaking, and she found it difficult to concentrate on driving.

During a roadside stop, while Tanya was in the restroom, Sue told Ellen that she'd texted Lexi about an emergency visit with her pastor. The pastor had agreed to meet them that evening at his church, which was in the same neighborhood as Lexi's house.

Once they were on the road again, Sue concocted a story for Tanya about wanting to see Lexi's place. It wasn't really a lie—they'd all wanted to see it before Tanya had become ill.

"That sounds fun," Tanya agreed, unplugging her phone from the car charger. "Something's wrong with my phone battery."

Ellen and Sue exchanged knowing looks in the rearview mirror.

The one-story bungalow was adorable. Lexi had her mother's good taste in interior decorating.

"This could be in a magazine," Ellen said, as she admired the farmhouse style that had become fashionable from *Fixer Upper*.

Lexi, playing along with Sue's plan, said she really wanted to show them her new church.

"I just love my new pastor!" Lexi said, feigning more enthusiasm than she probably felt—not that she didn't really love her pastor.

"I don't know," Tanya said. "I don't think I feel up to it."

"It's just around the corner," Sue said.

They all piled into the rental, including Lexi, who sat in the back seat with her mother. But when they arrived at the church, Tanya refused to go in with them.

"Maybe it's best you wait in the car," Sue finally gave in. "We'll just be a minute."

The pastor greeted them at the doors to the parish, shaking each of their hands and giving Lexi a hug. He was younger than Ellen and Sue—perhaps mid-thirties—with receding blond hair and green eyes. He was also short—about Sue's height—and a little round in the center.

"Thanks for meeting us on such short notice," Sue said. "We have a bit of a spiritual emergency."

"Come into my office," he said, leading them down the righthand aisle, through a doorway, and into a rectory. "It's just this way." He opened another door and motioned to a sofa and a chair opposite a desk, behind which he took his seat. "Lexi told me you're concerned about a possible demon attachment?"

"Yes," Sue said. "It's our friend Tanya. She's out in the car."

"She wouldn't come inside the church?" he asked.

"She said she didn't feel well enough," Sue replied. "But she was just in the hospital, where the doctors found nothing wrong with her."

Ellen cleared her throat. "Pastor, would you mind explaining to me what a demon is?"

Sue lifted a finger. "It's one of the fallen angels who sided with Lucifer."

"Not always," the pastor said. "In my experience, it's usually someone who doesn't want to let go of power after they've died. They latch onto a person who's been weakened by illness, depression, or addiction."

"Tanya recently had surgery," Ellen pointed out.

"And I think she still suffers from depression," Sue added.

"What makes you suspect a demon attachment?" the pastor asked.

Ellen and Sue recounted all they had witnessed in Tanya, including the peculiar odor, the nightmare, the nausea and dizziness, and the figure they'd seen behind her through the beveled glass of the bathroom door at Drummond Lodge.

"I see," he finally said. "Well, if this is, indeed, an attachment, you'll want to act quickly, before the demon takes possession of her. If that happens, well, saving your friend's life becomes much more difficult."

"Saving her life?" Sue asked.

Ellen's mouth dropped open. "She's in danger of dying?"

"Absolutely," the pastor said. "Demons—whether human or not—feed on the life energy of souls. It will eventually take possession of her body and use it until there's nothing left."

"Oh, my," Lexi cried, covering her mouth. "What can they do, Pastor John?"

"We need to bring her into the church and submerge her in holy water," he said. "But, if she does have a demon attached to her, getting her into the building will be no easy task."

"Can't we just squirt her with holy water, if she won't come?" Sue asked.

"You don't want to risk the demon attaching itself to *you*," he said. "Just bringing her into the church might be enough to get it to leave. The holy water is an insurance policy." Then he added, "I'll wait for you in the back of the church near the baptismal fountain."

"Now?" Ellen asked. "You want us to bring her in now?"

"The sooner the better," Pastor John replied.

Ellen and Sue returned to the parking lot and were startled to find Tanya vomiting in the grass just outside of the rental.

"Tanya?" Ellen rushed to her friend's side.

"I need to get back to the hotel," she said. "I feel like I'm going to pass out."

Sue and Ellen each took an arm and helped their friend to her feet.

"We need to tell you something," Sue said. "But it won't be easy."

Lexi stood on the church steps a few yards away, wringing her hands. "Mom?"

"Coming, darling," Sue said.

"What?" Tanya asked Sue. "Aren't we leaving now?"

"Not yet," Sue said.

Tanya pulled away from them with surprising strength. "I said I want to go back!"

"Easy," Sue said.

Ellen was too shocked to say a word.

"You have a demon attached to you," Sue explained. "We need to take you into the church to get rid of it."

"That's ridiculous," Tanya said. She turned to Ellen. "Do you believe this crap?"

Ellen nodded.

"Well, I think it's crazy," Tanya said with a laugh. "I'll be in the car when you're ready."

"Wait," Ellen said, finally finding her tongue. "Suppose it *is* crazy. What would it hurt?"

Tanya stood by the opened door of the passenger's side of the rental. "*Me!* You know I don't feel well."

"It'll just take a minute," Sue said. "In and out. Then we'll go get some Braum's ice cream. How does that sound?"

When Tanya began to climb into the rental, Sue surprised Ellen by grabbing their friend's arm. She couldn't recall ever seeing Sue move so swiftly. Ellen rushed over and took Tanya's other arm. Together, they tried to drag Tanya into the church, but her strength proved too much for them.

"Enough!" Tanya growled in a low, guttural voice. "Quit treating me like a child!"

Ellen and Sue released Tanya and glanced back at Lexi.

"Thank the pastor for us and come on," Sue said to her daughter. "This isn't going to work, after all."

Back at the hotel, Ellen and Sue sat on the bed opposite Tanya's, trying to think of a way to help their friend. Each time one of them asked how she was feeling, Tanya insisted she was fine and that they were making a mountain out of a molehill.

Then Ellen had an idea. "Maybe we should visit our old friends while we're here—you know, Carrie French, Eduardo Mankiller, and Miss Margaret Myrtle?"

"Good idea," Sue said, taking out her phone. "I'll see if any of them are available."

Tanya took out her phone, too. "Darn, my phone's dead again. Would you mind getting my charger for me, Ellen?"

"Not at all." Ellen crossed the room, unplugged Tanya's charger from the desk, and carried it over to her friend, whose face had returned to its pasty pale color. The dark circles had returned around her eyes as well.

Sue climbed to her feet. "I guess I'll turn in for the night. I'll let you know if I hear from any of our old friends."

"You aren't leaving me here alone, are you?" Ellen asked.

"Gee, what am I? Chopped liver?" Tanya shook her head. "See you in the morning," Tanya said to Sue.

Ellen gave Sue an urgent look and mouthed, *Don't leave me here.*

Then Sue said, "Maybe it would be a good idea for me to go get my stuff and move in here for the night, just in case Tanya gets sick again."

"That's crazy," Tanya insisted. "I'm fine."

"I think it's a good idea," Ellen said gratefully as Sue left.

Ellen was terrified to be alone in the room with Tanya and her demon. It was scary enough to be around benevolent spirits, let alone an evil one. The room was too dark and quiet as Tanya sat bent over her phone.

"What are you doing?" Ellen asked.

"Playing Solitaire. Why? Do you want to do something?"

"Do you mind if I turn on the television?"

"Not at all."

Ellen grabbed the remote from the bedside table and pushed the power button. Finding the guide, she looked for HGTV. She accidentally selected the wrong channel showing a gospel choir in blue gowns singing a lively hymn.

Ellen glanced at Tanya to see if the religious hymns affected her, but her friend was lying on top of the covers playing Solitaire on her phone and seemed unchanged.

Tanya looked up at her. "What?"

"What do you want to watch?"

"It makes no difference to me."

Ellen changed the channel to HGTV.

After an episode of *Property Brothers*, during which Ellen had continually glanced over at Tanya, except when she was occupied with trying to decide which brother she had the bigger crush on, Ellen received a text from Sue: *Carrie French is here. You and Tanya should join us downstairs for a snack.*

Ellen replied: *Okay.*

"I just got a text from Sue. Carrie French is downstairs. Want to join?"

"I don't know," Tanya said. "You go on without me."

"Oh, come on. Don't be a party pooper."

"I said go!" she growled.

Ellen jumped to her feet and slipped into her shoes. "If you insist. I won't be gone long."

"Take your time," Tanya said in her usual friendly voice.

But Ellen wanted the demon to know she'd be right back and said again, "I won't be long."

When she reached Sue and Carrie at the hotel bar, they wanted to know where Tanya was.

"She wouldn't come with me," Ellen said. "What should we do?"

"Carrie has some good advice," Sue said.

Ellen noticed an ambulance parked outside the hotel, its lights flashing without the siren. "What's going on out there?"

"A woman had a heart attack in the hotel lobby," Sue said. "I don't think she made it."

"Oh, no. That's awful." Ellen took a second look at Carrie, who'd cut her long, curly brown hair into a much shorter style. Ellen liked it. "Anyway, back to Tanya. How can we help her?"

"Before you do anything," Carrie said, "You and Sue need to get authentic gris-gris, but it won't be easy."

"What's that, and where do we get it?" Ellen asked.

"New Orleans," Sue replied. "Carrie says it will keep the demon from attaching to us."

"But what about Tanya?" Ellen asked. "What if the demon possesses her before we get the, what is it called?"

"Gris-gris." Carrie lifted a small cloth pouch from between her breasts. The pouch hung from a thin leather strap around her neck. "I wear one at all times. Everyone on my team does."

"I wish you would have mentioned this before," Ellen said.

"It probably wouldn't have done any good," Carrie said. "Authentic gris-gris aren't easy to come by. You need to visit an actual Voodoo high priestess in the Crescent City. And don't buy the crap in the French Quarter shops or online. It's fake stuff for ignorant tourists. Some of it might be authentic, but it's best not to take any chances."

"How long do we have before Tanya's possessed?" Sue asked Carrie.

"It's hard to know," the paranormal investigator replied. "But I wouldn't wait. I'd fly to New Orleans as soon as possible. Tomorrow, if you can. I'll give you the name of someone who might help you."

"Might?" Ellen asked.

"She's extremely skeptical about people who come to her for help," Carrie explained.

"I wonder why," Ellen said.

"Propaganda." Carrie took a sip of her drink.

"What kind of propaganda?" Ellen asked.

"Back in the day, Louisiana portrayed Voodoo as something evil and barbaric, either because of racism or because Voodoo threatened the spread of Christianity."

"You sure do know your history," Sue commented.

"The study of ghosts can't exist without the study of history," Carrie pointed out.

"I suppose that's true," Sue conceded.

"Anyway," Carrie continued, "Voodoo practitioners were portrayed in newspapers as primitive people who sacrificed animals, conjured zombies, and committed other depraved acts of superstitious nonsense. Even today, most people don't acknowledge Voodoo as a legitimate lifestyle or a true religion."

"We'll be nothing but respectful," Ellen promised.

"I'm not the one you need to convince," Carrie said as she took a card from her purse, jotted down a name and address, and handed it over to Sue. "Maybe if you tell her that I sent you, she'll listen to what you have to say."

Sue read the writing on the card aloud, "Priestess Isabel?"

"The tour guides make up all kinds of stories about her," Carrie said, "but she's the real deal."

"If she's the real deal, why do the guides make up stories?" Sue asked.

"Because the real deal is less interesting."

"What will we tell Tanya?" Ellen asked Sue.

Sue shrugged. "We'd better think of *something*."

CHAPTER THREE

The House on Chartres Street

Ellen and Sue were shocked when Tanya agreed to take a quick trip to New Orleans. Sue hadn't even had to use the excuse of finding a potential house to flip before Tanya said that *she'd* been looking at one in the French Quarter online. Ellen suspected that the demon *wanted* them to go to New Orleans, and this scared the heck out of her.

It was late afternoon the following day when they arrived at the Inn on Ursulines. Ellen was dragging after having had very little sleep the night before. Even though Sue had stayed in their hotel room and had even drawn a circle of protection around the two of them after Tanya had gone to sleep, they had tossed and turned in the too-small double bed in Tulsa all night long.

Fortunately, this place had queen-size beds.

As Ellen rolled her suitcase to one of the corners of the room, she said, "Anyone up for a nap?"

Tanya shook her head. "I'm anxious to show you the house that I found."

Ellen supposed she wouldn't get much sleep anyway—not with that demon still in the room. They needed to go see the Voodoo priestess as soon as possible, if any of them were to have rest and peace of mind.

"I promised Lexi I'd buy her a Voodoo doll while we're here," Sue said. "Let's do that first, to get it out of the way, and then, we can go and look at the house."

Leave it to Sue to think of a way to get Tanya to the temple.

But Tanya would have none of it. "Let's check out the house, and then I'll come back and rest while you do your shopping."

Since the house was only a block away from their inn, they headed toward Chartres Street on foot. On the way, Sue spotted a French bakery and sandwich shop.

"That place looks yummy," she said. "Why don't we rest for a minute and grab a bite?"

"The temple closes at six," Ellen said.

"What temple?" Tanya asked.

Ellen cursed herself. "The place Sue wants to go for the Voodoo doll. She Googled it while you were in the bathroom and said it closes at six, remember Sue?"

"That's right. We better wait and eat later."

Tanya asked no further questions, and Ellen sighed with relief, as they continued down Ursulines toward the vacant mansion Tanya had found online.

Without a real estate agent, Ellen didn't expect to see the inside. And she didn't care to, anyway, since they were only going to placate Tanya. But that was before she got a look at the outside of the house.

It looked exactly like the Mikaelson mansion in one of her favorite CW shows, *The Originals*. The two-story brick Creole house butted up to the property line, like most of the homes in the French Quarter. Four white French doors with green wooden shutters faced the sidewalk, and there were four more identical doors above on the second floor leading out to a narrow balcony with ornate cast-iron railings, from which four large potted ferns hung. Near the curb were iron posts cast in the form of horseheads, an icon on the CW show.

Sue turned to them with a look of glee on her face. "I can just imagine Klaus Mikaelson looking down at us from that balcony. Can't you?"

"Or Marcel Girard," Ellen said with a twinkle in her eye.

"Oh, my gosh, this place is amazing!" Tanya said.

"Breathtaking," Ellen agreed.

A realty sign above them provided the name and number of the listing agent, along with the words "Courtyard" and "Reduced."

Sue pointed to the sign. "Maybe we should give Lionel Hurd a call."

"Can we get a better look at the courtyard?" Tanya wondered out loud as she peered over a gate on the right side of the property. "Oh, look. The gate's open."

"Oh, wow," Sue said. "Let's check it out."

"Are you sure that's a good idea?" Ellen asked. "Isn't that trespassing?"

"We'll be quick," Sue insisted as she pushed the gate open and took the lead.

Tanya followed before Ellen could object. Ellen glanced around the empty street and darted into the yard, closing the gate behind her.

Inside the courtyard, the ornate cast-iron railing continued around both the balcony and the first-floor façade, where the white French doors and green shutters echoed the front of the building. Although the ground was mostly covered in brick pavers, there were flower beds lining the brick exterior walls of the mansion, creating a green border of lush palms, shrubs, and flowering vines around the courtyard. In its center was an elaborate fountain without water, and in front of a smaller house in back was an old-fashioned gas lamppost.

"How quaint!" Sue said.

"Look here," Tanya called from where she stood near the house. "This door is open."

"I don't think we should go inside," Ellen warned. "Clearly someone is taking care of this place. Look at these flowers. What if someone's at home?"

Sue went to the door beside Tanya. "Hello? Anyone here?"

When no one answered, Sue shrugged and pushed open the door. "What could it hurt?"

Ellen sighed but followed her friends, her curiosity winning over the moral high ground she'd been about to take. It had been one thing to investigate an abandoned building in Tulsa without an agent, but this place might still be *occupied*. Even so, she followed Tanya though the door.

Once inside, Ellen quickly changed her mind about the house being occupied. It stank to high heaven, and the only furniture in the front main room was a three-legged stool.

"At least the place isn't trashed," Sue said through a pinched nose. "Not like other places we've seen."

The ceiling was at least twelve feet high. Dusty drapes hung over the windows, and a gilded chandelier with elegant crystals hung from the center of the ceiling. There was an ornate brick fireplace on the back wall, and, on the other side of it was a smaller living area—or parlor— leading to the street. Light from the front doors showed wooden floors in good condition, though the plaster on the interior walls needed re-pairing, as did some of the brick around the fireplace, which was open to both the front and back rooms.

The parlor was flanked by a galley kitchen on one side and a library, still filled with books and a desk, on the other.

"That's a lot of books," Ellen murmured, glancing over the titles, which included both fiction and nonfiction. Most of the books were about medicines, plants, herbs, and apothecary. The library led to anoth-er room facing the courtyard. Light poured in through two windows, revealing an old hat rack near one wall and another fireplace on the oth-er. The ceilings were high in every room.

There was a small bathroom next to the library and office, and these rooms were perfectly symmetrical to the kitchen, dining room, and laundry room on the opposite wing.

Between the parlor and the kitchen was a staircase leading to the second floor.

"Shall we go up?" Tanya asked.

"Why not?" Sue shrugged. "We've come this far."

Tanya, usually the most cautious of their group, led the way, and Ellen couldn't help but wonder if it was the demon influencing her.

They passed an open door leading to an empty bedroom, also with a twelve-foot ceiling and a set of French doors facing the balcony overlooking the street. Beyond the bedroom was a bathroom. Tanya stopped short, covering her mouth. Ellen peered inside to see what had caught her friend's tongue. Sue gasped and covered her mouth, too. Ellen closed and opened her eyes to be sure she was seeing clearly.

A free-standing, claw-foot tub stood in the back of the room, and two hairy legs and feet hung over the side of it. The feet were pale, lifeless, and crusted with dirt.

"Is that a dead body?" Ellen whispered.

"Oh my God," Sue said. "Should we call 9-1-1?"

"How will we explain our presence here?" Ellen asked.

"And what if the police think we had something to do with it?" Tanya pointed out.

"We have to do something," Sue said. "We can't just leave him up here to rot."

"Where are his clothes?" Ellen wondered. "And his shoes?"

"Someone must have dumped him here," Tanya said. "Which means...someone must have murdered him."

Ellen peered over the tub to get a better look at the body. The man looked to have been in his forties. Curly dark hair covered his chest, legs, and arms. Straight brown hair, long and bushy, covered his head and hung to his shoulders. His face was unshaven—though Ellen recalled that body hair continued to grow after death. She wondered how long the body had been lying here.

Just then, the man opened his eyes.

Ellen jumped, nearly losing her balance. She had to grab a hold of Tanya to keep from falling.

"Are you the cops?" the man asked her.

Ellen shook her head, unable to find her tongue.

"Did Marie Laveau send you?" he asked.

Ellen shook her head again.

The man promptly closed his eyes and went back to sleep.

Ellen looked at her friends and whispered, "Let's get out of here."

Tanya led the way down the stairs, past the parlor, and out the door to the courtyard, where she and Ellen stopped to catch their breath and to wait for Sue.

"What do we do?" Tanya asked. "Shouldn't we report it to the realtor?"

"Are we sure he wasn't a ghost?" Sue asked as she caught up to them. "I mean, think about it. Where are his clothes and his shoes? Why would a naked man be lying in the tub of an empty house and asking about Marie Laveau?"

"Who's Maire Laveau?" Ellen asked. The name sounded familiar, but she couldn't place it.

"Only the most famous Voodoo queen in New Orleans," Tanya said. "We should visit her grave."

"She's dead?" Ellen asked.

Sue wagged her finger. "That's what I'm saying. Why would the living ask about a dead Voodoo queen?"

Ellen crossed her arms. "But why would a ghost care about the cops?"

Sue frowned. "Good point. Maybe we *should* call the realtor."

"Only if we're interested in the house," Ellen said. "Otherwise, I say we mind our own business."

"I'm interested," Tanya said. "This place is amazing."

"But we don't know if it's haunted," Sue said. "Our purpose is to heal haunted places, remember?"

"This whole city is haunted." Ellen took an EMF detector from her purse. "New Orleans is purported to have more ghosts than any other city in the country. There's bound to be a spirit in need of healing here."

"You carry an EMF reader in your purse?" Tanya asked with surprise.

"Don't you?" Ellen asked.

"I suppose we should, if we want to be serious paranormal investigators," Sue said.

Ellen noticed the meter fluctuating chaotically. "There's definitely activity here." She wondered if Tanya's demon might be the cause of it.

"Well, I'm open to doing some research on the place," Sue said. "But first, why don't we take a cab to that Voodoo shop, so I can buy Lexi's doll?"

"It's not that far of a walk," Ellen said, tucking the EMF reader back into her handbag. "Come on, there are lots of things to see on the way."

Sue mumbled a complaint about walking as she followed Ellen and Tanya through the gate to Chartres Street. A woman passed by but didn't pay any notice to them. Ellen headed toward Ursulines, and the others followed.

"Oh, look," Sue said suddenly. "That's the old Ursuline Convent. This is where the vampire lore is said to have originated from."

"I thought the vampire lore came from Anne Rice," Ellen said.

"Well, she helped it along," Sue said, "but it began way before her, in the seventeen-hundreds." Sue stopped in front of the convent to catch her breath. "When the French first came here, they considered this land to be strategic for trade but undesirable for living, because it's below sea level, swampy, and full of mosquitos."

"It does feel rather like a steam room," Ellen agreed—though, to be fair, it was August, she thought to herself, the hottest month of the year.

"To maintain territorial rights," Sue continued, "they settled the area with prisoners."

"Like a penal colony? Like Australia?" Tanya asked.

"That's right," Sue said. "But there were more men than women, so the governor wrote to the king of France asking for French virgins to be married off to the settlers here. They were to live here with the Ursuline Sisters until a match could be made."

"And what happened?" Ellen asked.

"The king sent about twenty French orphan girls. They arrived at night, pale from being below deck for two months. Some of them got tuberculosis and were seen with blood on their mouths. They each carried a small chest, called a casquette or cassette, resembling a miniature coffin, to hold all their things. Rumors quickly spread that vampires had arrived."

"I've heard of the Casquette Girls," Tanya said. "But there's a more interesting story this way. Come on."

"Wait," Ellen said, pointing at the house across the street from the convent. "I've heard of this place. Have you? The Beauregard-Keyes House?"

"No, but I definitely feel something strange about it," Sue said. "Is it haunted?"

"That's what they say," Ellen said. "By the ghosts of Civil War soldiers."

"Come on," Tanya said again, in a more assertive tone. "I want to show you why I brought you here."

Ellen and Sue exchanged looks of confusion.

"Why *you* brought us here?" Sue repeated.

"What?" Tanya kept walking. "Come on, slow pokes."

Alarmed, Ellen and Sue followed Tanya to the corner, where they turned up Governor Nicholls St.

"Did the demon bring us to New Orleans?" Ellen whispered to Sue.

"That can't be," Sue said. "Carrie French suggested it."

Ellen scratched her head. "The demon couldn't have known that you'd call Carrie."

Sue's eyes opened wide. "I thought *you* called her."

Ellen shook her head. "You texted her, didn't you?"

"Yes, but she never replied. When she showed up at the hotel, I assumed you had spoken to her."

"Here we are," Tanya said, stopping before a mansion similar in style to the one they'd just toured—except that this building had three levels and arched doors on the bottom floor.

"What is this place?" Sue asked.

"It was once a place of torture," Tanya said. "They call it the Lalaurie Mansion."

"A place of torture?" Ellen asked.

"Yes," Tanya said. "But not in the way most people believe."

"Where did you hear about *that*?" Sue asked.

Tanya blinked. "Where did I hear about what?"

"About this being a place of torture," Sue repeated.

"What are you talking about?" Tanya asked.

"Come on," Ellen said, her stomach forming a knot. "Let's get to that Voodoo temple."

CHAPTER FOUR

Priestess Isabel

The Spiritual Voodoo Temple on North Rampart was not what Ellen had been expecting. She had supposed it would be more like a church. Instead, it looked like a souvenir shop specializing in Voodoo dolls and other paraphernalia. It smelled of lavender and rose.

The fact that it resembled a shop more than a temple might have accounted for the ease with which Tanya walked into the building.

"Where are you all from?" a black woman in her seventies asked as they entered the shop.

"Texas," Ellen said.

"All my exes live in Texas," the woman sang and then laughed.

Ellen lifted her brows in surprise. A high Voodoo priestess who sang George Strait? Maybe this was just the shopkeeper and not the actual priestess.

"I see you brought a friend," the woman said to Tanya.

"Excuse me?" Tanya asked.

"Hello, there," the woman said, her dark eyes shining.

She seemed to be looking at empty space beside Tanya.

Ellen glanced at Sue and then asked the woman, "Are you Priestess Isabel?"

"That's me," the woman said, still smiling.

Ellen hid her surprise. With short, curly hair, dainty earrings, and a belted colorful dress, she looked like an average businesswoman from suburbia.

"We were hoping to tour your temple," Sue said.

"My body is the temple," the woman said. "This place is just a building."

"I like that," Ellen said, not sure what else to say.

"I'm shopping for a Voodoo doll," Sue said. "Can you help me pick the best one for my daughter?"

As Sue engaged with the older woman, Ellen distracted Tanya with some of the paraphernalia on the wall. They were being carefully watched by a younger, quiet woman in her twenties with fair skin, blonde hair, and dark eyes, from where she sat behind a counter in front of a computer.

"What do you suppose that represents?" Ellen pointed to an image of a snake biting its tail.

"Death and rebirth," Tanya said. "Don't you think?"

Before Ellen could reply, the priestess said, "That's one way of looking at it. Creation is another."

Sue, who had been talking with the priestess, said, "Priestess Isabel, these are my friends Ellen and Tanya."

"Today, you can call me Lucibel," the priestess said with a laugh as she looked up to the ceiling. "I'm feeling loose-y today."

Ellen wondered what the woman might have been smoking in the back room.

"I was just asking her what it takes to be a high priestess in the Voodoo faith," Sue said.

"I wouldn't call myself such a grand thing," Isabel said. "I'm just an old woman who pays her bills."

"What is a high priestess, anyway?" Ellen asked. "And what led you to decide to become one?"

"I didn't choose this life." The woman laughed. "It chose me."

"And what is 'this life?'" Ellen pressed.

"Well, if you really want to know, my ancestors were the psychologists of their time. They had an intuitive way of treating the ailments of the people when no doctors could. Even today, modern medicine doesn't suit everyone and everything. You can't read in a book what my grandmother knew. You can't learn that in school."

"It had to be passed down?" Tanya asked.

"Not passed down," the priestess said. "Understood intuitively, from the creator. The gift is inherited, so, I suppose, in a way, it's passed down, but not in the way you mean."

Ellen noticed that Tanya's foul odor had returned. She ignored it as best as she could.

"So, you don't see the ailments as spiritual warfare?" Sue asked her.

"Not warfare, no," the priestess said. "But it's spiritual, all right." She winked at Tanya.

"You don't believe in spiritual warfare between good and evil?" Sue asked with her brows furrowed.

The priestess smiled and closed her eyes. "You see, spirits are energy, and energy is *energy*. It's neither good nor evil."

Ellen felt even more certain that the woman was high.

"You really don't believe in good and evil?" Sue asked.

"I didn't say that," the priestess said with a laugh as she looked up to the ceiling again.

"Then what are you saying?" Ellen asked.

"We assign it, that's all. It depends on your perspective."

Ellen was beginning to wonder why Carrie French had sent them to this woman, who, in Ellen's opinion, was right to call herself Loosey Bell.

"Then what's the purpose of the gris-gris sachets, if not to protect one from evil?" Ellen pointed to the baskets of sachets marked $7 each.

"And what about this incense called 'Evil Away'?" Sue held up a small plastic pouch marked $8.

Tanya laughed. "Tricks for the tourists?"

"I pray over those," the priestess said. "And then people burn them or hold onto them and get a better feeling than they had before. I try to be a facilitator of peace."

"So, it's all in the mind?" Ellen was confused. It sounded like the priestess was admitting it was all a scam.

"I didn't say that," the priestess said, laughing.

Sue cleared her throat and put a hand on her hip—a posture that Ellen had come to recognize as "warrior ready." "Just suppose some of this *energy* attached itself to a living person, and that person wanted to get rid of it."

The priestess laughed again. "You can't get rid of it. The energy does what it will." Isabel stopped laughing and glanced suspiciously at Tanya. "Where'd you say you was from?" the priestess asked.

"San Antonio," Sue replied when Tanya didn't. "But we were just in Tulsa. Have you heard of Carrie French?"

"I don't remember Carrie," the priestess said. She turned to Tanya. "Do you know Carrie?"

Tanya nodded.

"What's your plan, friend?" the priestess asked Tanya with a laugh.

"What do you mean?" Tanya asked, turning pink.

"Come back tomorrow," the priestess said. "I'll be able to help you better then."

"Can we buy some authentic gris-gris and a Voodoo doll?" Sue asked.

"Over there." The priestess pointed to the baskets on the shelves.

Sue picked through the dolls. "These are all handmade. I don't know which one I like best."

Ellen picked up three sachets. "Do you have any we can wear around our necks?"

"Oh, you want my special stuff." Priestess Isabel disappeared into the back room and returned with three smaller gris-gris bags tied to thin, soft leather, like the one Carrie wore.

The quiet young woman behind the counter took Sue's credit card as the priestess disappeared into the back room again. Ellen had a feeling Carrie had sent them on a wild goose chase.

As they left the temple, Sue said, "Let's take a cab. I don't think my feet can endure the return walk to the hotel."

"But Bourbon Street is just a few blocks this way," Tanya said, taking the lead.

"A few *blocks*," Sue complained.

"Oh, Sue," Tanya said, dismissively. "You can do it."

Tanya called back to them. "Let's check it out. It's been so long since I've walked these streets."

"I thought this was your first time in New Orleans," Ellen said to Tanya.

"I grew up here," Tanya said.

Ellen and Sue stopped in their tracks and looked at one another. They knew for a fact that Tanya had not grown up there.

"Tanya?" Sue called to their friend.

Tanya ignored them and kept on walking.

Ellen stayed back with Sue as Tanya went on several paces ahead of them. When she seemed out of earshot, Ellen said to Sue, "What now?"

"Who the heck knows," Sue muttered. "I don't have much faith in Priestess Isabel."

"What was Carrie thinking?"

Sue shook her head. "I don't know, but let's put on one of those gris-gris bags, just in case."

Sue handed her one of the gris-gris bags, and they each put one on. Ellen had been hoping to feel more confident in its protection, but confident she was not. So much for getting peace of mind and a good night's sleep.

"Tanya!" Sue called to their friend, who was a half a block ahead of them. "Wait up! And put one of these sachets on, will you?"

"No, thank you," Tanya said as she waited for them on the sidewalk. "I'm good."

Ellen decided to send off a quick text to Carrie, to ask if she really had faith in Priestess Isabel and her gris-gris.

She was shocked by Carrie's reply: *I don't know what you're talking about. Who's Priestess Isabel?*

Ellen's mouth fell open as she showed Sue the text.

"Then who was that we talked to at the Mayo Hotel in Tulsa?" Sue whispered.

"Are you guys coming?" Tanya asked as she resumed walking.

"Slow down, Speedy," Sue said. "You know I have a bad foot."

"Are you okay?" Ellen asked Sue.

"I could use something to recharge my batteries and calm my nerves," Sue replied. "Oh, look. There's a bakery."

That evening, curious about the way Tanya had insisted on taking them to see Lalaurie Mansion and concerned by the cryptic way she had said that it was once a place of torture but not the way most people think, Ellen used her phone to conduct a Google search. Tanya seemed to have no memory of stopping there or of making her statement about torture, and this worried Ellen. What was that demon up to?

Ellen's Google search of Lalaurie Mansion brought up gruesome articles about Madame Delphine Lalaurie's mistreatment of slaves. Apparently, an 1834 fire revealed dozens of slaves chained in an attic, their limbs pointing in all directions, skin peeled, intestines tied around their waists, and other horrors that hinted to medical experiments. When the neighbors discovered the horrifying mistreatment, a mob descended upon the mansion that same night, and Madame Delphine Lalaurie fled with her children to France to avoid persecution.

Glancing over at Tanya, who was beneath the covers and on the verge of sleep, Ellen feared for her friend's life. What kind of evil thing had taken hold of her?

The following day, when they returned to the Voodoo Spiritual Temple, Priestess Isabel held a can of Sprite in her hand and was speaking with another patron as the three friends entered from the street.

They had taken a cab, because Ellen and Sue hadn't gotten a lick of sleep and were dead-dog tired. Ellen had kept her eyes trained in Tanya's direction, half-expecting to see the red glowing eyes of the demon she'd seen crouched behind Tanya in the bathroom at Drummond Lodge.

The other patron seemed to be conducting an interview, for Priestess Isabel was recounting her life.

"I worked as a domestic in Mississippi before going to Chicago, where I was an operating room technician in a hospital," Isabel said.

"Is that when you converted to Voodooism?" the young woman, who looked just out of college, asked.

"I don't like the word 'convert,'" the priestess said. "I've been talking to spirits since I was a little girl. I never changed. The label did."

"You met your late husband in Chicago, isn't that right?" the interviewer asked.

"Yes," Isabel said. "We built this congregation together, and, after he died, I carried it on in his name, as a tribute to him. It's his legacy, you see, and my inheritance. It's both my honor and my duty. It liberates me, but it's a great burden."

"A burden?" the young woman asked.

"Until you've walked in my shoes," the priestess said, "you have no idea what it means to be me. If you knew how many letters I receive, daily, from mothers whose sons are in jail, or in the hospital, or otherwise troubled...How do I begin to answer them all?"

Ellen was beginning to wonder if they'd come at a bad time. To Sue and Tanya, she whispered, "Maybe we should come back later."

"We're nearly done here," Priestess Isabel said.

Ellen hadn't expected to be overheard, especially by a woman in her seventies.

The interviewer asked a few more questions and then thanked the priestess for her time before leaving the shop.

"Can you believe that young thing is from *Time Magazine?*" Priestess Isabel asked.

"Wow," Ellen said. "We're so sorry to have interrupted."

"You must be pretty famous to be interviewed for *Time,*" Sue added.

"I'm just a woman who pays her bills," the priestess said.

"Evidently you're more than that," Tanya said.

"I can't see your friend today," the priestess said to Tanya, "but I can feel him."

"I don't know what you mean," Tanya said with wide eyes. "What friend?"

"Deep down, you know," Isabel said.

"Can you help us?" Ellen asked.

"First, there's something you need to understand," the priestess began. "I don't think you comprehended what I had to say yesterday."

"You're right," Sue said. "We didn't comprehend it."

Ellen wanted to add that it might have had something to do with how *high* the priestess was—and maybe that's what people meant when they said Voodoo *high* priestess. Ellen was tempted to ask if they were still speaking to Loosey Bell, but she bit her tongue.

"We assign words like good and evil to spirits, but they just energy," Isabel repeated. "Spirits can bring harm to people, and they can commit harmful acts, but the spirits themselves come from the creator and are not without the possibility of redemption. There's goodness in all of us."

"We think this demon is killing our friend," Sue said bluntly.

"Sue!" Tanya berated. "Why do you keep saying that?"

"Just hold on there, friend," Isabel said. "People never think of themselves as evil. From their point of view, their evil acts is justified. Sometimes it's because they sick. Or they have a narrow point of view. But most of the time, it's because they desperate."

"But…" Tanya began.

"Just hear me out," Priestess Isabel said to Tanya. "There's only two ways this can end. The spirit sucks you dry of life, or you help it."

"Help it?" Ellen asked. "How?"

"Find out what it wants, what it needs."

"And how do we do that?" Sue asked.

"We ask," the priestess said.

CHAPTER FIVE

Of Snake and Bone

Priestess Isabel turned to the quiet woman behind the counter. "Keep an eye on things, will you, dear?"

The young woman nodded as Isabel motioned for Ellen and her friends to follow her from the front gift shop, through a cluttered back office, and into a courtyard filled with plants, herbs, and other botanicals.

In the center of the courtyard was a table with two chairs. The table was covered in a green fibrous cloth with yellow and red markings. Priestess Isabel motioned to Tanya to have a seat in one of the chairs. Ellen and Sue sat on the brick pavers of a raised garden bed a few feet away. The priestess went to what Ellen now noticed was a glass aquarium, and, from it, the priestess lifted a large python, at least five feet in length, which she coiled around the top of her head.

"The snake is a powerful conduit between us and the other side," Isabel explained.

Ellen gave Sue a worried glance as the Voodoo queen sat opposite Tanya.

"Don't be afraid of Henry. He's been with me for over twenty years. He ain't venomous. My late husband brought him here from Belize in the nineties." Isabel took up a leather pouch and emptied its contents into Tanya's hands. "Shake the bones."

Tanya stared down at the items in her hand. "Are these real bones? What kind of bones? I see shells, but what kind of bones am I holding?"

Ellen recognized the real Tanya coming through. That wasn't the demon talking.

"Those are the bones of my spirit animals," Isabel said. "They were pets that died of natural causes over the years. They help me to speak with the ancestors on the other side. They may be able to tell us what your new friend wants from you."

"Oh," Tanya said with a tinge of disgust. "I didn't know you were going to ask me to hold the bones of dead animals."

The priestess adjusted the python, which had begun to uncoil and lift its head. "Shake them and then scatter them onto the table."

Tanya did as she was told. One of the shells landed on the ground beneath the table.

"If it landed face down, you can leave it. It's not important," the priestess said. "But if it's face up, I need to look at how it landed."

Ellen couldn't see it from where she and Sue were sitting, but Tanya leaned over and asked, "How can I tell if it's face down?"

"Can you see an x marked on it?" Isabel asked.

"No."

"Good." Isabel adjusted her snake. "Now lookie here."

Ellen stood up and moved closer to the table, so she could see what the priestess was pointing at.

"The position and placement of this bone means a sacrifice, an important sacrifice. The spirit attached to you is willing to give up something very important to be here."

Ellen wanted to say, "Yeah, our friend Tanya," but she didn't.

"This bone here gives another meaning," the priestess continued. "It has something to do with finding something hidden. The spirit wants you to find something. It's something he treasures, but it isn't where it's supposed to be."

"What does he want us to find?" Sue asked.

"This other bone means balance or justice," Isabel continued, ignoring Sue's question. "By finding what is lost, you will restore balance or bring about some kind of justice." She pointed to a shell and said, "And this balance will bring freedom, not just to the spirit, but to someone close to him."

"How can we figure out what the spirit wants us to find?" Ellen asked.

"Take up the bones," Isabel said to Ellen. "Take your friend's place and cast the bones."

Ellen felt her hands begin to tremble. She wasn't sure why she had become so nervous as she gathered up the bones and shells.

"Don't forget the one on the floor," Isabel said.

Tanya crouched down and picked it up and handed it over to Ellen.

"Shake," Isabel said. "And think hard about your question."

As Ellen shook the bones, she said in her mind, "What do you want us to find?"

Then Ellen dropped the bones onto the table and watched them land and roll, until they settled.

Ellen watched Priestess Isabel studying the bones and shells on the cloth. The red and yellow markings were lines and symbols that apparently meant something to the Voodoo queen.

"He's looking for a loved one," Isabel said. "Someone who has passed. He must be looking for his or her remains. For the bones. They haven't been consecrated."

Ellen's mouth fell open. "Can you give us a name? Who are we looking for? And why?"

"Where do we start?" Sue added.

"Let her take your place," Isabel said to Ellen. "Let her ask her question with the bones."

Ellen stood up, and Sue took the chair before taking the bones in both of her hands and giving them a shake.

Aloud, Sue said, "Where do we start?"

Then she scattered the bones across the table. Three of them fell off the table and rolled across the courtyard.

"Check if they're face up," Isabel said as Ellen and Tanya went to retrieve the fallen bones.

"These two are face down," Tanya said.

One of them had flown clear across the courtyard and landed on a piece of trash. Ellen bent over it to have a closer look.

"Do you see a mark on the bone?" Tanya called.

Ellen noticed an "x" marked on the edge of one side. "Yes."

Isabel stood up and crossed the courtyard. "Then it's face up and important." Holding the snake on her head with one hand, she pointed at the trash on the ground. "What does that paper say?"

Ellen picked up the trash. It was a brochure from a local ghost touring company. The bone had landed on a photo of the house Tanya had taken her and Sue to see just a short while ago.

"It says Lalaurie Mansion," Ellen finally said, with a lump in her throat.

The priestess's eyes grew wide. "Then you have your answer."

Sue stood up and put her hands on her hips. "Does this demon expect us to go snooping around someone else's property?"

"That's all I have time for today," Priestess Isabel said, as she returned the python to its aquarium. "Pay my assistant for three readings and make an appointment for tomorrow."

Ellen, Sue, and Tanya took a cab back to the Inn on Ursulines to rest and to think of what to do next. On the way, the driver asked if they'd heard about the dead body on Chartres Street.

It smelled like a dead body in the cab. Ellen wondered if it was the cab, or if Tanya had brought the odor in with her.

"No," Sue said. "What happened?"

"Some guy was found dead in a bathtub."

"Did he drown himself?" Ellen asked.

"No water in the tub, just the dude in his birthday suit."

With brows lifted, Ellen glanced at her friends.

"Where on Chartres?" Tanya asked.

"Just a few blocks over," the cabby said. "A real estate agent found him this morning."

"Was it the house for sale near Ursulines?" Ellen asked.

"I think so," the cabby said.

Ellen gasped. She noticed Sue was trembling.

"Who was the victim?" Sue asked.

"They don't know yet," the driver said. "No ID with the body. The police are treating it like a homicide, since the dude's clothes were missing."

"Do they have any suspects?" Ellen asked.

"That's all I heard," the man said. "Probably just a hobo who overdosed."

Once they were back in their room, Sue turned on the television, searching for the local news, and then sat in the one upholstered chair in the corner of the room, shaking like a leaf as she searched for news on her phone.

"Sue?" Ellen asked. "You okay?"

"If we'd called that agent, or even the police, that man might still be alive," Sue said.

Ellen's stomach formed a knot. Her friend was right.

"We thought we were helping him by minding our own business," Tanya pointed out.

Sue put her face in her hands. "What if the police find our fingerprints, and we become suspects?"

"That's not going to happen," Ellen said, trying to console her friend. "We didn't touch anything, did we?"

Tanya shook her head. "I don't think so."

"I did," Sue said. "I touched the back door when I opened it. I touched the railing on the stairs."

"I may have touched the railing," Tanya said. "I can't remember."

"I'm sure I did," Sue said.

"We've got no motive," Ellen said, though she sounded more confident than she felt. "We didn't even know the guy. Let's try not to worry about it. The cab driver was probably right. The guy OD-ed, end of story. An autopsy will prove it."

"But what if the guy *was* murdered?" Tanya said.

"And what if the murderer saw us there?" Sue said suddenly.

Ellen sat on one of two queen-sized beds with her back against the pillows and headboard. She stretched her legs out, trying to get comfortable. Not having slept for days, she was so very tired. "Let's cross that bridge if we come to it."

"At least we know that this demon attached to Tanya isn't necessarily evil," Sue said. "But evil or not, Tanya's life is in danger, if we can't give him what he wants."

Tanya, who sat on the other queen bed with her legs crossed, yoga style, leaned over her phone. "I'm searching up the Lalaurie Mansion. You won't believe what took place there."

"Is this you talking? Or your *friend?*" Sue asked.

"That's not funny, Sue," Ellen chastised.

"Sometimes when you're terrified out of your wits, humor is all you have left," Sue said.

Ignoring them, Tanya read, "'On April 10th, 1834, a fire broke out at the mansion, destroying part of it and revealing that at least seven slaves had been chained, starved, and tortured in the attic. The slaves were taken to the Cabildo Prison, where they were on display. When the town heard of what Delphine Lalaurie had done, a mob gathered. It is believed that she fled to France.' And listen to this: 'When the mansion was rebuilt by its next owner, workmen uncovered numerous human skeletons beneath the house. The authorities speculated that the remains belonged to former slaves of the Lalaurie family.'"

"Do you think there are more bones to be found beneath Lalaurie Mansion?" Ellen asked Tanya.

"I think so," Tanya said. "I think that's why we're here."

"We should go and buy another Ouija Board," Sue said. "Maybe Tanya's *friend* will give us more information."

"No need." Ellen crossed the room to her suitcase. "I brought one with me, along with all my paranormal investigation equipment." She'd begun to take it everywhere. "We *are* serious paranormal investigators now, aren't we?"

Ellen took out the board and planchette and brought it over to Tanya's bed. Then she helped Sue carry the one chair over. Once they'd muted the television and were settled, with Ellen on the bed beside Tanya and their fingers touching the planchette, they began.

Sue spoke first. "I'm addressing the ghost attached to Tanya. We mean you no harm. Are you here with us?"

The bedside lamp flickered as the planchette moved to "Yes."

Then, the planchette circled around and spelled out, "H-E-L-P-M-E."

Sue glanced at Ellen, with a look of concern on her face.

"What's your name?" Ellen asked.

They watched as the plastic indicator moved, and Sue said the letters, one at a time, "C-O-R-N-E-L-I-U-S-N-U-N-N-E-R-Y."

"Cornelius Nunnery," Tanya said.

"That's a mouthful," Ellen whispered.

"What should we ask next?" Sue asked.

"When did he die?" Ellen suggested.

Before anyone else could say anything, the planchette moved to "2-0-0-5."

"That's more recent than I thought," Ellen murmured.

"How old were you when you died?" Sue asked.

The television and bedside lamp both flickered as the planchette spelled out "1-6."

"Sixteen?" Tanya asked. "You were only sixteen years old?"

The planchette flew across the board to "Yes."

Ellen frowned. "He was a child."

"How did you die, Cornelius?" Sue asked.

The television turned off and didn't turn back on. The lamp flickered as the planchette spelled out, "K-A-T-R-I-N-A."

"*Hurricane* Katrina?" Tanya asked.

The planchette moved to "Yes."

"How did a ghost from Hurricane Katrina attach to Tanya?" Ellen wondered out loud.

The planchette moved, spelling out, "M-E-M-O-R-I-A-L-H-O-S-P-I-T-A-L."

"Memorial Hospital in Houston!" Tanya cried. "That's where I had my surgery a few months ago."

"So, Cornelius must have died there," Ellen speculated.

"It's strange that a ghost from 2005 would attach to a person thirteen years later," Sue said.

"And what does this have to do with Lalaurie Mansion?" Ellen wondered.

The bedside lamp flickered off, and they were left in darkness.

Ellen used the flashlight on her phone to turn on a second lamp before returning to the board.

Then Sue asked, "Is someone you love buried at Lalaurie Mansion?"

The three friends waited, but the planchette did not move.

"Cornelius?" Sue asked. "Are you there?"

"I don't feel so good," Tanya said, her face pale again.

"Maybe we should take a break." Ellen studied Tanya's face. The dark circles had returned.

"Priestess Isabel said it was a loved one," Sue said. "But I doubt people were still burying remains beneath the Lalaurie Mansion in 2005."

Ellen took up her phone. "Which means it must be an ancestor, right?" She Googled "Cornelius Nunnery 2005."

"That's my guess," Sue said. "What do you think, Tanya?"

When they looked at their friend, they saw her eyes were closed, and her head was hanging to the side.

Ellen touched her shoulder. "Tanya?"

She opened her eyes. "Huh?"

"Nothing," Ellen said. "Go back to sleep."

"I guess this means we aren't going out to dinner tonight," Sue said with a tinge of disappointment.

"Why don't you order something for delivery while I search up Cornelius?" Ellen suggested. "Order whatever you want. It doesn't matter to me."

Ellen was able to find Cornelius's 2005 obituary in the *Houston Chronicle*, but it gave her no leads into the possible ancestor that might be buried beneath Lalaurie Mansion.

The obituary read:

Cornelius Jamar Nunnery, born July 12, 1989, died on September 20, 2005 at the young age of sixteen from injuries sustained during Hurricane Katrina. He is preceded in death by his father, Jamar Collin Nunnery, who died on August 30th when his New Orleans home was destroyed in the same hurricane that fatally injured his son. Cornelius is survived by his mother, Maria, and his sister, Cecilia. A bright and happy boy, a lover of music, and an excellent saxophonist in the Alfred Lawless High School Band, Cornelius also sang and played a major role in his high school musical last year. He will be missed by family and friends.

Ellen fingered the gris-gris bag she wore around her neck. The spirit attached to Tanya did not sound like a demon. The boy must be desperate. Ellen was determined to help Tanya be free of him, but she also felt a responsibility to help Cornelius find peace.

CHAPTER SIX

Marie Laveau

The following afternoon, Ellen and Sue sat on the pavers of the raised garden bed in the courtyard of the Voodoo Spiritual Temple, wiping sweat off their brow, as Tanya sat opposite Priestess Isabel at the table. The priestess wore her snake, Henry, coiled on her head, as she had the previous day. Ellen had just finished recounting all they'd learned the night before using the Ouija Board and Google.

Ellen also told her that Carrie French had no memory of recommending their visit to the priestess. "She doesn't even know who you are."

"No wonder I couldn't remember her," the priestess said. "I usually remember people."

"If that wasn't Carrie who spoke with us in Tulsa, who was it?" Sue asked.

"The boy's ghost isn't strong enough to create an illusion or to possess someone while attached to someone else," Isabel said. "Someone more powerful is working with him."

"Who?" Tanya asked.

Isabel poured her bag of bones into Tanya's hands. "Shake the bones and ask."

Tanya's hands were trembling as she shook the bones and scattered them across the fiber mat.

The priestess leaned over the table and removed some of bones from the spread. "Since they landed face down, we don't consider these. Okay, let's see what we're looking at."

Ellen moved closer to the table, to get a better view.

"This bone says it's someone of great power from the other side," Isabel said. "Maybe a Loa."

"What's a Loa?" Tanya asked.

"A spirit guide," Isabel said. "Like a saint. Saint Jude and Saint Francis are two of my favorites."

"So, a saint could be helping Cornelius?" Tanya asked.

"It's possible," the priestess said.

Ellen wrinkled her brow. She doubted a saint would allow a spirit to threaten Tanya's life.

"Is there any way you can get a name?" Sue asked. "Or some clue to point us in the right direction?"

"The spirits decide how much to tell us," the priestess said. "Yesterday we were lucky to get the name of Lalaurie Mansion."

When Isabel blinked, only the whites of her eyes appeared. Ellen gasped in surprise and glanced over at Tanya and Sue, who also wore looks of concern on their faces.

"My name is Marie Laveau," Isabel said in a gravelly voice. "Find the devil child and consecrate his bones in my family tomb. The diary of Delphine Lalaurie will guide you."

"Diary?" Sue repeated. "Where is it?"

"Beneath the tub where the dead man lay."

Ellen gawked. "Do you mean the vacant house on Chartres Street?"

Ellen flinched when the limp body of the python fell from the priestess's head and landed with a heavy thud at her feet.

Isabel shrieked, her eyes no longer white but wide with despair. "Henry?"

"What happened?" Tanya asked.

Full of tears, the Voodoo queen crouched on the ground beside her beloved snake, lifting its limp body toward her bosom as she kissed its head. "Henry was a gift from my late husband. And now he's gone."

"How did this happen?" Tanya asked.

"I'm so sorry." Sue climbed to her feet. "Is there anything we can do?"

"Just go," Isabel said. "Leave me to mourn in peace."

Feeling terrible, Ellen and her friends paid for three readings and three Voodoo dolls inside the gift shop before walking onto North Rampart Street into the hot, sticky air.

"I feel so bad for Isabel," Tanya said. "Maybe we should buy her some flowers and make a donation…something."

"That's a good idea," Ellen said.

Sue started walking. "First, we need to call Lionel, the realtor."

"I guess we need to walk over to the house to get his number from that sign," Ellen said, following Sue.

Tanya quickly took the lead. "Do you think Henry died so that Marie Laveau could speak to us?"

Ellen stopped in her tracks. "Oh, my gosh. I just thought of something." Goosebumps spread across her arms, even though she was nearly sick with heat exhaustion. "The night Sue and I met Carrie in Tulsa, someone died of a heart attack. Do you think that was Marie Laveau's doing, too?"

"Sacrificing a snake is one thing," Sue said. "But a human being?"

"The man in the bathtub," Tanya began. "He asked if Marie Laveau had sent us, remember?"

"Oh, my gosh," Ellen cried.

"You think she killed him?" Sue asked.

"I don't know what to think," Ellen admitted.

Sue put her hand on her hip. "What do we know about Marie Laveau, anyway? Let me Google her."

As they walked toward the house on Chartres Street, Sue read them what she could find on the most famous Voodoo queen of New Orleans. "'Marie Laveau was a New Orleans Voodoo practitioner who lived from September 10, 1794 to June 16, 1881. She was born to a wealthy plantation owner, Charles Laveau, and his mistress, Marguerite, who was a free woman of color of Native American, African, and French descent. Marie was educated and raised in both the Catholic faith and in the principles of Voodoo by her maternal grandmother, Catherine.'"

Sue handed the phone over to Tanya. "I'm running out of breath with all this walking. Maybe you should read it."

Tanya picked up where Sue had left off. "'In 1819, Marie married Jacques Paris, a carpenter and free person of color from Haiti, just after the Haitian Revolution, when many refugees came to Louisiana and contributed to the Voodoo culture. After Paris went missing and was presumed dead in 1824, Marie became a hairdresser for the wealthy white and Creole women of New Orleans. She also did charitable works as a midwife, nurse, and prison minister.'

"'In 1826, Marie moved in with a free man of color named Glapion and bore fifteen children to him, only one of which lived into adulthood. Under Doctor John Bayou's tutelage, Marie became a Voodoo queen by 1830, merging, as she always had, her Voodoo and Catholic faiths.'

"'The social contacts she made as a hairdresser for the wealthy and as a nurse to the sick may have given her an advantage over other Voodoo practitioners, because she was privy to inside information, which was useful as an oracle in making predictions and instilling fear in others. This, combined with her beauty, her charisma, and her numerous charitable works, quickly made her the queen of Voodoo queens. Even today, people visit her tomb and leave her offerings.'" Tanya turned back to Ellen and Sue, who were working hard to keep up with her. "She doesn't sound like the kind of person who would sacrifice innocent people and animals."

"Sounds to me like she could have had something to do with her husband's disappearance," Sue said.

"Sue!" Ellen chastised. "There's nothing…"

"And she may have sacrificed fourteen of her fifteen babies," Sue added.

"Oh my God." Ellen shook her head. "Tell me you're teasing."

Sue shrugged. "What do we really know about this woman except that she might have killed two people and a snake to communicate with us?"

"The article said she did numerous charitable works," Ellen pointed out. "Maybe she's desperate, like Cornelius."

"Or maybe those people weren't innocent," Sue offered. "Maybe Marie Laveau only sacrificed bad people and babies that cried too much."

Ellen rolled her eyes. "You're impossible."

"Or maybe the woman in Tulsa and the man in the bathtub, and maybe even the snake, volunteered as tributes to Marie Laveau" Sue said.

"You sure have an active imagination," Tanya said.

They walked another few blocks in silence, so Ellen and Sue could focus on breathing, before they finally arrived at the house. Sue phoned Lionel, the realtor, and was told he could meet them there in an hour. So, they strolled over to the bakery and sandwich shop a block away and had a snack and read more about Marie Laveau.

"This website claims that she continues to practice her magic from beyond the grave," Sue said.

"Does it offer any proof?" Ellen asked.

"No." Sue took another bite of her pie.

"I wonder why only one of her children lived to adulthood," Tanya said before sipping her tea.

"I think that was common back then," Sue said.

"But only one out of fifteen?" Tanya asked.

"Like I said before, maybe she sacrificed them." Sue grinned.

"It says here that she once saved a man from death row," Ellen said.

"Some of these sources describe her as a witch and others as a saint," Sue pointed out. "I wonder if she was somewhere in the middle."

Ellen took a sip of her coffee. "Most people are."

"Marie Laveau said to find the bones of the devil child," Tanya said. "I Googled 'devil child New Orleans' and found an article called 'The Demon Baby of Bourbon Street' on *The Haunted Tours of New Orleans* website. Listen to this: 'A high society Creole family had a beautiful daughter named Camille who was eagerly courted by many suitors, but, preferring the Americans, Camille settled on Mackenzie Bowes, a Scotsman by birth. He was obscenely wealthy, and both Camille's family and Mackenzie's were pleased with the match. But one of her Creole suitors wasn't so pleased. In fact, he went to Marie Laveau to ask for a favor.'

"'Etienne, the Creole suitor, wanted Camille for himself. When Marie Laveau said it wasn't meant to be, he wished Camille dead. Marie Laveau took his offering, stamped her foot, and agreed, though she warned him it would cause him suffering, too.'

"'When the bride and groom returned from their honeymoon, Camille was already pregnant and quickly began decorating a nursery in her new home on Chartres Street.'" Tanya looked up. "Do you think it's possible that it's the same house we're…never mind, it can't be."

"That would be a crazy coincidence," Ellen said. "Read on."

Tanya continued, "'Both Camille's mother and her husband began to suffer from terrible dreams about the baby. Marie Laveau was called to the house to offer her remedies. She said she was worried for the child and asked that she alone be allowed to be present when the child came.'

"'Her request was honored, and Marie Laveau was with Camille when the time came. Her labor was difficult, causing Camille to wail and moan until she, at last, passed out and died. Marie delivered the baby from Camille's cooling flesh, only to find that the child was a monster.'"

"What?" Ellen gawked. "That's ridiculous."

Tanya read on, "'The baby had claws instead of fingers and toes and the nubs of horns on the top of his head. He was covered in scales, and his eyes bulged. Mackenzie Bowes was horrified and wanted nothing to do with the monster that had killed his beautiful wife, so Marie Laveau took the child to another woman of high society, Madame Delphine Lalaurie.'"

Tanya looked up. "Seriously?"

"Keep reading," Sue said before taking the last bite of her pie.

"'Delphine Lalaurie wanted to have the devil child baptized, and then she and Marie Laveau shared the responsibility of raising it. For years, Marie Laveau could be seen walking from her house on St. Ann, down Bourbon Street, turning at Governor Nicholls to the home of Delphine Lalaurie on Royal, either to retrieve or to deliver the devil child, its cries echoing throughout the quarter as she walked. To this day, people claim to hear the wails of the devil baby along Bourbon Street between St. Ann and Governor Nicholls, which is why it's come to be called the Devil Baby of Bourbon Street.'"

"That's so bizarre," Sue said.

"If Marie Laveau cared so much about raising that child," Ellen said, "she wouldn't have sacrificed her own."

"Unless she sacrificed her babies so that Satan would give her his," Sue offered. "Maybe to make her more powerful or more feared."

"'No one knows whatever became of the devil child,'" Tanya read before looking up from her phone. "Guys, this is crazy. I don't believe Satan gave Marie Laveau his baby."

"Of course not," Ellen said. "But there was a child, and Cornelius won't be allowed to rest until we find its bones and consecrate them."

When it was nearly time for their appointment with the realtor, they headed back on foot to the house on Chartres.

Lionel was waiting for them on the sidewalk beneath his sign when the three arrived. He was taller than Tanya and nearly as thin, with receding black hair, brown eyes, and dark skin. He was at least ten years younger, if not more.

"Good afternoon," he said as they caught up with him. "How are you ladies today?"

"Hot and out of breath," Sue said. "Can we see the inside?"

"Yes, of course," Lionel said. "But let me tell you a little about the house first, if you don't mind."

"Please, go ahead," Ellen said.

"This Creole-style mansion was originally built in 1828. It was updated some in the 1950's. Central air and heat were added in the eighties. The original character was maintained, as you'll see in a moment. It's a four bedroom, three and a half bath, with a living room, dining room, kitchen, library, office, and courtyard. There's also a guesthouse at the back of the courtyard with two additional bedrooms, a bath, and a kitchen, making a combined total living space of 3700 square feet. The house was originally listed for 3.5 million, but due to a recent death on the premises…have you heard about it?"

The ladies nodded.

"The price was dramatically reduced just this morning to 1.5."

"That's less than half," Sue whispered to Ellen.

Then he added, "They think the guy was a random squatter who overdosed. It happens, you know?"

"Sure," Ellen said through a dry throat.

"It's too bad, too," the guy said. "Rotten luck for the owner."

"Not to mention the dead guy," Sue added.

"I can show you all but the top floor…it's considered a crime scene and has been blocked off by the police."

"For how long?" Sue asked.

The agent shrugged. "I have photos of the upstairs on my website." He took out his phone. "Let me pull them up for you."

"But we can still tour the bottom floor?" Tanya asked.

"Certainly." The agent put his phone away. "Let's do that first."

He took out a key and unlocked the front door and led them into the parlor. To the right of the kitchen, yellow caution tape blocked access to the upstairs.

As Lionel took them through the rooms on the street level, Ellen and her friends pretended to be viewing the house for the first time—something they already had some practice in.

"Two famous people from New Orleans are said to have lived here," Lionel said. "Have you heard of Delphine Lalaurie or Marie Laveau?"

The women gawked.

"Apparently, you have," the agent said with a laugh.

Tanya asked, "They lived *here?*"

The real estate agent nodded. "Marie Laveau is said to have lived here briefly as a midwife and nurse to a wealthy woman who died in childbirth. Delphine Lalaurie is said to have lived here until she died in 1858. You've heard about the fire at the Lalaurie Mansion in 1834?"

"Yes," Sue said.

"Some people believe Delphine Lalaurie fled to Paris and remained there until her death," the agent said. "But others say she moved back from Paris into this house in 1842 and remained here until her death in the late 1850's."

"Do you have proof that she lived here?" Ellen asked.

"No proof. Only legend." Lionel led them to the living room. "Would you like to see the guesthouse?"

"Yes, please," Tanya said.

The guesthouse, which had a small kitchen, living room, and bath on the main floor and two bedrooms upstairs, appeared to have been more recently renovated. When asked, the agent said that it had been updated in the nineties.

"The people who owned the house before the current owner had planned to renovate while living in the guesthouse, so they renovated it first and then ran out of funds. The bank foreclosed on the estate in 2001. That's how the current owner got this property. He told me he had planned to renovate and move here, but his business dealings led him and his family abroad, so they rarely make it out here anymore. In fact, no one has stayed in the house for at least fifteen years."

"We'd like to make an offer," Sue said. "Wouldn't we, ladies?"

"Yes," Tanya said.

"Let's offer asking price," Ellen said. "No contingencies. Full cash."

The agent's mouth widened into a huge grin. "Wonderful. I'll draw up the paperwork and contact the seller right away."

CHAPTER SEVEN

The Lower Ninth Ward

Ellen and her friends wouldn't be able to close on the Chartres mansion until after the police declared the second floor was no longer a crime scene. Since they didn't know how long this would take, and since they couldn't search for the diary of Delphine Lalaurie until then, they decided to hunt down Cornelius's mother, Maria Nunnery.

But first, they each needed to break the news of their intentions to acquire the house to their husbands, who hadn't been consulted an iota before the ladies had made their offer.

Sitting alone in the shade of the courtyard at the Inn on Ursulines, which was surprisingly not like a sauna, Ellen reminded herself that it was easier to ask for forgiveness than for cooperation on opportunities such as this one. With her fingers crossed and a knot in her stomach, she dialed Paul's number.

"Hi, Honey," she said, once he'd answered. "How are you?"

"Good. Just finished a record round of golf. Wish you were here to celebrate with me."

"Me, too, Honey. I miss you."

"Miss you, too. How's it going in Tulsa?"

Ellen hadn't realized she'd not yet told Paul about her emergency trip to New Orleans. "I'm glad you asked. Something extraordinary happened to Tanya, and it brought us to the French Quarter."

She went on to tell him about the ghost attachment, about what had happened at Lexi's church, and about the strange visit with Carrie French. She told him how Carrie had either been possessed by Marie Laveau or had been an illusion altogether. She told him about the woman who'd died at the hotel in Tulsa on the very same night of their visit with Carrie, about the naked man in the tub, and about the beloved python of the Voodoo high priestess, all who seemed to be victims of the most famous Voodoo queen in history.

"You're in too deep," Paul said. "Why risk your lives for people who are already dead?"

That wasn't the response she'd been hoping for. "Honey, but this ghost, Cornelius, he's just a boy. He needs peace. And there might be another child who needs peace, too."

"The devil child."

"Yes."

"And you're the one who has to give it to them?"

"Tanya could die if we do nothing, Paul. If we don't help Cornelius, he'll use her up until there's nothing left. Don't you see? We had no choice."

"Well, maybe I should fly out there, keep an eye on you."

As much as she'd love to see him, and as much fun as she thought they'd have together on Bourbon Street, she doubted it was a good idea. "Honey, there's more. Sue and Tanya and I put an offer on the house where Marie Laveua said we'd find Delphine Lalaurie's diary."

"You what?"

"We put in a full price, all cash offer just today. I would have called you first, but it was an opportunity we couldn't afford to miss…"

The call ended.

Had he hung up on her? Or had the connection just gone out on them? Or, was it possible that Marie Laveau had interfered? Ellen was afraid to call back. If Paul *hadn't* hung up on her, he would call her; and, if he *had*, well, there was no use in her calling him. He'd talk to her when he was ready.

Her eyes filled with tears. She wished he'd understood. She wished he'd felt the same sense of urgency in solving this mystery as she did.

Upstairs in the room, Tanya lay curled on one queen bed, and Sue lay stretched out in the middle of the other. Both were sound asleep. Ellen took her phone and lay down on Tanya's bed, where she searched for Maria Nunnery on Google.

The search produced results on Maria Monk's book about her frightening experiences in a nunnery, but nothing came up for a *Maria Nunnery*.

Undeterred, Ellen searched up the number for Houston Memorial Hospital. She called the patient information desk and, pretending to be a reporter writing an article about where Hurricane Katrina victims were today, asked if there was any contact information for the family of Cornelius Nunnery, who died there on September 20, 2005.

"That information is confidential," the woman on the phone said. "Even if we had it, I couldn't give it to you."

Tempted to go to sleep, Ellen closed her eyes after ending the call, wondering what to do next. Tears of frustration slipped from the corners of her eyes, wetting her ears. She wouldn't be able to fall asleep even if she wanted to, so fixated was she on solving the mystery that had endangered Tanya's life.

A sudden gasping snore from Sue jolted Ellen from her pondering, causing her to flinch. Sue mumbled, "Huh?" before drifting off to sleep. Tanya, briefly awakened by Ellen's sudden movement, rolled over and went back to sleep.

Ellen had another idea. She called the Voodoo Spiritual Temple and, as expected, the quiet woman who always sat behind the counter answered the phone. First, Ellen asked if she knew what Isabel's favorite flowers were, to which the quiet woman replied, "Lilies." Next, Ellen asked if the temple had any contact information for Maria Nunnery. Ellen explained that the spirit of Maria's son was attached to Tanya.

"One moment, while I check," the quiet woman said.

Ellen crossed her fingers as her heartrate picked up speed.

Then the quiet woman said, "I don't have anything for Maria Nunnery, but I have a phone number and address for Cecilia Nunnery. Do you want that?"

"Yes!" Ellen cried so loudly, that she woke up Sue and Tanya. "Please!"

An hour later, Ellen and her friends rode in a minivan cab to the Lower Ninth Ward, about fifteen minutes away. Since the phone number given to them by the quiet woman at the Voodoo Spiritual Temple had not been a working number, they had no idea what to expect. They'd called the realtor for a status update on the Chartres property, but he had no news yet. They'd also ordered lilies to be sent to Priestess Isabel. Now, they fidgeted in the second and third seats of the van as they gazed out on the magnificence that was the Mississippi River.

But the magnificence was soon overshadowed by the poor state of the roads and buildings as they crossed the bridge over the canal and entered the Lower Ninth Ward.

"Oh, my gosh," Ellen said through a dry throat. "I hadn't realized the area was still so far away from being completely rebuilt."

"Oh, yeah," the driver said. "Over there was where the barge hit."

"Barge?" Ellen asked.

"Don't you remember?" Tanya said. "During Hurricane Katrina? When the levees broke, and that Casino barge destroyed all those homes?"

Ellen nodded. "Yes. I remember now. Oh, wow."

"Some of those houses look new," Tanya said. "The ones with the solar panels on the roofs."

"That's Brad Pitt's Make It Right housing," Sue pointed out. "Right?" she asked the cabby.

"Right. Lot o' folks wouldn't have homes if it weren't for him," the driver said. "That entire area was wiped out. And look over there. You'll see a nice, fixed up house right next to one that's about to fall down. That's how it is for my parents. They live across the street from an abandoned house full of mold and rats. The neighborhood stinks like rotten milk. The people here don't even smell it anymore. I think it's killing them, slowly, you know what I mean?"

"That's terrible," Ellen said.

The driver turned left onto Flood Street.

"Well, who named this street?" Sue asked with a laugh.

They passed a construction site on the right and a half-built shotgun-style house on the left. There were a few nice-looking brick homes and two-story Creole town houses, but past these nicer homes were empty lots, one of them with a foundation and steps where a house used to be. Construction crews lined some of the streets where they were repairing the roads. But amid the improvements were piles of rubble, discarded tires, and abandoned houses that looked unsalvageable, especially one that had been taken over by vines and brush.

"What do those markings painted on some of the houses mean?" Ellen asked.

"That's from the rescue crews," the cabby said. "They drew an x and put the date on the top, a note about gas leaks or other damages on the right, the number of dead bodies on the bottom, and the rescue worker's initials on the left."

"September nineteenth?" Ellen read. "The rescue workers didn't get there until twenty days after the hurricane hit?"

"It was bad," the driver said. "See that one? It says 4DB? That means they found four dead bodies in that house."

Ellen shuddered. "It's been thirteen years. Why hasn't someone painted over them?"

"Some people think of them as a memorial to their lost loved ones," the driver explained. "Others just never came back—or if they did, they turned around and went back the other way."

"I wonder why," Tanya said.

"The businesses didn't want to move back if there weren't no people, and the people didn't want to move back if there weren't no stores and gas stations. The schools were closed. Hell, it took forever for my parents to get electricity. They lived with me for two years in a FEMA trailer parked on my property, on account as I had electricity in my area."

"Do you or your parents know of a Maria or Cecelia Nunnery?" Ellen asked.

"I went to school with Cecilia," he said. "I haven't seen her around since Katrina."

They turned left on Law and passed the high school—Cornelius's high school, Ellen thought to herself, where he had played in the band and had sung in a musical—before coming to a stop.

"This is it," the cabby said. "Do you want me to wait for you?"

A set of posts, on which a house had presumably stood before the hurricane ripped it apart, protruded from the ground like tombstones in knee-high grass in front of a worn-down shack. A message spray-painted on the front of the shack read: "Don't demolish."

To Sue and Tanya, Ellen said, "Maybe we can ask around the neighborhood."

"More walking?" Sue complained. "I'd just as soon go back and ask Cornelius with the Ouija Board."

"He might not be able to help us," Tanya said. "He may not know where his mother and sister are."

"Are you talking about Cornelius Nunnery?" the cabby asked.

"Yes," Sue said. "We're paranormal investigators, and we've made contact with him."

"For real?" the driver said. "That's amazing. Tell him his old pal, Hank Jones, says hi."

"You knew Cornelius?" Ellen asked.

"We played in the band in high school together. I had a crush on his sister. They was good folks. I just realized this was where their house used to be. I only ever went over one time."

"You don't know what happened to their mother?" Tanya asked.

"No." He continued to gaze at the remnants of what once was the Nunnery residence. "I can't believe their house is completely gone."

"What about that building behind the stilts?" Ellen asked.

"I think that was their storage shed."

"Wow," Tanya said. "How sad."

"Well, maybe some of the neighbors know something," Ellen said.

"You seriously want to go door to door?" Sue asked.

"Come on," Ellen said to Sue. "We won't stay long."

"You can sit under that shade tree and wait for us," Tanya offered Sue.

"Yeah, right. I'd never get back up again." Sue said with a laugh.

"You want to wait in the cab?" Ellen offered.

"And miss out on the adventure? No way!" Sue handed money to the driver.

"You don't want me to stay?" Hank asked.

"If you have a card, we'll call when we're ready," Sue said.

Hank handed Sue his card. Then she, Ellen, and Tanya climbed from the van and stood before the abandoned stilts as the cabby drove away.

"Where do we start?" Tanya asked.

"I know it's a longshot," Ellen said, "but why don't we knock on the door of the shed, just in case?"

Tanya and Sue waited on the street while Ellen went to the shed. She knocked on the ruined door and waited for several seconds. As expected, no answer came. She turned back to Sue and Tanya.

"Now what?" Sue asked with her hands on her hips.

"There's a church down the road," Ellen said. "Let's start there."

Pastor Ronny at the Baptist church knew Maria but hadn't seen her for many weeks. He said that she couldn't have gone far, because she occasionally walked by to check on her property before she disappeared again. Her daughter, Cecilia, had moved to Houston.

"Her husband was one of my parishioners; but, Maria's Catholic, so I never got to know her very well," the pastor said.

"Can you think of anyone in the neighborhood who might be in touch with her?" Sue asked.

"There's a teacher at Lawless High," Pastor Ronny said. "They was good friends before Katrina hit. There's a chance they stayed in touch. Beatrice Leland is one of my parishioners and the band director at the high school."

"Does she live around here?" Ellen asked.

"Sure does." He pointed to his right. "Corner house, same side of the street."

"Thank you, Pastor," Sue said.

Ellen and Sue followed Tanya down the road to the corner to a pretty, blue townhouse with a wooden front porch and a red compact car in the driveway. When they knocked on the door, a black woman about their age answered.

"How can I help you?" the woman asked.

"Are you Beatrice Leland?" Ellen asked.

"I am."

"Pastor Ronny told us that you were a friend of Maria Nunnery's," Ellen said.

"I am," Beatrice said again, sounding as though she were a witness in a court of law.

"We're looking for her," Sue explained.

"May I ask why?" Beatrice asked.

"It's kind of…complicated," Ellen said.

"Do you believe in ghosts?" Sue asked bluntly.

"Sue!" Ellen chastised. "You can't just ask a person that. It's personal."

"Did Cornelius send you?" Beatrice asked.

Ellen's mouth dropped open. "How did you know?"

"Another woman came looking for Maria about seven years ago," Beatrice said. "And then another about three years ago. They both said the same thing."

Ellen and her friends gawked at one another.

"Seriously?" Ellen asked.

Beatrice Leland nodded.

"If you could put us in touch with Maria, we'd be very grateful," Tanya said.

"I can do better than that," Beatrice said. "Let me get my purse, and I'll drive you to her."

CHAPTER EIGHT

Maria Nunnery

Beatrice Leland drove Ellen, Sue, and Tanya six blocks to a shotgun-style house with a FEMA trailer, about fourteen feet wide and fifty feet long, sitting in the driveway. Ellen recalled hearing that some of the FEMA trailers were believed to contain toxic levels of formaldehyde. After parking by the curb in front of the house, Beatrice led them to the trailer and knocked on the door.

A woman in her sixties, who looked of both Native American and African descent, with long, straight black hair and round, dark eyes, answered and smiled down at Beatrice, revealing a missing front tooth. "What's going on, girlfriend?"

"Hi, Maria. Cornelius sent these ladies to see you," Beatrice explained.

Maria's eyes widened. "Really, Bea? Again?"

"Seems so," the high school band director said.

Maria shook her head as her gaze turned to Ellen and her friends. "Let me guess. He wants you to find the Demon Baby of Bourbon Street."

Ellen gawked.

"How did you know?" Sue asked.

"Come on inside," Maria said. "Just excuse the mess, ladies. We need to talk."

Ellen followed Beatrice, Sue, and Tanya into the small and crowded trailer.

Once inside, they were met with an L-shaped sofa, the back of which partly cut off the access to the tiny galley-style kitchen. The kitchen had a sink and stove on one side and a small table and fridge on the other, and the little bit of counterspace, including the table, was covered with dishes, books, trophies, statues of saints, framed photos, and baskets piled high with who knew what.

"I don't have a lot of storage space," Maria said. "That's why it's such a mess. Believe it or not, this is what it looks like when it's *organized*."

"No worries," Tanya said. "It's fine."

Sue and Ellen took a seat on the sofa with Tanya squeezed between them. Beatrice sat on the side of the sofa that partly blocked the kitchen.

"Can I get anyone anything to drink?" Maria offered.

"Maybe some water, if you don't mind?" Tanya asked.

"I wouldn't recommend it," Beatrice said. "We don't think the water is safe yet."

"I brewed some tea," Maria said. "That's all I drink anymore. The way I figure it, boiling the water kills the germs."

"Actually, I'm fine," Tanya said, before giving Ellen a glance that said, "Yikes."

Maria sat on the couch beside Beatrice. "So how did Cornelius lead you here?"

Ellen told her about their experience with the Ouija Board and how she got their contact information from the Voodoo Spiritual Temple.

"Cecilia used to go there to see Priestess Isabel," Maria said.

Sue told about their encounter with Pastor Ronny, which had led them to Beatrice.

Maria nodded, seeming unsurprised by any of it. "It's true what Pastor Ronny said about my Cecilia living in Houston. She just finished law school and got a job there at a prestigious firm. It took her a long time to get through college, but she did it, bless her. And when she can afford it, she's going to help me rebuild my house."

"Cecilia has offered for Maria to come and live with her in Houston," Beatrice explained. "But Maria won't leave New Orleans."

"This has been the home of my family for over a century," Maria explained. "And I have a lot of memories here. I can't leave."

"Cecilia will come through for you," Beatrice said. "She'll build you that dreamhouse."

"I know she will," Maria said. "But I guess we're not here to talk about Cecilia and my dreamhouse. We're here to talk about my Cornelius and the curse put on him by Marie Laveau."

"Curse?" Ellen asked.

"She visits me in my dreams," Maria said. "She's my great, great, great aunt. She says that if I can't help her bring peace to the devil child by consecrating him to our family tomb, then she won't let my child find peace, either."

"Maria has tried," Beatrice explained. "I've helped her. We've snuck onto the grounds of Lalaurie Mansion more times than I care to admit, praying to Marie Laveau to guide us."

"And we get nothing," Maria said. "No guidance. I'd come to believe my dreams were just dreams. Then about six or seven years ago, a woman found me and said Cornelius had sent her. But she had no further guidance than what we already knew."

"And then about three years ago, another lady came," Beatrice said. "But we never found anything."

"Apparently, the information we need is in the diary of Delphine Lalaurie," Sue said.

Maria nodded. "Maire Laveau speaks of it in my dreams, but I can't figure out what she's trying to say. It's in an old house beneath the floor. That's all I know."

"It's supposed to be in a house on Chartres Street," Ellen added. "We're trying to buy the house, so we can look for it."

"Really?" Maria cried. "How do you know it's there?"

Ellen told her about the dead man in the tub and Marie Laveau's brief possession of Priestess Isabel.

"If we can find the diary," Tanya said, "maybe we can find the devil child, and Cornelius can find peace."

"I sure hope so," Maria said, wiping tears from the corners of her eyes. "That would be such a blessing."

"Do you have any idea why the baby is called a devil child?" Ellen asked Maria.

"Well," Maria began, "the way I heard it, from my mama, was that the infant was a harlequin baby, born with a genetic skin disease. It's very rare, but Marie Laveau had seen it before. I think one of her own babies may have been born with it."

"Do you know what happened to the other thirteen?" Sue asked.

"Gah, don't believe what you read online," Maria said with disdain. "My mama said Marie Laveau gave birth to nine babies—two with Paris, a free man of color from Haiti, and seven with Glapion, a wealthy white man from a prominent French family. I'm descended from him, and the Glapion tomb belongs to my family. The other children died of yellow fever. The reason legend says she had more babies is because she took care of orphans that no one wanted. Most of the time, those babies were afflicted with an incurable disease. She did what she could for them, in their last days of life."

Ellen lifted her brows at Sue, as if to say, "I told you so."

"I thought both of her consorts were free men of color," Ellen said.

"Gah!" Maria said again. "Glapion was the descendent of French aristocracy. Everyone seems to get that mixed up with her father, Charles Laveau. Charles was a free man of color—not a wealthy plantation owner, like so many articles say."

"Wow," Tanya said. "The articles do seem to mix everything up."

"Legend has it that the devil child lived for some time," Sue said. "Long enough for Marie and Delphine to share in the responsibility of caring for it. Is that part true?"

Maria nodded. "My mama believed the child lived to be four or five years old, but no one knows for certain. There weren't no records kept. My mama said some people say the devil child was called Richie, after one of Marie Laveau's slaves. But others say he was called Charles, after Marie Laveau's father."

"Marie Laveau had slaves?" Ellen asked.

"A lot of successful free people of color owned them," Maria said. "Marie's biological father, Charles Laveau, had them, too."

"And you have no idea where the child is buried?" Sue asked.

"If I did, don't you think I'd have done something by now?"

"Of course," Sue mumbled. "I'm sorry."

"It's been very hard on Maria knowing that Cornelius hasn't found peace," Beatrice said.

Maria wiped the tears from her face and sniffled.

Ellen cleared her throat, trying not to cry. "He had a lovely obituary. He played the saxophone in the school band, right?"

"He was always first chair," Beatrice said. "So talented."

"And he could sing, too," Maria added as more tears fell to her cheeks. "I think he would have made it big one day."

"Is it still hard to talk about?" Sue asked.

Maria nodded. "Even after all this time. Maybe if the condition of the neighborhood didn't remind me of it every single day, it would be easier to move on."

"I'm so sorry," Ellen said.

"That Monday when the levee broke, we were all four together," Maria said. "We didn't have the money to evacuate, and we thought we could ride it out. We'd been through plenty of hurricanes and storms before. Our house was built on stilts, so we thought we were safe."

Ellen bit her lip, unable to imagine the pain Maria felt as she recounted her story.

"When the water started coming in and flooding the house, we ran upstairs into my bedroom. The kids and I laid down together on the bed and prayed while my husband stood watch near the window. The house felt like it was moving, like a rocking boat. The wind and the rain were so loud. When the water crept up to the second floor, I became truly scared for our lives. I remember my husband looking at me in a way that made me believe he thought it was the end for us.

"He kissed each of us on the head and told us he loved us and needed us to be brave. It wasn't seconds later that the house split wide open, and part of the roof landed on Jamar and took him under with it. I never saw him again."

"Oh, my Gawd," Sue whispered.

Maria fought hard to speak through her tears. "I held onto my children for dear life. We were treading water, trying not to get hit by the walls and furniture falling in on us. The water carried us from the house, and I remember I kept grabbing at trees and other houses with my legs, trying to find anything that would keep us from getting carried away. Because, you see, there were all kinds of things blowing around us in the water, and I was afraid we'd be killed if we didn't climb onto something.

"I thanked God when I gripped a tree with my legs, and, between the three of us, we were able to pull ourselves up into the branches and out of the water. But that's when I saw that Cornelius was bleeding from a gash beneath his ribs. He was bleeding bad."

Maria covered her face and cried for a moment as Beatrice patted her friend's back.

"You don't have to finish," Beatrice said after a minute.

"I do," Maria said. "People need to know."

Beatrice got up and found a paper towel in the kitchen and brought it over to Maria, who wiped her eyes and blew her nose before continuing. "Cornelius was only sixteen years old. Beatrice was seventeen. We were all three still in shock over seeing Jamar so brutally taken from us. And we saw dead bodies float past. I half expected one of them to be Jamar."

"How horrible," Tanya muttered.

"We were up in that tree for five days without food or fresh water," Maria said. "The sun was shining, yet the water kept on rising. A couple of helicopters flew by overhead, but they either didn't see us, or they didn't think we were worth saving. We ate leaves that we picked from the treetops. We took turns sleeping, because I was terrified we'd float away or miss seeing a boat. Finally, on the sixth day, a rescue boat got to us."

"Five days in a tree," Ellen repeated. "Geez."

"From the stories I heard about what happened at the Superdome, we were lucky," Maria added. "We were eventually taken there and put on one of the last busses out to Houston. Can you imagine what it must've been like for the 30,000 people in that Superdome, with hardly any food and water and very little medical aid or supervision? Sometimes I think we were better off in that damned tree."

"Maybe you were," Sue said.

"Cornelius was taken to Memorial, and even though he was so weak and so pale by the time they got to us, I never stopped believing he would make it," Maria said. "It was a shock when I lost him. I was crushed."

"I'm so sorry," Ellen said again.

"Don't be," Maria said. "Because you're here to help my boy, ain't that right?"

Ellen glanced at friends. "That's right. We are."

Maria went on to tell Ellen, Sue, and Tanya about the days after Cornelius's death, about the vague hope that Jamar might be alive, about having to stay in a hotel in Houston with Cecilia with nothing to live on and in such despair that some days she thought they would just go to sleep and never wake up. Jamar had been a brick layer, and Maria had been a substitute teacher, but they had nothing in savings.

"We were living paycheck to paycheck, like most of our neighbors," Maria said.

"Ain't that right, sister," Beatrice said. "And when the city decided to halt reconstruction until the people came back, well, that was a death sentence for the lower ninth."

"What do you mean?" Sue asked.

"People don't want to go back to a place that's got no electricity," Maria said.

"It was like a catch twenty-two," Beatrice explained. "Having no electricity kept the people away, and when the people stayed away, the city put its limited resources elsewhere."

"It felt like the government wanted to keep the poor and the black people out," Maria added.

Maria went on to say that it took nearly a year for them to get back to their property, and another year to go through the debris, salvage what they could, and organize it in the old shed that had somehow held up when their house had not.

Maria said that she checked on the property every so often to make sure her shed was still there. Anything small enough to take with her, she did—some of the kids' trophies from school, statues of her favorite saints, and a few framed family photos, all of which she dug out from the mud and debris. But larger things, like Cornelius's old bicycle, Jamar's lawnmower, her grandmother's rocking chair, and a few other things, she stored in the shed.

"They're all I have left," she explained. "I can't let them go. I refuse to sell my lot. It would be like selling part of my soul."

"I can understand," Ellen said.

"And when we did come back, we found the schools were closed," Maria said. "When they finally opened the schools, they fired most of the teachers and staff and hired new people—outsiders."

"I was lucky," Beatrice said. "I was one of the few to get hired back."

"Does that make any sense to you?" Maria asked Ellen and her friends. "To take jobs away from a community that was already devastated?"

"No, it doesn't," Tanya said.

"That's how I ended up here, in this FEMA trailer, all these years," Maria said. "Even getting on as a sub is hard. I take what I can get, but it's not enough. I don't have a car, so I'm limited in where I can go for work. If it weren't for my daughter helping me, I don't know what I'd do."

"Cecilia is a good girl," Beatrice said.

Ellen sucked in her lips, fighting tears. When she could, she said, "My friends and I are going to do everything we can to help your son find peace. As soon as we can get the house on Chartres, we will search every square inch for that diary."

"We promise," Sue added.

Tanya nodded. "You have our word."

Then Tanya did something strange. She stood up, leaned over Maria Nunnery, put her arms around her neck, and wept.

"Cornelius?" Maria asked through quivering lips.

Tanya stood upright and wiped her eyes. "What was I saying?"

CHAPTER NINE

The New Orleans Profiteer

The cab met Ellen, Sue, and Tanya in front of the FEMA trailer. Hank climbed out to give Maria and Beatrice a hug. He told Maria that he'd known Cornelius, and he asked about Cecilia. Maria's face brightened as she talked about the days when her children were still in high school, before Katrina. Beatrice asked how Hank and his family were doing, and he said fine. Then they said their goodbyes, and Ellen and her friends followed Hank to the van.

During the ride back to the Inn on Ursulines, Ellen and her friends seemed to be thinking the same ideas. Some of the most devasted areas of New Orleans still needed help recovering from Katrina thirteen years later.

"What can we do?" Ellen wondered out loud.

"Maybe we could donate to Brad Pitt's Make It Right foundation," Tanya suggested.

"That's a good idea," Sue agreed.

They hadn't been in their hotel room long when Sue received a call from Lionel, the realtor. She put him on speaker, so he could deliver the devastating news that the seller had rejected their offer.

"Did he say why?" Sue asked.

"We received a similar offer as I was drawing up your paperwork," Lionel said.

"What?" Ellen cried. "Oh, no."

"That can't be," Tanya said.

"It's not over yet, ladies. The seller rejected *both* offers," Lionel said.

"What a relief," Ellen said with a sigh.

"He's asked that you put your best and final offer forward by the end of the day today. Then tomorrow, he will make a decision."

"Can you tell us anything about the competition?" Sue asked.

Lionel was silent for a few moments before they heard him clear his throat and say, "Are you ladies available to meet with me in person sometime this evening?"

"We have reservations at Antoine's," Sue said.

"We do?" Ellen wrinkled her brow. She would have liked to have been consulted.

"Would you like to join us?" Sue asked, ignoring Ellen.

"That's my favorite restaurant," Lionel said with a laugh. "I'd love to."

"Great," Sue said. "I'll call and add one more to our reservation. We'll meet you there at seven."

White linens and fine china dressed each table at Antoine's. The patrons were also nicely dressed. There were no t-shirts or flip-flops or blue jeans. It was all elegance and glamor.

Ellen was a little worried when the foul odor followed them inside. She'd thought it was coming from the street, but she now realized it was Tanya.

Lionel met them at the front counter before they were taken to a table in the back of the restaurant.

Despite being a millionaire for nearly six months, Ellen gawked at the high-priced menu. She would always be a penny-pincher at heart, she supposed, and opted to have the gumbo.

Tanya seemed to be thinking similarly, as she ordered the same. Sue and Lionel, however, decided to share the Chateaubriand for two—the most expensive thing on the menu.

As they waited for their food to arrive, they shared a bottle of expensive wine, which took the edge off the competing odors in the room. Ellen was anxious to hear why Lionel wanted to meet with them in person, so, after taking another sip of the wine, she asked, "So, why did you want to meet with us?"

"There's an unscrupulous profiteer who's been buying up New Orleans," Lionel began.

"Unscrupulous? How?" Sue asked.

"He isn't breaking any laws, per se," Lionel said, "but he and his real estate agent are known for taking advantage of natural disasters and other calamities by buying property out from under the victimized all over the country."

"How can they do that?" Tanya asked.

"It's easy, really," Lionel said. "Think about it. The people who are most vulnerable to a natural disaster aren't the wealthy, right? The wealthy usually have well-built homes in safe areas and have good insurance. Even if their houses are wiped out, their property taxes are high enough for them to secure decent loans for rebuilding. That's not true for the poorer homeowners, whose houses are usually substandard in riskier areas. When their homes are wiped out, they can't get a loan to cover the cost of rebuilding, because the area they live in doesn't appraise for much. It would be easy for a developer to swoop in with an offer below market value, because the poor homeowner with no home and no resources to rebuild has no other viable option."

"But why would a developer want to buy land that doesn't appraise for much?" Ellen asked.

"If that developer improves the property with better drainage, better sewage, better amenities...if that developer builds several nice homes...well, suddenly the land becomes worth a lot more, you see? Especially if he plans to build short-term rentals for tourists. That's where the big money is in New Orleans."

"Is that what he wants to do with the house on Chartres Street?" Tanya asked.

"I'd bet my money on it," Lionel said. "There's a local housing commission that's been trying to get an ordinance passed for over four years to limit the number of short-term rental houses in the city."

"But isn't tourism the biggest industry in New Orleans?" Sue asked. "I would think the city would want the rental properties."

"Many do," Lionel said. "That's why the ordinance hasn't passed. But the short-term rental properties are making it hard for the people who live here. They shoot up our property taxes, making it too expensive for locals to live in their own city. And the people who own the rentals don't really live here or contribute to the community in any way. They don't care about the impact they have on the neighborhoods."

"I would think you would personally benefit," Sue said to Lionel. "If property values go up, so does your commission."

"Except that I live here, too," Lionel said. "It's a wash for me financially, but the sense of community is lost, and that's what I don't like. The character of New Orleans is at stake."

Their food arrived, and they were quiet for a few minutes as they dived into their entrees.

"This gumbo is amazing," Ellen said.

"Mmm-hmm," Tanya agreed.

"How's your steak?" Ellen asked Sue.

"Delicious, don't you think, Lionel?"

"Outstanding," he said.

After a few minutes of silence, save for the noises of smacking lips as they ate, Ellen turned to Lionel. "So, you're obviously rooting for us, Lionel. What do you recommend we do?"

"Keep in mind that I represent the seller," the agent said. "And it would be in my best interest to sell you the property at the highest possible price."

"We understand," Sue said. "What are you getting at?"

"I just want you to know that even if I were a disinterested party…"

"Which you aren't," Ellen said.

"Which I'm not," Lionel agreed. "I would still advise you the very same. Offer fair market value. The house was overpriced at 3.5. It's severely underpriced at 1.5, which is what drew the attention of this unscrupulous fellow. I doubt he will offer market value, because he's looking for a deal, not just an investment."

"What would you say is fair market value?" Sue asked.

"I'd say 2.7," Lionel said. "And I'd bet all my money that the other offer will be between two and 2.5."

"That's over a million more than our original offer," Tanya said.

"I think we should take Lionel's advice," Sue said before taking another bite of her steak.

Ellen sipped her wine. "We don't have much of a choice. Don't you agree, Tanya?"

"I feel like this is my fault. That's a lot of money."

"It's definitely not your fault," Ellen said.

"How could it be?" Lionel asked.

"It's a long story," Sue explained. "But just be assured that we'll do it. Our final offer is 2.7, cash, no contingencies."

Lionel grinned and lifted his wine glass. "Cheers, ladies."

They clinked their glasses together, but it wouldn't feel like a true victory to Ellen until the closing papers were signed.

As they left Antoine's, Ellen asked Lionel if they could view the house on Chartres again that evening. He agreed and even offered to drive them—perhaps because they had paid for his expensive meal and the bottle of wine.

Ellen wondered if the others were feeling as toasty as she was from the wine, as they parked near the corner and then walked the rest of the way to the Creole-style mansion.

When they neared the door, they found it ajar.

"What the hell?" Lionel murmured as he cautiously entered the front room and flipped on the light.

"Did you lock up after we left today?" Sue whispered to the agent.

He nodded and quickly put his fingers to his lips. The sound of a thud carried from one of the other rooms—perhaps the library.

The thud came again.

"What is that?" Tanya whispered.

"I'll call 9-1-1," Sue whispered, taking out her phone. "Great. My phone's dead."

"Mine is, too," Tanya whispered.

"I still have a charge," Ellen said, fingering the gris-gris bag around her neck. Maybe the thud was coming from something supernatural.

The agent shook his head and lifted his hand. "Wait by the door."

Ellen picked up a loose brick from the fireplace hearth. "I'm going with you."

Sue and Tanya waited by the door as Ellen followed Lionel through the front room toward the library.

Light poured into the hallway as another thud echoed through the house. Lionel peered inside and stopped short.

"Curtis, what the hell are you doing?" Lionel asked.

"Hello, Lionel."

Ellen followed Lionel into the room. "You know each other?"

"This is Curtis James," Lionel said. "He's the agent representing the other interested buyer."

He was shorter and thinner than Lionel and completely bald. Calculating blue eyes narrowed at Ellen through black-rimmed spectacles before glancing at her friends, who had hurried in to join them.

"I see," Ellen said, noticing the books he'd been dropping onto the floor. "I hope you weren't planning on removing those."

"Of course not," Curtis said, taking offense. "I'm merely assessing their value before I call Lionel with our final offer."

"Do you think they're worth anything?" Sue asked.

"Probably not," Curtis said as he dropped another with a thud.

Tanya picked up one of the books and turned it over. "I would imagine they are. Some of these are over two centuries old."

"Do the books come with the house?" Ellen asked Lionel.

"Everything stays," Lionel said. "The furniture, the drapes, the fixtures, and the books."

Curtis dropped another book onto the floor with a thud.

"Why are you doing that?" Ellen said without hiding her frustration.

"They're full of dust," Curtis explained. "I'm just bouncing the dust out before I examine them, so I don't die of an asthma attack when I open them." He laughed.

"I think you ought to treat them more carefully," Sue said. "After all, they aren't your client's property, yet."

"*Yet* being the operative word," Curtis sang merrily before dropping another book.

Sue put her hand on her hip, warrior ready. "Sir, if you don't stop, I'm afraid I'm going to have to call the police."

"Fine," Curtis said. He gathered up the books he'd dropped. "Don't you folks have someplace to be?"

"We'll talk later," Lionel said as he left the room.

Ellen followed, glancing back at Curtis with disdain. She was afraid to leave the building lest he carry some of the rare books out in the dark of night.

Back in the parlor, Sue asked, "Do you think we could have a quick look at the upstairs if we promise not to disturb anything?"

Lionel shrugged. "I'm not allowed to show it to you, but what you do on your own is your business."

Ellen smiled at her friends, returned the loose brick to the hearth, and followed Sue past the crime scene tape and up the stairs, with Tanya on her heels.

They glanced into the other rooms—two unremarkable bedrooms and a bath—before they returned to the scene of the "crime," where the body had been found.

Ellen was shocked to see that some of the floorboards beneath the empty tub and been pulled from the subfloor, exposing rotten plywood.

"Someone else is looking for the diary," Sue cried.

"Oh, no," Tanya said. "Do you think they found it?"

"Who else would have known that it was hidden here?" Ellen wondered aloud. "Priestess Isabel?"

"She wouldn't!" Sue said angrily. "Would she?"

Tanya covered her heart with her hand. "I think I'm going to be sick."

"Are you okay?" Ellen asked.

"I think so. I just need to sit down."

Sue wagged a finger. "Unless Marie Laveau has spoken to someone else about it, Isabel is the only person I can think of, but what would her motive be? Revenge on Marie Laveau for killing the snake?"

"Maybe she wants to find the devil child first," Tanya offered.

Ellen kicked around a few of the boards, afraid to get her fingerprints on anything. "We don't even know if the diary was found."

"I think we should pay the priestess a visit," Sue said.

Before heading downstairs to rejoin Lionel, Ellen and her friends heard voices down below—more than just those of the two real estate agents.

"I wonder what's going on?" Sue mumbled as she gripped the railing and made her way down, with Ellen and Tanya following.

When they reached the parlor, they found two police officers in uniform questioning Lionel and Curtis, who were explaining their presence.

One of the officers—a heavy-set black man with a wiry beard—noticed the three friends as they neared the landing and asked, "You do know that you just contaminated a crime scene, don't you?"

"It was contaminated way before we got here," Sue said. "Someone vandalized one of the bathrooms."

The other police officer—a short black woman with a single French braid that fell to her waistline—said, "We need to close up the house and bring you all down to the station for questioning."

CHAPTER TEN

Interrogations

Ellen sat alone at a table in an interrogation room at the police station for half an hour before the female officer with the long braid entered and sat across from her. The officer opened a manila folder and pulled out a photograph of the man Ellen had seen in the bathtub at the Chartres house while he was still alive.

"Have you ever seen this man before?" the officer asked.

Ellen wanted to lie. She wondered if Sue and Tanya had lied. She didn't want to get them into trouble if they had. She wanted to lie, but she couldn't. It just wasn't in her. "Yes."

"Under what circumstances?"

Ellen couldn't hide her trembling. "Should I have a lawyer present?"

"That's up to you. You haven't been charged with anything. You aren't under arrest. We're just gathering information right now. But if you have something to hide…"

"I do, but I won't."

"I'm listening."

"Two days ago, my friends and I went into the house…"

"The house on Chartres Street? Where we found you tonight?"

Ellen nodded.

"Were you with a real estate agent?"

"No. The back door was unlocked. We called out, in case people still lived there, and, when no one answered, we went inside to look around."

"You trespassed on private property?"

"Yes." Ellen felt blood rush to her cheeks. "When we were looking around upstairs, we saw a man naked as a jay bird in the bathtub. We thought he was dead, but he wasn't. He talked to us."

"What did he say?"

"He asked if we were the cops. I shook my head. Then he asked if Marie Laveau had sent us. I shook my head again."

"And then what happened?"

"We left. And he was alive when we left."

"Did he seem drunk or high on drugs? Could you smell liquor or drugs of any kind in the vicinity?"

"He seemed sleepy," Ellen said. "He smelled of body odor. I can't recall if I smelled alcohol or anything else."

"Do you know of anyone who might want to do harm to this man?"

"I'd never seen him before. I knew nothing about him. I don't know of anyone that would want to harm him, except…" Ellen dropped off, not wanting to mention that a dead Voodoo queen could be responsible.

"Except who?"

"You're going to think I'm crazy."

"I'll be the judge of that. Just answer the question, please."

"Marie Laveau."

"The Voodoo queen who died in the late eighteen-hundreds?"

"Like I said, it sounds crazy. My friends and I are paranormal investigators, and after hearing what happened to the man, considering that he'd asked us if Marie Laveau had sent us, we came to suspect that maybe she used his death to invoke the energy she needed to communicate with us."

"You believe that's possible?"

If Ellen had been asked the question two years ago, she would have laughed and had said it was a ridiculous notion, but now she was dead serious when she said, "Yes."

"And why would the Voodoo queen want to communicate with you?"

"She wants us to find her devil child," Ellen admitted. "To consecrate his bones to her tomb."

"You just lost me right there," the officer said with a laugh. "Now you've gone too far."

Ellen wanted to explain that the child wasn't of the devil. She wanted to say that "the devil child" was just a name given to an innocent baby that had been born with a serious condition. But she didn't have the chance. The officer stood and said, "Come with me."

She led Ellen to another interrogation room where Sue and Tanya were already sitting across the table from the other officer—the one with the wiry beard.

"Have a seat, Mrs. Mohr." The officer with the beard motioned to a chair next to Sue. "I'd like to get your opinion on something, if you don't mind."

Wondering if the real estate agents had already been released, Ellen took her seat. "I don't understand."

"The owners of the house on Chartres installed surveillance cameras throughout the property," the female officer said. "Including one in the bathroom, where the victim died."

"Did you see what happened?" Ellen asked.

"Not long after you and Mrs. Graham and Mrs. Sanchez left the premises, the victim passed away," the officer with the wiry beard explained. "The surveillance doesn't show how, but an autopsy may. We're waiting on the report."

So, the police had known that she and her friends had seen the victim before his death. Ellen was glad she hadn't lied—not that she was capable of it. She wondered if Sue and Tanya had also been truthful, or if they'd only admitted to being there after the officers told them about the cameras.

"I don't understand how my opinion can be helpful to you," Ellen said to the officers. "I've told you all that I know."

"Once we found the cameras, our tech guy fed them to our monitors," the female officer explained. "We want to show you some recent surveillance to see what you make of it."

"The sooner you stop asking questions, Ellen," Sue mumbled, "the sooner we can get started."

"Sorry." Ellen felt her face grow hot.

Sue patted her leg, to let her know she was only teasing her.

The officer played back the footage on the television that was mounted in the corner of the room, near the ceiling. Ellen covered her mouth in shock when she saw the quiet woman from the Voodoo Spiritual Temple enter the bathroom with a hammer, which she used to pry up the floorboards beneath and around the bathtub. After half an hour, the sound of footsteps from the floor below alerted the woman. She stood up with her hammer and fled the scene.

"Cameras located in other areas on the property reveal that the trespasser eventually left through the courtyard," the officer with the wiry beard said as he turned off the television. "Do you ladies have any idea who this person is and what she was doing there at the scene of the crime?"

Ellen glanced at Sue and Tanya, relieved to learn that the diary hadn't been taken; however, she was also alarmed. Had Priestess Isabel sent the would-be thief, or had the young woman acted of her own accord?

"She works at the Voodoo Spiritual Temple," Sue said.

"We don't know her name," Tanya added. "But she works for Priestess Isabel."

"And why was she there?" the female officer asked.

Ellen fidgeted in her chair, wishing she could be the kind of person who could lie—or, at the very least, who could withhold the truth. "She may have been searching for the diary of Delphine Lalaurie."

A few minutes after they'd walked out of the police station on Royal St. to meet their cabby, Hank, Ellen received a call from Lionel. She put him on speaker as they climbed into the second and third seats of the van.

"The seller is still considering both offers but wanted me to ask each potential buyer a question before he makes his decision."

"Okay," Ellen said into the phone. "Go ahead."

"What are your intentions for the property?" he asked. "Will it be a vacation home? A rental property? Both? Or do you plan to renovate and resell?"

"We haven't had a chance to discuss it yet," Sue said, "but after what you told us about the locals getting squeezed out and the city losing its character, I was going to propose that we turn the mansion into three condos for long-term rental only. We could also hire someone locally to manage the condos for us, and we could house that manager in the guesthouse. This would also provide someone local with a job, in addition to providing long-term housing to three local families."

Ellen lifted her brows. "You've put a lot of thought into this, Sue. I think that's a sweet idea."

"I agree," Tanya said. "But how will the seller feel about it, Lionel? Do you think he's looking for a different answer?"

"He's here on conference call with us," Lionel said. "I'll let him answer for himself."

"Hello, ladies," the voice of an older gentleman sounded through the phone.

"Hello," they all three said at once, as Hank pulled up in front of the Inn at Ursulines.

"I'm pleased to hear of your intentions," the older man said, "and am also pleased to accept your offer."

Ellen covered her mouth to stifle her squeal of joy. "Thank you!"

"Great news!" Sue said.

Tanya smiled with relief and looked like she was about to faint.

Lionel said he would call soon with a date and time for closing and wished them a goodnight.

After they hung up, they paid and thanked Hank, and then climbed out of the cab into the dark night.

"Thank goodness!" Ellen cried as they walked toward the inn. "I can't recall ever feeling so relieved."

"Tanya? Are you okay?" Sue asked her.

Before Tanya could reply, she collapsed and would have fallen face-first on the sidewalk if Ellen and Sue hadn't broken her fall.

CHAPTER ELEVEN

The Search

Three weeks after their offer was accepted by the owner of the Chartres mansion, Ellen, Tanya, and Sue returned to New Orleans from San Antonio to sign the closing papers and to accept the keys.

While in San Antonio, Tanya had received medical care from her regular doctor and was now feeling much improved. Her health problems had distracted her husband, Dave, from the frustration felt by Sue and Ellen's husbands, Tom and Paul, over the investment of millions of dollars on what appeared to them to be an impulsive whim.

It was a miserable three weeks at home with Paul in San Antonio, so Ellen was glad to get away in mid-September from the stone-cold stares and awkward silence to the vibrant French Quarter to begin the search for Delphine Lalaurie's diary.

They returned to the Inn on Ursulines, this time sharing connecting rooms so each had her own bed. But their stay would be short, because they planned to move into the guesthouse as soon as possible.

And that, of course, meant shopping.

But before they could enjoy shopping for new beds and pretty furniture, drapes, and linens, they had to finish what the quiet woman from the Voodoo Spiritual Temple had begun and pry up every last floorboard beneath the bathtub where the dead man had been found.

It had been a relief when the autopsy had confirmed the cause of death to be an overdose and the case had been closed. The quiet woman from the temple had been charged a five-hundred-dollar fine for breaking and entering and vandalism. Ellen, Tanya, and Sue were anxious to learn if she still worked at the temple or if the scandal had lost her the job.

They met with Lionel and the title company representative on Tuesday morning to complete the paperwork, hand over a cashier's check for 2.7 million, another for title, license, and fees, and receive the keys. After a delicious celebratory lunch of shrimp po-boys and fries, they drove to the house on Chartres.

Carrying the shiny, new crowbars they'd recently purchased at a local hardware store, Ellen followed Sue and Tanya through the courtyard of their new house. One thing they'd learned as new homeowners in the French Quarter was that the side of the house that faced the street was usually considered the back, and the side facing the courtyard was the front. This explained why so many of the houses looked plain along the sidewalk, and why garbage could often be seen in cans by the doors. Most people drove their vehicles into a bay area that led into the courtyard. Sue had parked their rental in the bay attached to the mansion. Ellen had been relieved to see that there was room for two more vehicles. This meant their three future renters would have parking spaces, but the manager, who would stay in the guesthouse, would have to park on the street.

Ellen had forgotten how lovely the courtyard was. Thanks to the company the previous owners had hired to maintain it, it was lush and beautifully manicured. She couldn't wait to fill the fountain with water and listen to its rustling flow while sitting beneath the canopy of vines and palms on a cool evening.

Sue led them into the living room of the main house and flipped on the lights. "Can you believe it's finally ours?"

"I'm glad the previous owner had the house professionally cleaned," Tanya said. "What a difference."

"Now if only your ghost will continue to behave himself and not stink up the place."

Tanya blushed.

"She's teasing you," Ellen said with a laugh. "Just think: It's going to be so much fun fixing this place up. I can't wait to get started. If only we had the Property Brothers here to help us."

Tanya chuckled. "Yeah, but first things first."

"Of course." Sue led them to the stairs.

"I can't believe no one came to remove this." Ellen pulled at the crime scene tape and rolled it into a ball before following the others upstairs.

Tanya wasted no time getting on her hands and knees near the tub and pulling up boards. Ellen and Sue quickly joined her. The boards that had been previously removed had been neatly stacked in one corner of the room. Ellen was glad because she'd been hoping to reuse them.

Fortunately, the previous owner had kept the electricity and utilities on during the fifteen years that he'd never visited, and central air conditioning had been added in the eighties. Otherwise, the three friends might have fainted from heat exhaustion as they crouched on the floor, putting the crowbars to good use. However, there was still no sign of a diary.

After fifteen minutes, Sue said, "Why don't you two keep searching while I take the rental and get us some refreshments?"

Ellen, who'd been surprised to get even fifteen minutes of hard labor from Sue, laughed and said, "Refreshments sound good. Why don't you stock up the fridge and pantry in the guesthouse?"

"Oh, I was just going to swing by the bakery for cupcakes and iced tea," Sue said. "Why don't we do the major shopping *together*?"

Tanya gave Ellen a knowing glance before saying, "Okay, missy. But then you have to help here. You can't just stand there and supervise."

Sue scoffed. "I know that. What kind of cupcakes do you like?"

Sue took their order and left. Ellen and Tanya kept at it. But even after prying up every floorboard in the bathroom, they came up empty.

"What now?" Tanya asked.

"I'm at a loss," Ellen admitted. "But those boards are still in good condition, so let's not throw them out. I think all of the floors can be refinished, don't you?"

"I haven't given it much thought, to be honest."

Ellen felt guilty for thinking beyond finding the diary. Naturally, her friend, whose life was in jeopardy, hadn't thought about refinishing the floors. "I'm sorry. That was insensitive of me."

"You don't have to apologize. I appreciate all you and Sue are doing to help me."

When Sue returned, they took a break in the courtyard. It was hot, but at least there were places to sit—the brick pavers that lined the raised gardens, like those at the Voodoo Spiritual Temple.

"If the diary isn't under the tub, why did Marie Laveau say it was?" Tanya wondered out loud before taking a bite of her cupcake.

Ellen took a sip of her tea. "Do you think it could have been an act?"

"You think her snake's still alive?" Sue asked. "Because if her snake died, I doubt it was an act."

"Unless the death of the snake was Karma," Ellen said.

"Why *would* she, though?" Sue licked icing from her finger.

Ellen shrugged. "Maybe to seem to be more powerful than she is?"

"But she didn't know about the dead man in the bathtub, did she?" Tanya asked.

"Maybe she heard it on the news," Ellen said.

"She kept saying she was just an old woman who paid her bills," Sue pointed out. "She doesn't strike me as the kind of person who would create a ruse to seem more powerful."

"Why don't we pay her a visit?" Tanya suggested. "We can find out if that quiet woman—what was her name?"

"Julie, I think," Sue said.

"We can find out if Julie still works there and whether she was sent by Isabel or was working on her own," Tanya said.

"I doubt Isabel would admit to it, if she was in on it." Ellen finished off her cupcake, wishing it had lasted longer.

"We need to furnish the guesthouse," Sue said, "so we have a comfortable place to rest while we're working on this house."

"And it would be nice to save in hotel costs," Tanya said. "I hate throwing money away."

"Speaking of which," Sue began, "the longer we go without renting this place out, the more money we lose. We need to get the architect started on some plans as soon as possible."

Ellen agreed, so it was decided that they would fit out the guesthouse with furniture and groceries and meet with the architect before seeking an interview with Priestess Isabel.

That night, they gathered in Ellen and Tanya's hotel room at the Inn on Ursulines after dinner to discuss their plans, but before they talked about furniture and linens, Sue wanted to read them more information she'd found about Delphine Lalaurie.

"Listen to this," Sue said. "'Madame Delphine Lalaurie was born Marie Delphine McCarty in 1787 and was thrice widowed, though the cause of death of her late husbands was never documented, nor were their bodies ever found. Many believe Delphine Lalaurie to have been a notorious serial killer who married wealthy and killed her husbands for their money while tormenting her many slaves as she lived a lavish lifestyle in the public eye. Before the 1834 fire that destroyed most of her home on Royal Street, Delphine was viewed as a high-society lady who threw luxurious parties and was loved and envied by other Creole aristocrats. But her private life was sadistic, twisted, brutal, and perverse.'"

"Oh my God," Tanya said.

Sue looked up. "It gets worse. Listen to this: 'Because her last husband, Dr. Louis Lalaurie, was rarely at home, most people believe that she was solely responsible for the mistreatment of the slaves, which came to light that fateful day of April 10, 1834. Although she showed kindness to them in the public eye, even requesting that two of her slaves be freed when they reached middle age, behind closed doors, she tortured them for her own pleasure. One slave girl not twelve years old jumped from the second-floor balcony to her death to escape Delphine's cruelty. It's also believed that the old cook, Rachel, chained to the stove so she couldn't flee, was the one responsible for starting the fire that finally revealed Delphine's wicked secrets.'"

"This is making me sick to my stomach," Ellen said, fingering the gris-gris bag she still wore around her neck. "I'm not sure I believe what the priestess said about evil being a matter of perspective. This woman sounds like pure evil."

"Maybe she was insane," Sue said.

Ellen shook her head, "If she were, wouldn't people have noticed before 1834? By then, she would have been in her late forties."

"People can be good at wearing masks in public," Sue said.

"Does it say anything more?" Tanya asked.

"I haven't even read the worst of it yet," Sue said. "Listen to this: 'Perhaps a morbid curiosity drove Delphine to experiment on her slaves. The day of the fire, they were found in the garret chained to the walls. One wore an iron collar with spikes digging into the flesh of the neck. Another had his sex organs removed and sewn onto the woman chained beside him. A fourth slave was found with her limbs sewn on at odd angles, so that she resembled a crab. A fifth slave had her skin peeled from the flesh in a spiral pattern. A seventh had her intestines removed and tied around her waist. Beside the weakened slaves, who'd been starved in addition to their torment, was a bloody bucket of organ parts. It was unclear to the rescuers that night whether the organs belonged to those still living or to slaves long dead and dumped into the swamp or buried beneath the house.'"

Sue looked up. "And listen to this: 'Delphine Lalaurie was also believed to have a monstrous, deformed child, known as the Devil Baby of Bourbon Street, who lived in a small, dark room at the back of the house. The child was given to Delphine by Voodoo Queen Marie Laveau, who wanted to keep the devil child alive to add to her own fearful reputation. Delphine's motives are less clear. People suspect she found his screams and spasms amusing as she petted him and fed him raw bits of meat.'"

Ellen clutched her stomach. "How disgusting. I don't think I can listen to any more."

"I'm almost to the end," Sue said. "'On the morning of April 10th, neighbors spotted the smoke and rushed over to help. Instead of fleeing, Madame Lalaurie was busy saving her jewels and treasures. When someone asked about the slaves, Delphine urged them to save a valuable painting instead. Soon the fire brigade arrived, and, at the urging of Delphine's neighbor and cousin, Montreuil, they found the locked garret door. They busted it open only to be sickened by what they discovered. The seven slaves were rescued and taken to the Cabildo Prison, where they were on display for the citizens to view. An outraged mob rushed to the Lalaurie Mansion, and Delphine, along with her children, fled with her driver, a slave named Bastien, to Bayou St. John, where she and her children boarded a boat to Paris. The mob descended upon the driver, Bastien, and beat him to death.'"

Sue cleared her throat. "'Delphine is believed to have been accidentally killed by a boar in a hunting accident in 1842, after which her body was secretly returned to New Orleans to St. Louis Cemetery #1.'"

"But Lionel said she moved to the house on Chartres Street and died later," Ellen said.

"There are a lot of discrepancies in the articles I've found," Sue said. "It's hard to know what to believe."

"What a cruel, malicious woman," Tanya said. "There's no discrepancy about that."

"I'm almost afraid to find and read her diary," Ellen added.

"We have no choice," Sue said.

Ellen frowned. "I know. But still…"

"If only we knew where to look," Tanya muttered.

"Why don't we try the Ouija Board?" Sue suggested.

"Cornelius doesn't know where the diary is," Tanya said. "He would have told us by now."

Sue wagged a finger. "But Marie Laveau does."

"She obviously doesn't," Ellen pointed out.

"Maybe we misunderstood her," Sue said. "It won't hurt to ask. What do we have to lose?"

Ellen sighed. As much as she wanted to help Tanya and Cornelius, she was terrified of Delphine Lalaurie and Marie Laveau. Yet, Tanya's life was at stake. "Okay." She got up from the bed and dug the board out of her suitcase.

Sue lit a candle and found a half-eaten muffin to sit beside it, since food, light, and warmth attracted ghosts. Then she moved her chair to the foot of Tanya's bed, where Ellen and Tanya sat yoga-style, on the bedspread with the Ouija Board resting on their knees. With their fingers touching the planchette, Sue began:

"Oh, spirits of the other realm, we mean you no harm. We are looking for Marie Laveau, the Voodoo Queen of New Orleans. Please help her to find us. Marie Laveau, we call upon your help and guidance. Look for our light and our humble offering."

Ellen sighed, doubting that this would work. The Voodoo queen had likely sacrificed two humans and a snake to communicate with them; if an Ouija Board was all it took, she would have spoken to them by now.

The lights flickered, and the three women smiled.

"Oh, spirits of the other realm," Sue repeated. "Is anyone with us today?"

Ellen felt a chill in the room as the planchette moved to "Yes."

"What is your name?" Sue asked.

The planchette spelled out "P-H-I-L-O-M-E-N-E" before pausing and spelling out "L-E-G-E-N-D-R-E."

Ellen glanced with confusion at her friends before asking, "When did you die?"

The planchette spelled out "1-8-9-7."

"Eighteen ninety-seven?" Sue repeated.

The planchette flew to "Yes."

"Did you know Marie Laveau?" Sue asked.

The planchette circled around and returned to "Yes."

One of the bedside lamps went out.

The planchette spelled, "D-A-U-G-H-T-E-R."

Ellen lifted her brows. "Are you Marie Laveau's daughter?"

The planchette circled the board and stopped at "Yes."

"Do you know where Delphine Lalaurie's diary is?" Tanya asked.

The planchette moved to "No."

Tanya frowned and whispered, "Great."

Then Sue asked, "Can you ask your mother where it is?"

The planchette moved to "No."

"Great," Tanya whispered again.

"Can you help us?" Sue asked.

The planchette spelled "M-A-Y-B-E."

Then it spelled, "M-O-T-H-E-R-S" before continuing with "T-I-G-N-O-N."

"Mother's tignon?" Ellen repeated. "What's a tignon?"

"Marie Laveau wore a turban," Sue said.

The planchette flew to "Yes" before spelling "M-U-S-E-U-M."

"Museum?" Tanya said. "Is your mother's turban in a museum?"

The planchette flew to "Yes."

"Which museum?" Ellen asked.

The planchette spelled "H-I-S-T-O-R-I-C-V-O-O-D-O-O."

"The Historic Voodoo Museum," Sue repeated. "What do you want us to do with the turban?"

"S-T-E-A-L."

Ellen gasped. "She wants us to steal it? Why?"

"P-O-W-E-R."

"It has power," Tanya said. "Maybe with the turban, we can communicate with Marie Laveau herself."

The planchette flew to "Yes."

The flame on the candle went out.

"How do we use the turban to communicate with your mother?" Sue asked.

The planchette did not move.

"Philomene, are you there?" Sue asked.

Again, the planchette did not move.

"She's gone," Tanya said, pulling her hands form the planchette and sitting back on the bed. "But at least we got a lead."

"I don't like the idea of stealing," Ellen said, recalling the guilty feeling that had bothered her for months after taking the last can of cranberry sauce from the grocery store one Christmas eve.

Sue glanced at Tanya, whose dark circles had returned beneath her eyes. "I'm not sure we have a choice."

CHAPTER TWELVE

Louis Lalaurie

The next morning, Ellen, Sue, and Tanya spent the day outside of the French Quarter shopping for beds, linens, and furniture for the guesthouse. They had agreed that Sue and Ellen would take the bedrooms upstairs, and Tanya, wanting to be close to the bathroom, would sleep on a sleeper-sofa on the main floor. This would also make it easier for Sue and Ellen to keep an eye on Tanya and the effects of Cornelius's ghost.

Picking out a pretty shower curtain, soap dispenser, and towel set for the guesthouse bathroom, along with some basic dishes, pans, bakeware, and utensils for the kitchen, took Ellen's mind off the threat to Tanya's life. Sue, who had a flare for decorating, found an area rug that tied in perfectly with a set of drapes, linens, and other items they'd picked out together. After a morning of shopping, they celebrated their success at Antoine's, where they found the lunch menu to be significantly less expensive than the dinner.

Because they're appointment with the architect wasn't until two o'clock, after lunch they decided to stop in at the Historic Voodoo Museum.

"There's no way we're stealing it," Ellen said as they parked the car a block away.

"Neither of us *wants* to do it," Sue said in an exasperated tone. "But if it will help save Tanya's life..."

Tanya averted her eyes and took the lead toward the museum.

The front room was a tiny giftshop—even smaller than the shop at the Voodoo Spiritual Temple. For seven dollars each, they were permitted to enter the museum, but the narrow hall leading to the back rooms was so small that Sue had to walk sideways, and even then, she brushed against the walls, nearly pulling off posters and photographs along the way.

"This is ridiculous," she complained.

Ellen, also on the chubby side, felt claustrophobic and wished Sue could manage to speed things up. "We're almost there."

But the next room offered little relief for Ellen's feelings of claustrophobia. The eight-foot-by-eight-foot room was packed full of Voodoo relics, paintings, sculptures, candles, and other cultural artifacts—including a temple to Marie Laveau covered in offerings of dollar bills and coins. However, Ellen saw no sign of the Voodoo queen's turban among the artifacts.

The next room was just as small and housed African masks, musical instruments made of wood and leather, dolls in the shapes of crosses, along with paintings, photographs, and newspaper clippings on the wall. One of the photographs was of Priestess Isabel with her late husband. She was smiling jubilantly as she and her husband held a python—presumably Henry—over their shoulders.

"There it is," Tanya whispered.

Tucked away in the corner was a wooden hat rack. Several brightly colored textiles draped from it, and it was crowned with an African head wrap with a label attached to it. The label read *Marie Laveau's, circa 1859*.

There were two other people in the room with them, and at least three others behind them in the other room. There was no telling how many more were around the corner, and whether one might step back in at any moment.

"What's the worst thing that could happen to us?" Sue whispered. "We'd be charged a fine. And guess what? We're millionaires."

"We could do jail time," Tanya said.

Sue bent her brows at Tanya, as if to say, "You aren't helping."

"What?" Tanya whispered. "We need to be prepared for the worst."

"There's got to be another way," Ellen whispered back. "This doesn't feel right."

"We'll bring it back," Sue said. "We're not stealing it—just borrowing it."

"Never mind," Tanya said. "I don't want you to do anything that doesn't feel right. Just forget it."

Tanya left the room before Ellen or Sue could stop her.

"Now look what you've done," Sue said, before following Tanya out.

Ellen took a deep breath and glanced around. While the other two patrons were bent over an ancient musical instrument, she lifted the turban from the coat rack and stuffed it into her purse. The label dropped to the floor. In a panic, Ellen bent over and picked it up and stuffed it into her trouser pocket before leaving the museum.

Her friends were ahead of her at the rental by the time she made it out to the street. Ellen said nothing until Sue had pulled from the curb and had headed toward their meeting with the architect.

"I got the turban," Ellen finally said.

Tanya's mouth fell open. "You did not."

Ellen pulled it from her purse as proof.

"Well, call me shocked!" Sue cried.

Tears streamed down Tanya's cheeks.

"Don't cry," Ellen said. "Everything's going to be okay. We've got your back."

"Thank you, Ellen." Tanya wiped her cheeks with the back of her hand. "I know you didn't want to do it but thank you for doing it anyway."

Ellen took a deep breath and forced back tears.

"I'm glad it was you and not me, Ellen," Sue said with a laugh. "I think you'll fare better in prison. Those inmates would get one look at these babies," she glanced down at her breasts, "and they'd lose all self-control."

"Now who's having lesbian fantasies?" Tanya teased.

Ellen laughed. "Just keep your eyes on the road, will you? And get us to the architect's office in one piece."

Michael Rouchell's office was located on the other side of Highway Ninety outside of the French Quarter. Their real estate agent, Lionel Hurd, had recommended him. The architect's website and reviews emphasized his commitment to historical preservation and traditional style, which was exactly what they were looking for.

As soon as he entered the foyer to greet them, Ellen recognized him from HGTV.

She shook his outstretched hand. "Weren't you on *Property Brothers Take New Orleans?*"

Michael Rouchell, who was about Ellen's age but slightly taller and well-built, smiled, revealing dimples and perfect teeth. He had a twinkle in his dark brown eyes that mesmerized Ellen.

"That was me," he said. "That show brought me a lot of business."

"Are the brothers as nice in person as they seem on TV?" Sue asked.

"Even nicer," Michael said. "And just as goofy."

"Do you keep in touch with them?" Ellen asked, not sure whether she was more fascinated by his connection with celebrities or by his incredible good looks.

Michael shrugged. "We meet for drinks every time they come into town, but that's not too often."

"I'm impressed," Sue said with a laugh. "You must be pretty good at what you do to warrant their trust and friendship."

"Thank you, ma'am. That means a lot."

They followed him to his office. The view of Michael Rouchell from the back was as interesting to Ellen as the one from the front. As soon as the thought had entered her head, she chastised herself. She was a married woman, after all.

Then she chastised herself for chastising herself. For heaven's sake. She wasn't dead.

Michael offered them each a chair in front of his desk before moving to the other side and taking his seat. "What can I do for you ladies?"

"We just purchased a Creole-style mansion in the French Quarter on Chartres Street," Ellen explained. "It was built in 1828."

"We'd like to convert the mansion into three condos," Tanya said. "Do you think you can help us with that?"

Michael clapped his hands together and smiled. "Boy, can I! That's just the kind of project I've been looking for. Did you bring the house plans with you?"

"We weren't given any," Sue said. "Should we have been?"

"Only if the house had been renovated in modern times," Michael explained.

"I think some updates were made in the fifties," Ellen said. "But they weren't significant."

"Central heat and air were added in the eighties," Tanya mentioned.

"No problem," he said. "I can come out, take some measurements, and draw up the plans as they are. Then I'll create some preliminary sketches for the new plans and schedule another meeting with you, so you can look them over. Does that sound good?"

"What kind of timeline are you thinking?" Sue asked.

"I can take the measurements as early as tomorrow and have the original plans plus my renovation proposal ready in two weeks."

"That's awesome," Ellen said. "We're looking forward to seeing what you come up with."

"As far as the exterior goes, I'll be sure to get everything approved by the VCC before I present my plans to you."

"What's the VCC?" Tanya asked.

"The Vieux Carré Commission," Michael explained. "They're responsible for preserving the historical character of New Orleans. Any changes made to the exterior of a historical building must be approved by them before a building permit can be granted by the city."

"I see," Sue said.

"That's a good thing," Ellen said. "We care about preserving historical character, too, don't we, girls?"

"We do," Tanya agreed. "That's what we're all about."

Ellen wanted to add "That and *ghosts*," but she held her tongue.

After their meeting with the architect, Sue drove them to the Voodoo Spiritual Temple. Ellen was nervous about seeing the priestess again. She wasn't sure how they'd be received. Did Isabel blame them for what had happened to her snake, Henry? And had Julie, the quiet woman from behind the counter, been acting independently when she broke into the house on Chartres Street, or had Isabel put her up to it? There would be some awkward conversations in store for Ellen and her friends when they arrived.

But when they pulled up in front of the shop, they saw a large group of people pouring from the door. From what Ellen could tell from the curb, the inside was also crowded.

"That must be a tour group," Sue said. "Let's come back tomorrow."

As nervous as Ellen had been, she was disappointed that their visit with the priestess would be put off for another day. "What do we do now?"

"We could try to use Marie Laveau's turban to communicate with her," Sue said.

"That doesn't sound horrifying," Ellen said sarcastically. "Are you sure we shouldn't wait and ask Priestess Isabel for help with that?"

"Yeah, maybe we should wait," Tanya agreed.

Sue lifted her brows. "Okay, but let's not put it off for *too* long. That smell is beginning to mess with my appetite."

"And that's the very worst thing that could happen to either of us," Ellen said with more sarcasm.

"I think we should go through all those old books in the library," Tanya said. "Some of them could be quite valuable, don't you think?"

"Good idea," Ellen said.

"Let's pick up some more of those cupcakes from the bakery on the way," Sue said as she drove from the curb. "That kind of work is best done with plenty of carbs."

"Your appetite sounds pretty healthy to me," Ellen teased.

"And it's a good thing," Sue said, "considering all the manual labor you expect of me tonight."

A few hours later, Ellen and her friends sat in the folding camping chairs they'd bought that morning as they poured through book after book in the library. The shelves and spines had been dusted by the professional cleaning crew, but the inside of the books left a lot to be desired, and a cloud of dust seemed to float around their heads, reminding Ellen of the character Linus from *Peanuts*. They had formed stacks on the desk, sorting the books by topic. Although some of the books were written in French, Tanya sorted those, because she had majored in French literature in college and was fluent in the language.

"Here's another one in French." Ellen added a book to the pile on the desk near Tanya before climbing up the shelves to reach the highest books in the twelve-foot room.

"Honestly, we need a ladder," Sue complained. "You're making me nervous, Ellen."

Ellen laughed. "Just put 'Determined Investigator' on my headstone if I fall down and break my neck."

"That's not funny," Tanya said without looking up from her book. "Hold on a minute. I think I've found something."

Ellen reached for another book on the highest shelf and climbed back down. "What is it?"

"This reads like a medical journal," Tanya said. "And I think the author is Dr. Louis Lalaurie."

"Dr. Louis Lalaurie?" Sue repeated. "Wasn't that the name of Delphine's third husband?"

"Yes." Ellen sat between Sue and Tanya. "What does it say? Anything about Delphine or her diary?"

Tanya shook her head. "It's a very dry recounting of his medical experiments."

"What kind of doctor was he?" Sue asked.

"He opens with a reference to his degree in dental medicine in France, and how the education served him well as a surgeon, but that he endeavored to learn more through a series of experiments, which he conducted on slaves, both those he owned and those owned by others."

"I thought Delphine was the one who conducted the experiments on their slaves," Ellen said.

"Maybe they did it together," Sue said.

"I don't think so," Tanya said. "He makes a reference to his dire need for an assistant, because his beautiful wife has proved a disappointment, unable to stand the sight of blood."

"What?" Ellen was confused. "That can't be right."

"He goes on to say that he has resorted to soliciting another slave to aid him in the procedures, which one pair of hands cannot possibly undertake alone."

"What else does he say?" Sue asked before taking a bite of her unfinished cupcake. "Keep reading."

Tanya scanned through the pages. "This is disgusting. He gives a detailed report on three sequential surgeries that attempt to curve the spine in two different subjects which, he says, although ultimately failures, provided great insight into future success for curing hunches."

"I thought you said he went to dental school," Sue said. "But he operated on spines?"

"Not just spines," Tanya said. "He writes for several more pages about relieving pressure in the brain for chronic headaches by drilling holes in the skull."

Ellen shuddered. "Geez Louise."

Tanya covered her mouth and gasped.

"What does it say?" Sue asked.

"He discusses the effects of a powder, which he calls Zombie Powder, made from the crushed seeds of a Borrachero tree, dried glands of a puffer fish, and dried entrails of a tree frog. It was intended to make slaves more cooperative and help patients suffering from chronic pain or mental instabilities. He writes that his experiments have shown that less puffer fish and more Borrachero ensures a higher survival rate."

"I can't believe doctors were allowed to do such things," Ellen said.

"I read about a similar drug, I think," Sue said. "It's used in cases of date rape. I think it's called Devil's Breath."

"What?" Ellen smirked. "Were you worried someone was going to use it on *you*?"

"Of course. You can't be too careful when you look like this."

"Well, I suppose we have Dr. Louis Lalaurie to thank for inventing it," Ellen said.

Tanya shook her head. "He didn't invent it. According to his notes, he first procured the Zombie Powder from Marie Laveau."

"What did Marie Laveau use it for?" Ellen asked.

"Dr. Lalaurie doesn't say." Tanya looked up from her book. "But if Delphine couldn't stand the sight of blood…"

"Then maybe she was innocent," Ellen finished.

"Why would the legends say otherwise?" Sue asked.

"We need to find her diary," Tanya said. "Marie Laveau sent us here to find it. It's got to be here somewhere."

Ellen stood up and went back to work on sorting the books. "Maybe with Marie Laveau's turban, Priestess Isabel can help us find it."

Sue lifted a finger in the air. "What if, when Marie Laveau said to look beneath where the dead man lay, she didn't mean the floor? What if she meant the room below?"

Tanya jumped to her feet. "Good idea, Sue. Let's go look."

Ellen followed Tanya and Sue through the front parlor to the stairs.

"Go up to the bathroom and stomp on the floor," Sue said to Ellen. "Tanya and I will try to figure out what's directly below you."

Ellen did as Sue had asked. Standing beside the clawfoot tub, Ellen stomped on the plywood subfloor they'd exposed when they'd removed the hardwood planks, hoping she wouldn't fall through.

"Can you hear that?" Ellen shouted.

She couldn't hear them answer, so she stomped harder a few more times and then took the stairs down to meet them in the dining room, where Tanya had already begun prying up the floor with a crowbar. Ellen fetched another to help. Together, they crouched on their hands and knees and lifted a few planks of the hardwood floor, one by one.

"What is that?" Tanya said, pulling up another plank.

It was a small wooden chest. Engraved on the lid was the name Jeanne Blanque De Lassus.

"Oh, my gosh!" Ellen cried. "Open it up!"

CHAPTER THIRTEEN

Jeanne Blanque De Lassus

Tanya lifted the lid of the wooden chest they had found in the dining room floor and sifted through the papers. "They're letters, I think."

"In French or English?" Ellen asked.

Tanya opened another folded paper. "Both. They're addressed to Jeanne. This is her box, so these must be her letters."

"It's not Delphine's diary?" Sue asked.

"No, I don't think so," Tanya said. "They're letters written to Jeanne from different people."

"The chest wasn't anywhere beneath the bathtub upstairs," Sue pointed out. "Which means, there may still be a diary somewhere."

"Let's go back to the library," Ellen suggested, "and Tanya can read what we've found."

Tanya unfolded over a dozen yellowed papers and smoothed them out on the desk in the library, where she and Sue and Ellen bent over them.

"Let's see," Tanya began. "This one is dated April 11, 1845, and it's signed Auguste De Lassus."

My Dear Jeanne,

I suppose you might be wondering why it has been so long since I have written. Please give my love to our children and to your sister and to Placide, and to their family. I will never be able to repay Placide for his generosity to you and to our children. I still feel homesick when I think of all of you there together, without me.

That is why I pour myself into my work here in founding this Missouri township in my father's footsteps. Unfortunately, it has required more time and money than I had anticipated, and I have exhausted my savings. If I am ever to hope you will take me back, it cannot be as a poor beggar. I work tirelessly to turn my situation around, so that I may one day win your heart again.

Please send me news of our darlings, though it breaks my heart to hear what I have missed. Is it true that your mother has taken over our old residence, and that you and the children intend to dwell there with her?

My aunt sends her love, as do I, your faithful servant.

Auguste De Lassus

"I wish we knew who these people were," Sue said.

"Oh, check this out!" Tanya said, excitedly. "This one is signed 'Dr. L. Lalaurie.'"

"As in Louis Lalaurie?" Ellen asked. "Delphine's husband?"

"Read the letter," Sue said.

"It's dated October 9, 1842 from Havana," Tanya said.

Ellen sat back in her chair. "Havana, Cuba?"

"What other Havana is there?" Sue teased.

"Listen," Tanya began.

Dear Jeanne,

I do not like to trouble you, but I have written to Auguste and have received no reply. You have in your possession some works of mine that I could not bring with me. These are my medical journals and books of medicine (some belonged to my father). I would like to have them delivered to me, along with two of my possessions—two diplomas, one of master mason and the other of the Lodge of the Friends of the Bourbons of Villeneuve-sur-Lot.

Please deliver them to the captain, who will deliver them to me by hand, since they cannot pass through customs. If you will do me this favor, I would be most grateful. If you believe that I can be of some assistance to you here, make use of me in all surety.

Give me some news about your husband and children, above all, about your oldest, who is also mine. He will not remember he who rendered him into this world, though I cannot forget. He was the first baby I delivered, and so he is marked in my mind forever.

Believe me your all-devoted servant and friend,

Dr. L. Lalaurie

"He must be referring to the books we found here," Ellen pointed out. "Obviously, Jeanne never sent them to him. I wonder why."

"Maybe because he was a psycho," Sue said.

Ellen laughed. "At least we know that Jeanne is somehow connected with the Lalauries."

"Oh my God!" Tanya held up another paper. "I think this one was written by Delphine."

"What makes you think that?" Sue asked. "Did she sign it?"

"Listen. It's dated May 20, 1838."

My Dearest Jeanne,

How I miss you and your sweet children. These six long months since your visit have been dreary. Please tell De Lassus I am not satisfied. You must come again soon. I know he was miserable. My in-laws are insufferable. Your sisters and brothers and I must abide their rude and queer manners for a few more years, until my finances are sorted, and we can return to New Orleans. How I miss my city!

Paulin, Pauline, and little Jean Louis miss you as much as I do, but your siblings believe me insane for wishing to return to my home after what happened that dreadful day four years ago when the flames engulfed our house and so much of what we held dear. I refuse to live in exile for the rest of my life. Am I to miss out on Borquita's adult life entirely? I have yet to see little Octave, whom she writes has nearly recovered from the measles. And now she is pregnant again. And Laure will soon be pregnant, too, I imagine. How difficult it is to be away at such important moments in a daughter's life. The presence of young people in a house always fills it with more gaiety and liveliness. I had once imagined I would have my grandchildren at my feet, not miles away across the sea.

Kiss your children for me. Urge your husband to look into that matter of which we spoke. I have been obliged to put my signature out. I don't know what to attribute the delay in the money he promised to send me. If my affairs have become too burdensome to administer, I pray he turn them over to Placide. After waiting in vain for the various steamships, which have arrived many times, I fear that my signature could be protested and my promissory note ineligible for renewal. I see no reason why my money has not yet arrived.

Give my love to Borquita and Laure and know that you are, as always, in my heart and on my mind.

Your loving mother.

"Jeanne De Lassus was the daughter of Delphine," Sue said. "Let me search her up on Google. Okay, yes. Marie Louise Jeanne Blanque was the daughter of Jean Blanque and Delphine Marie McCarty De Lopez."

"Ramon Lopez was Dephine's first husband, right?" Tanya asked.

Ellen nodded. "She married Don Ramon Lopez first, then Jean Blanque, and finally Louis Lalaurie."

"That's right," Sue said. "Here's a genealogy site with a list of Delphine Lalaurie's children. Borquita was her oldest daughter and the only child she had with Don Ramon, a Spanish officer. After he died, she married Jean Blanque and had four children from him. Jeanne was the oldest. Then later she married Dr. Lalaurie, and they had one son. So, these letters are to Delphine's second child."

"Oh, gosh!" Ellen cried, filling with hope. "We may be onto something. Are there any other letters from Delphine? Maybe she mentions the devil child."

Tanya sifted through the papers. "Here are two more, also written in French in the same handwriting and signed 'your loving mother.' One is dated June 23, 1834, and the other is dated September 19, 1834."

"Isn't that the year of the fire?" Sue asked. "The fire was in April of 1834, wasn't it?"

"Yes, that's right!" Ellen's heart picked up its pace. "Read them in chronological order."

"Okay. Here's the first one."

My Dearest Jeanne,

We are safe in New York City. We met Auguste and Placido in Mandeville two months ago and signed over power of attorney. Tomorrow, we leave on the ship Poland for Le Havre. We will remain there briefly before we journey on to my in-laws' at Villenueve-sur-Lot. Please send news there as soon as possible. I must know if Bastien made it home safely.

Poor Rachel. I shall miss her dearly, despite her evil deed. Pray for her, will you? And for the souls of your stepfather's slaves. Unlike the doctor, I do believe they have souls.

As soon as he has helped the children and me to settle down, your stepfather shall find another place to build his practice. We will finally live separate lives, as I have wished. But I shall never be happy again until I am home in New Orleans with you.

Please give Borquita and Laure my love and kisses.

Your loving mother.

Ellen sat up. "She wrote, 'Unlike the doctor, I do believe they have souls.' Maybe this explains why he treated the slaves like guinea pigs."

"I think so," Tanya said.

"It's unfathomable that anyone could believe that another race of human beings didn't possess souls," Ellen said.

"People say that today about animals," Sue said. "But I believe they have souls."

"I do, too," Tanya said.

"That doesn't stop me from enjoying a good steak," Sue admitted.

"I wonder who Rachel is," Tanya said. "Didn't we read something about a Rachel?"

"And Bastien," Ellen said. "I think those were the names of two of her slaves."

"I wonder what deed she refers to," Sue said.

"Starting the fire," Ellen said. "Didn't we read somewhere that Rachel was the cook, and she started the fire?"

"That's right," Tanya said. "And Bastien is the driver who was killed by the mob after Delphine and her children escaped."

"I wish I had a notepad, so I could take notes," Ellen muttered.

"Read the next letter, Tanya."

"Okay. Here it is."

My Dearest Jeanne,

The receipt of your letter caused me both happiness and pain. I am overjoyed by the news of your pregnancy. I am also satisfied to hear that De Lassus and Placido were able to complete the dispensation of what remained of my property.

I am pained to hear what people are saying about me on the streets and in the papers. On the ship to Le Havre, the rumors had already been received by many of the other passengers. I was at first confused by their reserve and their rude glances, but I overheard an American poet talking about it to his companion. He did not know I was standing not four feet away from him.

It is beyond my comprehension that I shall be blamed for the very thing I endeavored to prevent. If only I could go back in time to those days when your stepfather first began to treat Pauline. I was grateful for his promises, enamored by his charms, and so naïve. Marie Laveau warned me, and I did not listen. If it hadn't been for the help he gave to our Pauline and to the poor, unfortunate Charles, I might have stood up to him.

"Wait!" Ellen interrupted. "Charles! Didn't Maria Nunnery say that some people said the devil child was called Charles?"

"Yes!" Tanya cried.

"Keep reading!" Sue urged Tanya.

His family is worse. Our first night at their estate, Louis and his father ex-
changed violent words, and your stepfather left us for a hotel. I finally understood why
Louis is the way he is. He wants to be accepted by his father, but that man can never
be satisfied. He is a cruel tyrant with impossible standards and expectations. He let
me know that I, too, was a disappointment. I suppose he saw me as a vehicle to his
son's ascent up the social ladder and nothing more.

His mother claimed she had no clean beds and had us sleep on the floor. We slept
there for two nights before the linens were ready for us. They offer us nothing to eat. I
am forced to ask for anything we need, on behalf of the children. The servants ignore
us. I will soon be forced to read monsieur the riot act.

Enough of my trouble and woes. My heart aches for your sweet face and for those
of Borquita and Laure. Give them my kisses, and take mine into your heart, and
know that I will be home as soon as I can.

Your loving mother.

"No more mention of Charles, unfortunately," Tanya said.

"She said she was blamed for the very thing she tried to prevent," Ellen said.

"Do you think she's referring to the treatment of the slaves?" Tanya asked.

"I think so," Ellen said. "No one blamed her for the fire, did they?"

"Not anything we've read so far," Tanya said.

"Marie Laveau warned her," Sue said. "Delphine should have listened."

"I wonder what prompted Marie Laveau to advise her against marrying Louis," Tanya said. "She must have known something."

"Maybe Marie Laveau didn't like him using the Zombie Powder on slaves," Ellen offered.

Sue sucked through her straw but got nothing but air. "I'm out of Cherry Coke. Why don't we discuss these revelations over dinner somewhere?"

"I'd rather finish reading these letters," Tanya said. "I'm really anxious to see if there's any mention of Charles or the devil child. But if you want to go without me…"

"I want to see what the other letters have to say as well," Ellen said. "But why don't we take them with us? This camping chair is cutting off the circulation in my legs."

"Okay. I guess we can do that." Tanya folded the letters and returned them to the chest and followed Sue and Ellen to the bay, where the rental was parked. Since it was late and few places nearby were open, they returned to their favorite bakery for sandwiches.

In a corner booth, Tanya and Ellen sat across from Sue. After they gave their order to the waitress, Tanya unfolded one of the letters.

"This one is dated August 15, 1842."

Dearest Sister,

I just learned that our mother wrote to your husband about her intentions to return to New Orleans. This news will undoubtedly surprise you. She has been thinking about this for a long time, speaking about it in a vague manner, but we have thus far comforted ourselves in the impossibility of her finding a pretext on which to return, considering public opinion in the wake of the catastrophe of 1834.

This has continued for five years, but, more recently, everywhere we go, she makes announcements about our upcoming departure and gives the reason of her bad state of affairs in Louisiana. I bemoan (as we must all bemoan) the fate that awaits us if ever our mother puts feet in that country again. Her talk of it has caused us to shed many tears.

I truly believe that our mother never had a true idea of the evil of which she has been accused since she is thinking of returning to that country again.

When De Lassus receives her letter announcing her intention to return, please don't let the fear of displeasing her cause you to recoil from what you know you must

do. You must urge your husband to convince our mother of the impossibility of return-
ing to New Orleans. And you must also write to her with the same hard sentiment.

I know that the truth is sometimes painful to speak, but when it can prevent
great evils, it is a duty to divulge it. If Mother does indeed return to that country, our
lives and hers will be miserable ever after.

I will do my part here. The truth, as painful as it is for a son towards a loving
mother, must be said. I will tell her that her idea is insane. She will never be accepted.
The rumors took root long ago, thanks to that heartless doctor who calls himself our
father, and have grown and blossomed into a deadly vine that strangles the reputation
of our family, one which shall never be cut away but shall remain ever thick and
thorny. We are better off to stay away. In fact, Pauline and I are prepared to insist to
her that we will not go with her.

My task will be painful, as will yours, but we must do it, dear sister, so there will
be nothing to reproach us with later.

Ever your loving brother,
Paulin Blanque

"That's interesting," Sue said before taking a sip of her drink. "So, *Louis* was the slave abuser, and Delphine was innocent."

"She allowed it to happen in her house," Tanya said. "She could have reported him, but she did nothing. She was going to let the slaves die in the fire."

"Perhaps as a mercy," Ellen offered. "She called Rachel's deed 'brave,' remember? Maybe it was the only way out."

"She's not innocent," Tanya said again.

"Well, she may not be," Sue said. "But she doesn't sound like the monster history has painted her to be, either."

"Let's see if we can find any mention of Charles in the rest of the letters," Tanya said, barely touching her food.

Tanya read the remaining nine letters. One was another written by Jeanne's brother Paulin, one was written by her older sister Borquita (who was also called Delphine), and three were written by her younger sister Pauline. The rest were from Jeanne's husband, Auguste De Lassus. None of them made any mention of a devil child or shed any light on the atrocities that took place in the Lalaurie mansion before the fire of 1834.

Exhausted from a long and exciting day, they returned to the Inn at Ursulines for bed, but Ellen was anxious and lay there, tossing and turning, for most of the night. There were so many unanswered questions, and Tanya's life was no closer to being freed from the desperate ghost of Cornelius Nunnery.

CHAPTER FOURTEEN

Special Rites

After breakfast, Ellen, Tanya, and Sue returned to the house on Chartres to meet the architect. When the others were as eager as Ellen to help Michael Rouchell with his measuring tape, Ellen suspected she wasn't the only one enamored with him. His charismatic personality, sparkling dark eyes, and adorable smile bewitched them.

After they finished upstairs and had returned to the parlor, Michael asked, "How set are you on making this into *three* condos? What I mean is, would you be open to two bigger condos, instead?"

Sue crossed her arms. "I was just thinking three smaller condos would be more affordable for locals."

"But there aren't many places for *families* in the French Quarter," Michael pointed out. "They could be your target market."

"I'm open to that," Tanya said. "How would you do it?"

"We would have one face the street and another face the courtyard. We would add another set of stairs there by the office, so the back condo has access to the second floor. Both condos would have a living, kitchen, and dining room downstairs, with two bedrooms and two baths per unit. We might get a third bedroom for each unit, since the rooms are pretty big."

"I think that sounds awesome," Ellen said with too much enthusiasm.

Michael smiled.

"I'm good with that," Sue agreed.

"Great! Do you mind if I stay here for a bit and work on my preliminary drawings?" Michael asked.

"Stay as long as you like," Sue said, beaming.

Ellen tried not to roll her eyes. "We're on our way out for an hour or so, but we're expecting furniture for the guesthouse this afternoon and will be back after lunch. Will you still be here then?"

"It's possible," he said. "I'd like to make notes about the existing architecture as I go."

"Take your time," Sue said with another bright smile. "There's a desk in the library, if you need it."

As they returned to the rental parked in the bay, Tanya said, "What is the matter with you two?"

"Sue's the one who was beaming at him like a high school crush."

"Not just Sue."

Sue mimicked Ellen, "I think that sounds awesome!" Then, she added, "You may as well have said, 'I think *you're* awesome, Michael Rouchell. How about a kiss to seal the deal?'"

"Oh, hush," Ellen said.

"Excuse me, ladies?"

They turned toward the house and were horrified to see Michael Rouchell standing there with a huge grin.

"Yes?" Tanya replied when Ellen and Sue couldn't.

"If I leave before you get back, how do I lock up?"

"Um," Ellen didn't think she could finish her sentence as the blood rushed to her cheeks and her mortified heart pounded in her ears.

"I'll show you." Tanya rushed off to help Michael.

As Ellen climbed behind the wheel of the rental, she said, "I don't think I can ever make eye contact with him again."

"I'm sure he was flattered. Don't make it worse by making it awkward."

Ellen was pretty sure it was too late for that.

When they arrived at the Voodoo Spiritual Temple, Priestess Isabel was with another woman, black and in her late twenties, with tears streaming down her face. The quiet woman, Julie, wasn't there. Isabel and the sobbing young woman stood at the counter, and there was no one else in the room.

"I don't know," the sobbing young woman said. "The doctor didn't say. Mama Isabel, he's just a baby. Help me, please!"

"What hospital he at?" Isabel asked.

"Children's. Will you come with me? Say a prayer over him? I don't have any money, but I'm desperate. I'll do anything for you. Please?"

"You got a car?" Isabel asked.

"Yes, parked right outside. Does that mean you'll come?"

Isabel turned to Ellen. "What can I do for you, ladies?"

"We can come back another time," Ellen said.

"I'll be back in an hour," Isabel said. "Can you mind my store 'till then?"

"Huh?" Ellen wasn't sure if she'd heard the woman correctly.

"You trust us with it?" Sue asked.

"Would I ask if I didn't?"

"Sure," Tanya said. "What do we need to know?"

Isabel took Tanya behind the counter. "Enter the amount of each item like this. When you're done, push this button to add the sales tax. Then, if they pay cash, you push this and enter the amount of cash they give you. It will show how much change to give back, if any. If they pay with a card, you swipe it here. The computer will ask if you want a receipt printed, so just push yes, got it?"

Tanya nodded. "I think so."

"I keep the shopping bags down here, if they need one."

"Okay."

"If you get a tour group, keep your eyes open. Don't let anyone take anything without paying for it."

"We won't," Ellen said.

"I'll be right back."

"Thank you," the young woman said to them as she followed Isabel through the front door.

When they were alone in the shop, Sue said, "Can you believe that? I can't believe she left us in charge."

Ellen fingered the handmade Voodoo dolls. "Maybe this means she fired Julie."

"She could just be sick today," Tanya said. "Let's not assume."

"And even if she fired the girl," Ellen said, "that doesn't mean Isabel wasn't in on it."

Sue walked toward the back room, which led to the courtyard. "I want to know if the snake is still there."

Ellen glanced around the back room, feeling nosey. Papers and boxes littered a desk and shelves that lined two walls.

Sue disappeared and returned a moment later. "The aquarium's empty. Henry must be dead."

"What's this?" Tanya held up a booklet that had been sitting behind the counter. "Voodoo Rituals. Oh, wow. I don't think Isabel has been completely honest with us."

"What makes you say that?" Ellen asked, peering over Tanya's shoulder to get a look at the booklet.

"Listen to this," Tanya said. "'Anvwa Mo, or Sending the Dead, is a ritual used to either send mo after an enemy, or to rid a client of mo attachment or possession, a mo being a spirit of the deceased.'"

"There's a ritual for getting rid of a spirit attachment?" Ellen couldn't believe it. She'd taken Isabel at her word.

"Why did she lie to us?" Sue wondered out loud.

"Oh my God," Tanya muttered. "It says here that victims of the mo become violently ill, may spit up blood, become thin and pale, hear voices, grow crazy, and sometimes die." Tanya looked up at them with tears welling in her eyes. "Guys, I don't want to die."

"You aren't going to die," Ellen said. "We won't let that happen."

"I wonder what Isabel will have to say for herself when she gets back," Sue said, with one hand on her hip, warrior ready.

Just then, a woman not much younger than they, with long red hair, pale skin, green eyes, and a look of desperation, entered the shop. "Where's Mama Isabel?"

"Children's Hospital," Tanya said. "Can we help you with something?"

"My husband just died," the woman said.

"What? Where?" Sue asked.

"Oh my gosh," Tanya muttered.

"My house, two blocks away. I ran here as fast as I could. I need her to perform the rite of reclamation, to protect his soul from getting lost. This was very important to my husband."

"She won't be here for at least another half hour," Ellen said.

The woman broke down into tears.

"I'm so sorry for your loss," Ellen said. "Do you want us to call someone for you?"

The woman shook her head. "I'll wait here. I don't know who else to go to. His mother is there with him. She will be very upset if I return without Mama Isabel."

"Did your husband die suddenly?" Sue asked. "Or has he been sick?"

"Cancer took him," the woman said through her sobs. "I knew we were close, but…"

Ellen patted the woman on the back, not sure what to say. "I'm so sorry."

They were interrupted by the arrival of a large group of people—at least a dozen—and a short brunette in her twenties encouraged the last few people to squeeze inside.

"Where's Priestess Isabel?" the short brunette asked Tanya.

"Children's Hospital," Ellen answered. "Can we help you?"

"Oh, no," the brunette said. "I promised these people they'd have the opportunity to meet the most famous Voodoo queen in New Orleans. When do you expect her back?"

"In about thirty or forty minutes," Sue said. "Can you come back then?"

"This is our last stop on the tour," the brunette said. "At least I can take them to the courtyard and show them her famous python, Henry, who acts as her conduit between the living and the dead, much like Le Grand Zombie, the snake belonging to Marie Laveau, once did in the mid eighteen-hundreds."

Ellen glanced at Sue and Tanya, wondering which of them would break the news.

Sue spoke up. "Henry isn't with us anymore. He died about a month ago."

Disappointed faces in the crowd stared back at her.

"Seriously?" the brunette said with increased frustration. "That's just great."

Ellen felt sorry for the girl and for all the disappointed tourists, who'd been hoping for an experience.

"Did you hear how he died?" Ellen asked the tour guide, who shook her head. "We were with Priestess Isabel when it happened."

Everyone turned their eyes on Ellen, eager for a story.

"My friends and I came to her for help a month ago because our friend Tanya here has a mo attached to her," Ellen explained. "A mo is a spirit of the deceased."

Tanya turned bright pink and muttered, "Ellen!"

Several people backed away from Tanya.

"It's okay. It won't hurt anything to tell them about it," Ellen said to Tanya. Then she turned to the crowd. "Our friend became terribly ill and had to be hospitalized. She has a foul odor that follows her wherever she goes. She has nightmares and says things, and later forgets them. Once, we found her sleeping upside down. We eventually discovered that a sixteen-year-old boy who died in Hurricane Katrina has attached himself to her."

"Why?" someone asked.

"Marie Laveau, an ancestor of his, won't let him rest until we help her," Ellen continued. "The python died when Marie Laveau possessed Priestess Isabel, so she could tell us what we have to do to free our friend from the mo."

"We think Marie Laveau sacrificed the snake to create enough energy for the dead Voodoo queen to possess the priestess," Sue explained.

Many of the people in the group gasped, wide-eyed, and others shook their heads in disbelief, chuckling.

Someone in the crowd asked, "What did she say you have to do?"

"Find the bones of the Devil Baby of Bourbon Street," Ellen said. "The spirit attached to Tanya won't be allowed to rest until the spirit of the devil child is finally at peace."

Some of the tourists looked fascinated, but at least half of them smiled or laughed, their faces full of skepticism. Ellen remembered the feeling.

"And have you found the bones?" someone asked.

"Not yet," Sue said. "But we're working on it."

Ellen noticed a kid about nine or ten years of age slide a gris-gris bag into his pocket.

"Are you going to buy that?" Ellen asked.

The kid turned red and put it back.

His mother narrowed her eyes at him and said, "Keep your hands to yourself."

The boy started crying.

About that time, someone pushed through the crowd from the front door. It was Isabel. She was early.

"Well, well, well," she said. "Look at all these folks. How are y'all doin' today? Where are y'all from?"

The redhead rushed to Isabel's side. "Chuck died, Mama Isabel. Please come and bless him with the rite of reclamation before his soul is lost forever." The woman covered her face with her hands and sobbed again.

"When did he die, Sylvia?" Isabel asked.

"Not an hour ago. Doris is with him, and she wants you to come."

"Tell Doris we have time," Isabel said. "You go home and be with her, and I'll be by in a few hours, okay? Wash his body and prepare the govi, you understand?"

"Thank you, Mama Isabel," the redhead said before she ran from the shop.

Isabel turned to the crowd. "Why don't you all buy yourself a gris-gris bag or a Voodoo doll, and then make your way outside to the court-yard. I'll be happy to answer your questions out there, where there's more room."

Then Isabel walked over to Tanya and said in a quieter voice. "I'll take over from here, thank you."

"How's the baby?" Ellen asked.

"The doctors are running tests. We won't know for a few more days."

Tanya pointed to the booklet. "Why didn't you tell us about the Anvwa Mo ritual?"

Isabel sighed. "That should only be done as a last resort."

"You could have mentioned it, though," Sue accused.

"It's dangerous," the priestess said. "Not everyone survives it. It's better to cooperate with the spirit than to shun it. Safer for everyone involved."

"But what if we don't find the devil child?" Ellen asked. "What if we can't give the spirit what it wants?"

"Only then should we consider the Anvwa Mo," Isabel said.

"You still should have told us," Tanya said.

One of the tourists approached the counter with a Voodoo doll and a twenty-dollar-bill. Isabel helped the customer and then turned back to Ellen. "Why did you come here today?"

"We were hoping you'd try to communicate with Marie Laveau again," Sue said.

Isabel shook her head. "Without Henry as a conduit…"

"We have something else," Ellen whispered, close to Isabel. "We have something that once belonged to Marie Laveau."

"Are you sure?" Isabel asked.

Another customer approached the counter, and Isabel helped them as Ellen and her friends waited.

"Pretty sure," Ellen said, once the transaction was completed.

"That ain't good enough," Isabel said.

"What if we go to a place where Marie Laveau once lived?" Sue suggested.

"People ain't allowed to do that no more," Isabel said. "That house on St. Anne's, you mean? It ain't allowed."

"Not there," Ellen said. "We bought a house where Marie Laveau is said to have lived when she delivered the devil baby."

Isabel sighed again. "So many stories and legends. You can't believe everything you hear."

"Will you at least give it a try?" Tanya asked. "I don't want to die."

A third customer approached the counter.

Isabel turned to Tanya. "Write down the address. I'll meet you there tonight, when I'm done with the widow's husband."

CHAPTER FIFTEEN

A Paranormal Investigation

Because Priestess Isabel hadn't been clear on what time she would arrive at the house on Chartres, Ellen, Sue, and Tanya returned after lunch, having checked out of the Inn at Ursulines, to await the delivery of their new furniture, to wash the linens, and to prepare for the evening. Ellen was relieved to find Michael Rouchell gone.

The hour was approaching seven o'clock when Ellen, who was re-moving the last load of sheets from the dryer in the laundry room of the main house, heard a knock at the door in the parlor facing the street.

Ellen balled up the sheets in one arm opened the door with the oth-er. "Priestess Isabel. You came."

"I said I would, didn't I?"

"Thank you. We really appreciate it. Please, come in."

Isabel stepped into the parlor. "It's been a long day, and I haven't sat down once."

"Would you like to rest for a bit? Maybe have a bite to eat?"

"I want to get this over with, so I can go home."

"At least, let me get you something to drink. Let's go to the guest-house and discuss how we want to do this."

Ellen led Isabel across the courtyard to the guesthouse, where Sue was making sandwiches in the kitchen and laying them out on a platter that she had picked out at Home Goods. Sue had rearranged the furni-ture and Tanya had hung the drapes. Although it needed new paint and a kitchen makeover, the guesthouse already looked much improved.

"You're here!" Sue cried.

"Why is that so surprising?" Isabel said.

"Would you like a sandwich?" Sue asked, as way of apology.

"Since they're already made." Isabel lifted one of the halves and took a bite. "This is good. Thank you."

"Can I get you something to drink?" Tanya asked. "Some iced tea or soda?"

"Iced tea sounds nice," Isabel replied.

Ellen had quickly folded the clean linens and had draped them over the stairwell banister.

"Come have a seat." Ellen offered the priestess the new upholstered chair.

As Isabel crossed the room to sit down, she said, "So what is this thing you believe was once owned by Marie Laveau?"

Ellen went to her purse on the kitchen counter and pulled out the African head wrap.

Isabel gasped. "You either stole that, or someone sold you a fake."

"I stole it," Ellen admitted.

"Borrowed," Sue corrected. "We have every intention of returning it when we're finished with it."

"Marie Laveau's daughter told us we needed it," Tanya explained as she delivered a glass of iced tea to the priestess.

"What makes you think you communicated with Marie Laveau's daughter?"

Ellen recounted what had happened with the Ouija Board. "We looked up her name online—Philomene Legendre. It matches the name of one of her daughters."

"Did you look up that name before or after you consulted the Ouija Board?" Isabel asked.

"After," Sue said.

Ellen didn't blame the priestess for being skeptical.

Then Sue said, "Is Julie no longer working for you?"

"I fired her, on account of what she done."

"Why did she do it?" Tanya asked.

Isabel took a sip of her tea. "She says she wanted to sell the diary to a touring company. She needs money, poor thing. I feel sorry for her, but I can't trust her no more."

"Did you have any idea what she was up to?" Sue asked.

"Of course not." Isabel climbed to her feet. "Maybe I should go. I'm tired."

"Wait, please!" Tanya cried. "We didn't mean to insult you. We had to ask, only because we don't know you."

"Please stay and help us," Ellen said. "We'll compensate you for your time."

"Add insult to injury," Isabel said with disdain.

Ellen glanced at her friends as her face grew hot. "I'm sorry. I thought you meant to be paid."

"That's to be discussed *after*. That's not how it's done."

"Forgive me," Ellen muttered, afraid to say anything more, lest she make a bad situation worse.

"It must be frustrating working with ignorant people like us," Sue said. "Can I bring you another sandwich?"

Isabel returned to her seat and accepted another sandwich. It was decided that it would be best to hold the session in the main house, so, while Isabel rested, Ellen and Tanya set up their investigative equipment in the library.

Ellen's equipment included her EMF detector, EVP recorder, motion sensors, geophone vibration sensor, infrared camera, infrared thermometer, dousing rods, Ouija Board, and pendulum. Having learned from Carrie French and her team, Ellen and Tanya took temperature recordings and made other observations about the room in Ellen's notebook.

Sue and Isabel soon joined them. Sue created a circle of protection around them using common table salt and candles lit at each of the cardinal points. Isabel added a sandwich on a white napkin to the center of the circle—an offering to the spirits.

Ellen knew Isabel was in a hurry to get home, so she wasted no time getting started. Sue and Ellen sat in the circle in camping chairs. Ellen offered the third chair to Isabel. She went to the chair but didn't sit in it. The priestess held the turban from the Historic Voodoo Museum in both hands as she closed her eyes. Ellen pointed her camera at her. Sue monitored the thermometer while Tanya held the dousing rods.

Priestess Isabel began to stomp her feet in a pattern—slow…fast, fast, slow…fast, fast. She nodded her head, as she clung to the bright-colored fabric of the turban, which fell in folds over her arms.

"St. Peter, open the door, and let me in," Isabel said as she continued to stomp her feet—slow…fast, fast, slow…fast, fast. "St. Peter, open the door, and let me in."

Ellen felt a chill in the air as the candles flickered and one went out.

Then Isabel's eyes opened, but only the whites showed. She shouted something Ellen couldn't understand. The priestess seemed to be speaking in tongues. She repeated the same line, urgently, before her body convulsed, and she collapsed in her chair.

"Isabel?" Sue asked. "Are you okay?"

Ellen continued to record with her video camera as Isabel opened her eyes and asked, "What happened?"

"You spoke in tongues," Sue said. "Do you know what you said?"

Isabel shook her head.

"It was French," Tanya said. "Creuser plus profond. It means 'dig deeper.'"

Isabel's eyes widened in surprise. "That hasn't happened to me in a very long time. This head wrap must be Marie Laveau's. You *are* going to take it back, aren't you?"

"We promise," Sue insisted.

"What do you suppose the spirit is trying to tell us?" Tanya asked. "How do we dig deeper? Does it mean literally or figuratively? I don't understand."

"If literally, does the spirit mean for us to dig under the house?" Sue wondered.

"I know you're tired, Priestess Isabel," Ellen said. "Would you like me to help you out to your car?"

"I don't have a car. I took a cab."

"Then let us drive you home," Sue said. "And we need to pay you. How much do you charge for this kind of thing?"

"You pay what you think I deserve," the priestess said.

Ellen mouthed, "Five hundred dollars," to her friends while Isabel wasn't looking.

Sue and Tanya nodded.

"Can I help you out to the car?" Ellen asked Isabel.

Isabel's eyes had closed. "Let me just sit here for a while, okay?"

"Sure." Ellen picked up her camera. "Is it okay with you if we continue our investigation while you rest?"

"Mmm-hmm."

Ellen pointed her camera at Sue and Tanya. "Sue? Tanya? Y'all ready?"

The girls nodded.

"Spirits of the other realm," Ellen said. "We mean you no harm. We call on you to help us. Is anyone here?"

The chill in the air became cooler. To Ellen, the room seemed at least five degrees cooler than it had been previously. The overhead light flickered, and a second candle blew out.

"Spirits of the other realm," Ellen said again. "We're looking for the diary of Delphine Lalaurie."

Ellen felt something brush up against the back of her leg. She flinched. The hair on the back of her neck stood on end.

"I felt something," Ellen said. "Something touched my leg. I'm trying not to freak out."

"It's freezing in here," Tanya muttered with a shiver.

"It's sixty-one degrees," Sue said, reading the thermometer. "Down from seventy-two."

Ellen swallowed hard. "That's a big drop."

"Someone's here with us," Isabel said.

Ellen heard a very subtle scratching sound coming from behind Tanya.

"Did you hear that?" she whispered to the others.

Tanya and Isabel nodded.

"We mean you no harm," Sue said. "We want only to help."

The overhead light flickered and then turned off. The only remaining light in the room came from two candles and the French door to the street. It was dusk outside, but there was enough light to see by.

"It's fifty-eight degrees," Sue said. "Make that fifty-five and dropping."

Ellen shuddered, wishing she'd worn a jacket.

One of the books on the desk fell to the floor with a thud. All four of them jumped.

"Shit," Ellen whispered. Then she said. "Excuse my French."

"We're looking for the diary of Delphine Lalaurie, so we can help Cornelius Nunnery and Marie Laveau," Tanya said. "We want to help the devil child find peace. Please help us, if you can. Is this Cornelius? Marie Laveau?"

"Or Philomene?" Sue asked.

Ellen said, "Tanya, try to use the dousing rods."

"That curtain moved," Sue said, pointing to the drapes around the French door that faced the street.

Ellen pointed the camera in that direction, in case it could pick up anything. Then she moved the camera back to Tanya.

Tanya stood up, holding the rods out from her body parallel to one another. Ellen could tell her friend was frightened, because her arms trembled uncontrollably. Ellen understood the feeling. She could sense something there with them, something other than Cornelius.

She hoped and prayed that Marie Laveau wouldn't sacrifice one of them to get her message understood.

"Spirits of the other realm," Tanya began, "as I move, please use these rods to point me in the direction of Delphine Lalaurie's diary. If I'm going toward the diary, please point the rods toward one another, like this." Tanya touched the rod tips together. "If I'm moving away from the diary, please pull the rod tips apart, like this." Tanya spread her arms out. Then she returned the rods to a parallel position, her hands trembling uncontrollably. "Spirits of the other realm, help us to locate the diary of Delphine Lalaurie using the rods."

Tanya moved around the room, but the rods remained parallel.

Tanya dropped her arms to her sides. "It's not working."

Another one of the candles went out, leaving only the one at the northern point alight.

"Try saying it in French," Isabel suggested.

"Good idea." Tanya repeated her directions in French. Then she slowly turned around. When she faced the door leading out into the hall, the rods moved closer together.

"It's working!" Tanya whispered.

"The temperature is now forty-two degrees," Sue commented.

Tanya crossed the room. Ellen followed her with the camera, with Sue and Isabel at her heels. As they stepped outside of the circle of protection, a chill crept down Ellen's back.

"Please don't be evil," she whispered.

Tanya crossed the parlor and went toward the front door. The rods moved apart. She turned toward the fireplace, and the rods moved slightly together.

She walked around the fireplace to the dining room. The rods moved closer together. She pointed the rods toward the ground below the upstairs bathtub, but the rods pushed apart.

"Huh?" Tanya mumbled. "I was sure this would be where the diary would be."

"Try pointing them up," Sue suggested.

Tanya lifted the rods above her head, and the tips flew together.

"Let's go upstairs," Ellen whispered, full of excitement.

Tanya led the way, the rod tips moving closer together as they ascended the stairs. Ellen felt something brush the back of her other leg, causing her to nearly miss her step.

"You okay?" Sue asked from behind.

"Something touched me again."

Another chill moved through Ellen.

"Please don't be evil," she whispered again.

"Energy is energy," Isabel repeated from behind. "As long as we do what they want, all will be well."

Ellen wanted to say, "Tell that to Henry," but she held her tongue.

Although she had her infrared camera, which could switch modes automatically, Ellen flipped the light-switch on as soon as they reached the top floor. Within seconds of turning on, the light flickered out.

It was darker upstairs, where less light came in through the windows, and colder. Sue confirmed this when she announced that it was thirty-nine degrees. It was September in New Orleans before nightfall, and the room was thirty-nine degrees?

When they reached the claw-foot bathtub, where the man had been found dead, the rods pointed toward the floor and crossed tips.

"We already pulled up all the floors," Sue said with furrowed brows.

Isabel tilted her head to the side. "What about the subfloor? You didn't look beneath the plywood."

"Huh?" Tanya's eyes brightened. "I thought this was the ceiling of the lower level. If we make a hole…"

"No, it's not," Isabel said. "There's at least six inches between the subfloor and the drywall below it—enough room to hide a book."

"Why didn't we know that?" Ellen said. "We're HGTV junkies, and we didn't know that?"

Tanya dropped the rods and ran downstairs to get one of the crowbars that had been left in the dining room. She returned and used the crowbar like an axe, but it wasn't working.

"I need a better tool," Tanya said. "What can we use?"

"Let's use the crowbar like a chisel," Sue said. "We can hit it with another crowbar."

"Take the camera." Ellen handed the camera to Sue before rushing down the stairs to fetch another crowbar.

She ran through the rooms to the dining room, scared to be alone. Then she rushed up the stairs, breathing heavily, realizing she could move quickly when she needed to.

Tanya held one crowbar steady against the plywood while Ellen hammered against it with another, until they'd chipped a hole. Then they turned the crowbar around and pulled until they ripped a chunk of the subfloor up. It was somewhat damaged from water, so it came up easily, now that they had some leverage. They pulled up two more pieces when they came across a leather-bound book.

"Oh, my God!" Sue cried. "There it is!"

Tanya dropped her crowbar and took up the book. She opened it.

"Well?" Isabel asked.

Tears poured down Tanya's cheeks as she smiled up at them. "This is it. The diary of Delphine Lalaurie."

"What are you going to do with it?" Isabel asked.

"Read it," Ellen said. "Try to find out where the devil child was buried."

"We think he was called Charles," Tanya said.

"And after that?" Isabel asked.

Tanya shrugged. "I guess we should give it to the local historical society."

"That's the right thing to do," Isabel said. "But I'd like to read it, too, when you're done."

"Of course," Sue said. "We'll give it to you, since you helped us, and then you can turn it in."

"Let's take Isabel home," Ellen said as she turned off the camera. "We can stop by an ATM machine on the way, to get her cash. Then we can come back and read the diary together."

"Let's go by Starbucks on the way back," Sue said. "I need a latte with extra chocolate syrup to calm my nerves."

When they returned, lattes in hand, they gathered in the living area of the guesthouse on Chartres, where Tanya translated, aloud, the pages of Delphine's diary.

CHAPTER SIXTEEN

Delphine Lalaurie

August 30, 1834

Nothing went as planned.

Whether it was extreme agitation or a miscalculation, Rachel set the fire on Thursday morning, the tenth of April, while Louis and I were still finishing our breakfast in the dining room.

Perhaps it was an accident. Perhaps she was experimenting and did not intend for it to spread. Or perhaps she meant to trap us all.

Regardless, her screams haunt me still.

Why did she not keep to our plan?

And then there was the insufferable Montreuil, whose part in the catastrophe only worsened the results. I should have counted on his interference.

How shocked I was when passengers aboard the *Polish* refused to return my smiles and salutations. They did not look me in the eyes, but I felt their stares on my back.

I have never in my life been treated so poorly. I count among those instances those days when I was but twelve, and Don Ramon seduced me. When my parents forced him to marry me, to protect my virtue; his parents accepted me with opened arms—even after Don Ramon was stripped of his office by the Spanish king. They loved me as a daughter, better than my own father.

Louis's family are disrespectful to their son, to me, and to the children. They are cruel and ill-mannered, the sort of people who want to appear better than they are and yet insult those both above and below them in station.

To mourn is difficult enough. To be ostracized while in mourning is heartbreaking. I have been in tears since we landed, and my in-laws are no help to me with their rude comments.

Louis has gone to a hotel to escape his father. He left me and the children behind. If I never see him again, I shall be happier. But Jean Louis wants his father.

September 17, 1834

The rumors have spread to Paris. I have had to introduce myself with another name, to protect the children. The first name I thought of was D'Arcy.

I was devastated to learn that, while Louis managed to save his medical books and journals, the children's and mine are gone. The diaries I have kept since I was a girl are no more.

I should not cry for my books when so many lives were destroyed that night—mine among them. I am so very low that I doubt I shall ever reach the light of day again.

Why did Rachel not keep to our plan?

September 30, 1834

My money has, at long last, arrived from De Lassus. How weary I had grown of meeting the steamships. The children and I have moved into better rooms on Rue Le Sage, outside of Paris. I am careful to introduce us as D'Arcy. Although the people are friendlier here, they are old and boring. The children and I have little to keep us occupied.

Since my diaries have turned to ash, I shall entertain myself by recounting much of what I had previously written. It helps to dwell on better days, when I was loved and respected in my own city.

My father and mother doted on me and gave me everything I wanted. My aunts, my uncles, and my cousins adored me. All but my father continued to love me through my ordeal with Don Ramon. My father never looked at me the same again.

Don Ramon was the new Spanish *intende*, who had just arrived from Spain after losing his wife to an outbreak of yellow fever. Although he was twice my age, he was youthful and full of charm and vitality. I found him to be extremely handsome. I was used to men giving me attention. I had learned to be polite but distant. Yet in the case of Don Ramon, I could not keep my distance. His dark eyes and curly black hair and beard, his strong, wiry form, and his husky laugh attracted me.

He had been drinking with the other officials at our home on the plantation, celebrating the start of a new year and a new century, the first time he kissed me. We met in secret many times at the parties of my family. I had never been happier until my mother caught us in the south garden on midsummer's eve.

Don Ramon was apologetic to my parents and tender to me. When they insisted that we marry, he agreed, even though he knew he would not be granted permission from the king in time to satisfy my parents. Since two other officers had married without permission before us, he took a chance and was sorely disappointed when the king dismissed him from his office.

For years, he worked tirelessly to petition the king. During that time, I rarely saw him. Never again was our relationship like it had been in those first six months. Don Ramon worried constantly about money and position and had little time for his young bride. I continued to be the center of much attention among the friends of my parents, and many gentlemen continued to admire me even after I was wed. Sometimes, out of boredom, I let down my guard and admired them back, but I never went too far. I had learned the art of beguiling others while remaining respectable. It is a fine line to walk, indeed.

In the spring of '04, when I learned I was pregnant, I made a journey to Spain to speak to the king on my husband's behalf, believing the sight of Don Ramon's pregnant wife might move the king to pardon my husband and reinstate his office. The night before I was to be presented to King Charles, I was kneeling in a courtyard of the Spanish palace praying for strength and favor from the Almighty, when the queen happened upon me. She told me that I made a lovely picture beneath the moonlight. She caressed my long, hair, which fell, unbound, to my waist, and kissed my cheeks, saying she would grant me whatever I came to ask. I told her my story. She said she would speak to the king on my behalf.

The next day, the king pardoned Don Ramon.

I immediately wrote to my husband, who was on his way to meet me in Havana. But fate prevented our happy reunion when his ship was caught in a storm, killing him and several other passengers and crew.

When I arrived in Havana to bury Don Ramon, I gave birth to our sweet and beautiful Borquita, named for his beloved grandmother, who was always kind to me. It was both a joyful and somber time for me, to give birth to a daughter and to bury a husband within a few days.

October 4, 1834

I met Jean Blanque at one of the parties my parents hosted for the dignitaries of Louisiana, before Don Ramon's death. He was among the young officers and politicians who admired me and whom I deigned to admire back. In the year after my husband's passing, Jean continued to admire me with some reserve and constraint, but his charms and good looks grew on me, and by the end of '05, I was in love with him.

Whereas Don Ramon was tender and sensitive, lean and wiry, gentle with words, and constantly worried about money, Jean Blanque was the opposite. Jean was never tender, and his body was thick and massive. He had a boisterous, loud laugh that could bring a room into hysterics. Don Ramon found humor in the silly and ridiculous, but Jean Blanque found it in human foibles and at the expense of the weak. His dominance and authority were never questioned. His wit was sharp and cut deep, and I loved it. He proved a worthy opponent to my own sharp tongue. More than once we drew the attention of an audience with our banter.

Jean's tall and broad frame added to the authority he wielded in any crowd. Whereas Don Ramon cupped my cheeks and gently caressed my lips with his, Jean Blanque grabbed me roughly, pressed his mouth hard to mine, and crushed me in his arms.

It was exhilarating.

Jean's shrewd business dealings and his association with the pirates Pierre and Jean Laffite, who could obtain anything one might need from anywhere in the world, gave Jean a remarkable economic confidence. I did not worry that he might pursue me for the money I would inherit from my father, because he had more than enough of his own.

For three years, Jean and I kept our love affair a secret. When I turned twenty-two in 1808, he surprised me with a proposal, and we were married that same year. My sweet Borquita was nearly four years old.

My darling mother died within a year of my second marriage. Her loss was felt by the entire city. I was soon to learn that my mother's responsibilities of hosting dignitaries fell to me.

Jean and I spent our time between two households—our charming Ville Blanque on the Mississippi River, and our stylish Royal Street brick house in the Vieux Carre. We had the most exotic soirees, in the vein of my parents, but even more spectacular because of Jean's more colorful associates. Because we relied so heavily on their abilities to get us what we could not otherwise obtain, we happily ingratiated ourselves with them as readily as we would the highest dignitaries in the land.

Jean had a rule that all guests must put aside their stations and political differences to revel in the moment. Along with the lively sailors, we entertained the likes of Governor Claiborne, Commander Wilkinson, the Surveyor General Trudeau, Bosque, Marigny, Destrehan, Suave, Derbigny, Macarty, de la Ronde, Villere, and all the well-known leaders of the greatest city in America.

Except for the loss of my mother, those days were some of the best in my life. They were made ever more joyful by the birth of our children, who merged seamlessly into our grand lifestyle, with the help of our many slaves. Jeanne came first in 1810, before the slave revolt in Haiti. Laure was born a year later, just after that dreadful night when our great city saw its own slave revolt, and in which my beloved cousin, Francois, was killed. That marked the day Jean and I began to lock all but our most trusted slaves into their rooms at night, for fear they might kill us in our sleep.

For the next two or three years, Jean traveled more than I wished, and each time he returned home, we were embroiled in our passionate lovemaking, wishing less and less to share our time with the rest of society. Paulin was born in '15, and a year later, Pauline. As an infant, she was perfect, and there was no sign of the deformity that would plague her in later years.

Within a year of Pauline's birth, another epidemic of yellow fever struck Louisiana—the worst yet—and my strong, virile, irascible Jean was struck by it, too, turning him into a helpless infant until his death, six months later. It was a terrible time for me, but not the worst.

The worst was still to come.

October 15, 1834

We have taken rooms on the Rue St. Agnes, with the hope of better entertainment from gayer neighbors. The children had become restless and insufferable with their complaints of boredom. They and I dearly miss their older sisters.

Paulin and Pauline have already found friends nearby to keep them company, and even Jean Louis, when he is not at his lessons, has a playmate who comes to visit often. Only I am without companions. I have never felt so alone.

My loneliness reminds me of those days in the wake of my dearest Jean's death. The world will never know a livelier, more boisterous character—of that, I am certain.

My father died nearly a year after Jean. I had just been to the governor's house to emancipate my oldest slave, Jean Louis, who was well over fifty years of age and had been loyal and kind during his service to our household. I returned home to the awful news that Baba had died of heart failure.

I mourned the days when I was a child and my father had doted on me—before my marriage to Don Ramon. My father had never treated me kindly again, and it had left a hole in my heart.

His death brought me great fortune, however. This made me a desirable match in the eyes of the older unmarried men in my family's circle. At thirty-one, I was still something of a beauty.

For four years, I kept them at bay, occupied by the marriage of my oldest daughter and by the birth of my first grandchild.

In 1825, when Pauline was ten years old, her deformity had long since made its appearance. She walked bent over, doomed, I feared, to become a lonely old hunchback. When I read Dr. Lalaurie's notice in the *Courier* advertising a cure for hunches, a new hope blossomed in my chest for my sweet and gentle Pauline.

The first time I met Louis, I felt an instant attraction to him, perhaps because I saw him as my hope and savior. He was kind and gentle and very optimistic about Pauline's treatment. She would need to undergo at least three operations over the course of a year, with long hospitalizations.

Louis and I began our affair not long after Pauline's first operation. By the time Pauline had endured her final surgery, I was pregnant. I didn't love Louis. Our relationship was formed by my gratitude and by his lust. But a pregnancy introduced a complication. My family would not tolerate the birth of a child outside of marriage.

The doctor had traveled to France when I realized my condition, so I went to his uncle and asked that he send a discreet message to his nephew as soon as possible. My scandalous condition disappointed my favorite aunt and uncle, and enough pressure was put on Louis by both my family and his to force him to return to New Orleans and marry me in June of '28. A few months later, our son was born.

We were miserable from the beginning. By then, I was forty, and he but twenty-five and in the prime of his life. He had hoped to travel to different places to study and learn from other doctors and to try his treatments in many parts of the world. He was ambitious, and our marriage destroyed his dreams.

Although I maintained rights to my property and real estate, in case our marriage should not last, he took charge of my household as if he owned it and everything in it. He could be kind, gentle, and charming when he wanted to be, but when he was irritated, he took it out on everyone around him.

In the first year of our marriage, he was rarely at home, and when he was, we walked on pins and needles.

November 8, 1834

Reading back over what I have written, I recall the fun the children and I had in the weeks that Louis was away. Because we knew his arrival would mean we would once again be forced to walk the straight and narrow, we took advantage of his absence. We danced and ate and drank with the slaves, holding private parties for the household. Rachel taught us an African dance, and she and Devince entertained us with it for hours.

But by 1830, our little house parties ended when Louis opened his practice in our home—my home. I legally owned it. He promised it was temporary. He planned to have a new house built that would afford him a proper office. I told him I would agree to move and to invest in the estate with him if he would agree to host the wonderful parties for which I was once quite famous in my days with Jean. Perhaps because he could not afford such a grand house on his own, he agreed.

Around this time, I was visited by Marie Laveau, a Voodoo practitioner who was acquainted with Louis, having supplied him with various tonics and powders to try on his patients. She came to me in desperation with a newborn baby who was grotesquely deformed. His skin resembled the scales of a tortoise, and his little eyes bulged. His nose was malformed. He looked like a monster. Marie Laveau called him a "devil child" and said the mother had died and the father had abandoned it to her care. But the baby continuously screamed in pain and would not eat from her breast (she had her own baby to nurse). She begged me to beseech the doctor to help the unfortunate child, for even if he was born of a demon, he himself was innocent.

Not wanting to turn my back on an innocent, and imagining it would not live long, I took the baby to Louis, where he was bent over his journal in his office. He seemed pleased for the opportunity to observe and practice on the rare condition. He gave the baby an injection to put him to sleep, and he studied the infant's unusual deformities. I argued that the baby had a soul and must be baptized before he died, lest his soul remain in purgatory. I did not want my own soul besmudged by guilt and sin.

We called Father Antoine to our home for a private baptism, and the devil child was baptized "Charles" after Marie Laveau's father. Louis and I stood in as the baby's godparents.

Louis applied an ointment to the devil baby's skin, which eased his pain for many hours. During that time, the child's nose grew more normally, and he began to look less devil and more angelic—not quite normal, but the human features were visible. When he wasn't in pain, the child cooed and gurgled and smiled, like any other baby. But the reprieve from his pain never lasted more than a few hours. The misery would overtake him, and he would scream until we reapplied the ointment and fed him a calming tonic. In addition to the ointment and tonic, the doctor performed many operations. The child surprised us every day that he thrived.

For reasons I never understood, Marie Laveau came to love the devil child. She could not bear to be away from him for long. More than once a week, she walked to our house to retrieve the child and his medications, and she would keep him for as long as she could before returning him to the doctor's care.

Our new house was complete in the fall of '31. It was a beautiful two-story mansion, with an interior courtyard, six bedrooms, many balconies, and a galley of rooms at the back of the house with a kitchen for the slaves.

I spent months decorating the new house with gorgeous furnishings and the finest art, all at the height of fashion. The children helped and were pleased with their new rooms.

We moved into the mansion in February of '32. We threw a lavish party within a week to introduce our home to my family and friends. Our party received a mention in the society pages, and many more of our gatherings did, thereafter.

The doctor's practice benefited immensely from my parties, so he supported them, though he was never the charismatic host that Jean had been. I should credit Louis, perhaps, for his ability to conduct moving speeches.

Soon he was asked to perform procedures for which he was unstudied, and this was when he began to practice on his slaves. I would not let him touch mine, but I could not prevent him from abusing his own, because I feared the consequences the children and I would face if I tried.

CHAPTER SEVENTEEN

Curses

November 14, 1834

The winter holidays are nearly upon us. The children are anxious for their gifts from the beloved Mother and her Son, our Savior, Jesus Christ; however, I continue to feel lonely, angry, and depressed. I wish I could accept my situation and move on. Instead, I continually wonder how different our lives would be had Rachel stuck to our plan.

In the spring of '32, one of my slaves told my ill-bred cousin and neighbor Montreuil what the doctor was doing to his slaves in the garret. Instead of reporting *Louis*, Montreuil came after *me*, because he was resentful of the property that was bequeathed to me but that he felt was rightfully his. (Montreuil was never pleasant, but, after that transaction, he had become intolerable.)

I was called to the governor's court to be tried for violating the Code Noir, which protects slaves from excessive abuse. I spoke truthfully about my relationships with my own people, but when asked about my husband's behavior, I said that, if they wished to put him on trial, they should summon him to court. I could not speak on his behalf.

I was afraid to reveal the truth because I knew what would happen. Louis would be fined. Perhaps his slaves would be taken away. But then he would simply procure more slaves and carry on as before. Meanwhile the children and I would be made to suffer for my disloyalty.

The judge found me not guilty, and I returned home, vowing never to speak to Montreuil again. I wasn't angry at the slave who betrayed Louis, because he was trying to help his people. I was angry at Montreuil for not having the guts to go after the doctor and for using the opportunity to besmear my good name.

The coward. I hate him.

I hoped the court would follow my suggestion and summon my husband, because I wanted Louis's practice on his slaves to end. My slaves were upset by it and feared they would be similarly treated. The entire household suffered. The moans from the attic weighed on our hearts and our minds. But no charges were ever brought against the doctor.

November 29, 1834

Last Saturday, I went to Paris to shop for Christmas presents for my children and grandchildren. Yesterday, I shipped gifts for my dearest ones in New Orleans, though I know they will not arrive in time. As my favorite uncle often says, better late than not at all.

My joy was short-lived. Tonight, when I opened this diary and reread what I have written thus far, I began to dwell on how much more joyful our Christmas would be together with our family and friends in Louisiana. Tears fell from my eyes and smeared the ink on this very page.

If only Rachel would have staid her hand until the agreed upon time!

Rachel had been a gift from my parents. Short, thin, and missing two teeth, she was at least fifteen years older than I. For as long as I can remember, she had been in my life. She was a talented cook, a kind woman, and a loyal servant who, before Louis's practice in the garret, would have never considered fleeing.

After I returned from court, I told Rachel I would petition for a separation from Louis, offering to buy his share of the estate. The doctor would be forced to move and to take his unfortunate patients with him. I told her this to discourage her from running away.

Although Rachel was comforted by this plan, she revealed her fears for her cousin, Devince, who had been asked by the doctor to assist him in an upcoming procedure on young Armand, a slave belonging to Louis. Louis had previously asked for my assistance, but I had refused, unable to stomach the sight of blood and innards. Devince did not belong to my husband. Louis had no right to solicit his help without my permission, and I had no intention of granting my permission if Louis had deigned to ask.

I immediately took measures to have Devince emancipated. Louis was furious with me and made a scandalous scene on the steps of the courthouse. I used his mistreatment of me as supporting evidence for the petition I submitted a few weeks later, requesting our legal separation. The judge signed an order permitting me to go forward with my suit against Louis.

However, the events that followed rendered that endeavor impossible.

December 20, 1834

We had a miserable visit with the Lalauries. Why did I think the Christmas spirit would move them to be kind and polite? They were hardly civil. I have upset my children by forcing them to make the visit. I have ruined their Christmas and mine.

January 10, 1835

I had hoped a new year would bring a fresh start to my household, but we are all in a foul mood, especially Jean Louis. His father came to visit on Christmas day and left two days later. Jean Louis has been in tears ever since.

Paulin resents his stepfather and told him, just before he left, that his random visits were too upsetting to Jean Louis. Paulin will be twenty years old next month, and he fancies himself the man of the house. Louis merely forced a grin and said through gritted teeth that he would do as he pleased.

It was two years ago that I said similar words to my husband. I showed him the petition that had been granted by the judge and revealed my plans to sue for the separation. Louis had the same reaction to me then, gritted teeth and all.

Not long after this declaration to my husband, I was visited by Marie Laveau. As often as she came and left this house, to deliver or to receive her devil child, I rarely spoke to her. She usually dealt with Anne or Lucille, the young negresses who helped Rachel in the kitchen when they were not caring for the children.

But on this day in January two years ago, she asked for a private interview with me. I offered her a chair in the parlor, where no one would disturb us. She had just left the devil child with Anne, who had taken him to see the doctor in his office on the other side of the house.

By this time, the devil child was three years old. He could walk and speak. Although he was still plagued by his skin condition, and his facial features looked abnormal, he was otherwise like any other child of his age. Unfortunately, the other children shunned him. Even Jean Louis was afraid to look at him and would cry in the boy's presence. I felt sorry for the child, and I sometimes tried to comfort him with candies and gifts.

That day Marie Laveau sat across from me and said that the spirits had warned her of my intention to separate from the doctor. She threatened to curse me, my children, and my property if I went through with the lawsuit. She needed the doctor to remain close by, so he could continue to care for the devil child. She said she would bless us with great prosperity if I allowed the doctor to stay.

I asked why she thought he would leave New Orleans if we separated. She said the spirits had told her he would.

I had heard rumors of the Voodoo queen's powers. I was frightened by her threat. If she had threatened me alone, I might have risked it; but, she included my children and slaves.

I asked her why she referred to the boy as a "devil child" when she clearly loved him. She said she did it for his own protection. She wanted people to fear him so that they would leave him alone and not act cruelly toward him. There was power in being feared, she said. How right she was.

That night, I confided in Rachel what Marie Laveau had said in our private interview. Rachel's dark eyes widened with fear. She believed in the Voodoo queen's magic and advised me not to go through with the lawsuit.

By this time Devince had still not been emancipated, and the doctor had already solicited his help behind my back in two operations on slaves in the garret. Rachel told me that same night after Marie Laveau's visit that she was afraid for Devince. He had spoken to Rachel about running away, because he could not bear to play a role in the doctor's experimental procedures upstairs. She feared, if he ran, that he would be caught and lynched. I promised her I would ask the court to expedite Devince's case, but I knew the gesture would prove futile.

Later that night, I asked my butler, Bastien, to keep an eye on Devince. I told him what Rachel had shared with me. He agreed to lock Devince in his sleeping quarters at night and to keep a watchful eye on him during the day.

This practice continued until October, when Devince's papers, stating that he was a free man, finally arrived.

Devince had not been gone but one week when it was brought to my attention that the doctor had coerced my slave Bastien to assist him in Devince's place. Bastien was like an uncle to me. Like Rachel, he was a gift from my parents when I married Don Ramon. It pained me to know the horrors he was being forced to endure at the doctor's hands. I argued with Louis nearly every day, reminding him that he had no right to my slaves. I threatened to expose his vile treatment of his own slaves to the authorities. But these fights were for naught; he did as he pleased.

My fear of Marie Laveau prevented me from following through with my threat to expose the doctor. Instead, Rachel and I solicited the help of her cousin Sarah Lee, a free woman of color.

January 30, 1835

Recalling my dealings with Sarah Lee has prompted me to file a suit against her. I mentioned it in my letter to De Lassus requesting more money. I fear I should have signed power of attorney to Placide, as the doctor did. De Lassus has proven unreliable.

Rachel's idea to approach her cousin, Sarah Lee, initially seemed a sound one.

Marie Laveau had threatened to curse me, my children, and my property if I took measures to remove the doctor from my household, but she could not fault me if another made accusations against him. Rachel spent the following Sunday with her cousin Sarah (and Devince, who planned to live with Sarah until he could afford his own rooms). During her visit, Rachel petitioned Sarah to bring charges of slave abuse against the doctor. I would pay Sarah five hundred dollars, if she agreed to come forward and testify against the doctor.

When Rachel returned, she said that Sarah would consider my offer. Within a week, Sarah accepted, on condition that I give her the money immediately. I sent the funds with Rachel the following Sunday, along with a contract specifying that if services were not rendered, the money must be returned. Sarah signed the contract and returned it with Rachel.

In the following days, I noticed a change in the morale of the household, leading me to suspect that the other slaves knew of my arrangement. I dreaded what might happen if Louis were to get wind of it. With each passing day, I became more and more nervous and anxious. When four months went by and no letter from the court arrived, I went to see Sarah Lee myself.

I was shocked to learn that Sarah had been visited by Marie Laveau and threatened in a similar way as I. Sarah confessed that she had already spent the money but was terrified of the Voodoo queen. Sarah would not bring charges against the doctor.

I asked her how Marie Laveau came to know of our arrangement, and Sarah replied, "The spirits told her."

I decided to go to Congo Square on Sunday night to witness, firsthand, Marie Laveau in action. Every Sunday, people, both slaves and free, attend, in large numbers, a celebration of the sabbath in the way of their African ancestors. I had never been, though I had heard of other Creole and whites attending.

I was astonished to discover that almost as many whites as colored were in attendance, and equally astonished that they participated in the wild dancing, drinking, and prayer led by the Voodoo queen, who stood in the center of their circle near a large bonfire with a python draped around her shoulders. It was June of '33, when nights were intemperate. At one point in the ceremony, the drums stopped, the dancing came to a halt, and people were invited to make offerings to the Voodoo queen in exchange for a favor.

I watched in silence for an hour, screwing up the courage to speak to Marie Laveau, to petition her with my offering. But before I had decided what I would do, she noticed me standing there, alone, on the outskirts of the ring of multitudes. She narrowed her eyes at me, stomped her foot, and hurled her snake into the fire.

The snake shrieked and writhed. I had never heard a sound more haunting—not until the day of the fire, when Rachel screamed as the flames consumed her.

February 15, 1835

One year ago, on this day, the devil child died while under the doctor's care.

As saddened as I was by the death of the child—as one would be to hear of the passing of any child—I was elated by the prospect of finally being free of Louis and his abhorrent ways.

I took it upon myself to personally notify Marie Laveau. She was hesitant to receive me in her home on St. Anne's, but when I told her slave that I had important news, the Voodoo queen met me at the door and beckoned me to enter.

She did not offer me a chair. We stood in the foyer, where I told her what had happened. The child had not survived his operation.

The look of horror that flashed across her face frightened me. Then she wailed and moaned and pulled at her hair. Fearing for my life, I ran to the door, but she grabbed my arm and stared at me with wide, hateful eyes.

"Where is he now, my debil chile?" she asked.

I replied that he was in the doctor's office, being prepared for burial.

"I'll come for him tonight," she said.

I lifted my chin. "Promise to remove your threat to me, to my children, and to my household. Promise to release me from any future threat. Only then will I allow you to take the child from my home."

The Voodoo queen was not pleased that the tables had turned. She narrowed her eyes at me and told me that I would hand over the child tonight, or else.

"Or else what?" I asked.

"You'll be cursed, and your chillen 'll suffer, too."

March 11, 1835

I had come to realize that Marie Laveau intended to curse me whether she received her devil child or not. She had been the cause of great anxiety in my household, and I could not allow myself to give in to her threats a moment longer.

When I returned from Marie Laveau's house, I told Louis that I would personally see to the burial of our godchild. The doctor had already prepared and wrapped the body. Bastien helped me to find a crate, and then he loaded the crate with the body into the carriage and drove me out to my parents' old plantation, where the Voodoo queen would never find her devil child.

I chose a place on high ground—one I could easily find if Marie Laveau ever swore to release me from her threats. It was the Etienne de Bore Oak, which grew on the lower riverside of my parents' sugar cane plantation and was named for Jean Etienne de Bore, the first mayor of New Orleans. It was also the spot where Don Ramon and I first kissed and where Jean Blanque and I first declared our love to one another.

We reached the tree by nightfall. It was easy enough to find, being less than a quarter of a mile from the river. I held the lantern while Bastien shoveled the earth and buried the child. I marked the grave with a circle of stones. I said a prayer, asking the Almighty to forgive me for not giving the child a proper burial and to receive the child into His heavenly kingdom. I hoped my little prayer would be answered, but a nagging feeling in the pit of my stomach made me fear that it had not been.

CHAPTER EIGHTEEN

The Tree of Life

Ellen gawked at Tanya, who sat beside her on the couch with Delphine's diary in her lap.

Tanya looked up from the diary with tears in her eyes. "We'll never find the devil child. Guys, what am I going to do?"

"If it's not buried at the Lalaurie Mansion," Sue said, from where she sat in the chair opposite them, "why did Marie Laveau say it was?"

Ellen threw up her hands. "Obviously, she didn't know."

"I don't want to die." Tanya wiped her tears with the inside of her shirt.

"Don't get your panties in a wad," Sue said as she tapped on her phone. "I just Googled Etienne de Bore Oak, and you'll never believe what I found."

"Well, don't keep us in suspense," Ellen demanded.

"Listen to this," Sue said. "'The Etienne de Bore Oak, dubbed "The Tree of Life" by locals, was named after the first mayor of New Orleans. The tree stands on what was once part of de Bore's massive sugar cane plantation and is now Audubon Park.'"

Tanya's face brightened. "Oh, my God! Where's Audubon Park?"

"According to this website, it's in uptown, about thirty minutes away."

Ellen climbed from the couch and slipped on her shoes. "Is the tree marked?"

"It's on Google Maps," Sue said. "What are you doing?"

"We need to drive out there tonight, while it's dark, so we won't be seen," Ellen said.

"And do what?" Sue asked.

"Dig up the devil child," Ellen said. "Come on, guys. Get your shoes on. Let's go."

"What?" Tanya looked at Ellen like she was crazy.

"Do you think there will be anything left to dig up?" Sue asked. "It's been nearly two hundred years."

"There has to be," Ellen said, grabbing her purse from the kitchen counter. "Otherwise, the spirit of Marie Laveau wouldn't be after us to find it."

"But we don't have any shovels," Tanya said.

"Walmart does," Ellen pointed out. "Sue, can you find the nearest one?"

"On it." Sue tapped on the screen of her phone. "But think about this, Ellen. The child could be anywhere beneath that tree. We could be digging all night. We need to ask Delphine Lalaurie to guide us."

"Good idea," Ellen said. "Let's get our gear from the main house. Tanya, bring the dousing rods and Delphine's diary. Sue, you grab the salt. We should take along our camping chairs, too."

Sue grabbed the carton from the kitchen counter. "Okay, but you don't expect *me* to dig, do you?"

"Of course not," Tanya said. "If we're really going to do this, I'll do the digging."

"I'm just kidding, Tanya. Of course, I'm going to dig."

Ellen lifted her chin and guffawed. She laughed so hard that her belly hurt.

Sue gave her a hurt look.

"Sorry," Ellen said, feeling hysterical. "I'm not laughing at you. I'm laughing at all of us. None of us is really equipped for this, but I love that we're doing it anyway."

"For Tanya," Sue said.

Ellen smiled, still feeling a bit hysterical. "For Tanya."

Tanya's eyes filled with tears again, and, this time, they fell down her cheeks. "Thanks, guys. I owe you big time."

"Yes, you do," Sue said as she slipped on her shoes. "Now wipe those tears and let's go. Walmart is on the way."

They went to the main house to get their chairs and some of their other gear and then hauled it out to the bay, where the rental was parked. They loaded up the vehicle and climbed in, Ellen drove while Sue navigated from the back seat.

As Ellen turned off Chartres and headed east, she said, "You know we're not just doing this for you, Tanya. We're doing this for Cornelius and for Maria Nunnery, for the devil child and for Marie Laveau, so they can find peace. You don't owe us anything for helping. You're helping them, too."

"In fact," Sue said from the back seat. "You're helping more than any of us, even if it wasn't by choice."

Ellen almost said, "And you have the most to lose if we fail," but, fortunately, she caught herself.

"Thanks, guys," Tanya said. "I guess it's a good thing I'm fluent in French." She chuckled. "And when this is all over, I want to finish reading Delphine's diary. I want to know what really happened on April 10, 1834."

"Me, too," Sue said. "I hope Delphine reveals what the real plan was—the one that Rachel didn't follow."

"Me, too," Ellen said.

Twenty minutes later, they entered Walmart and headed straight to the garden center in search of shovels. They picked up flashlights and batteries, too, and, at Sue's insistence, a dozen glazed donuts and bottles of cola, to keep their energy up. Tanya, the healthy one in the group when she didn't have a ghost attachment, insisted that they also take bottled water.

At the checkout, the cashier—a young man in his twenties with a round belly, glasses, and pretty, green eyes—arched a brow as he rang up the shovels.

"Burying a dead body?" he asked playfully.

"Something like that," Sue said.

The young man's eyes widened. "I hope not."

"I'm just kidding," Sue said. "We're treasure hunters."

The cashier furrowed his brows. "Treasure hunters, huh? Along the river, or what?"

"Yeah," Ellen said. "Along the river. Our metal detectors went wild this afternoon, so we're going back tonight to dig deeper."

"Okay," he said with skepticism. "That'll be eighty-four twenty-seven."

Tanya handed over her credit card, and, as they left, the cashier said, "Good luck."

"Thanks," Tanya said.

Sue added, "We'll need it."

Ellen took Tchoupitoulas Street toward East Drive for about twenty more minutes and turned right. She hadn't gone far, just past the tennis courts, when Google Maps indicated that their destination was on the left. Ellen pulled into a spot on the edge of the park, glad the place seemed deserted.

The three of them unloaded their gear and hauled it, along with their camping chairs, across the grass toward the tree. There was a little light from the moon and stars and a distant lamppost—enough to make out the silhouette of the tree and of the wooden fence behind it, but not enough to clearly see the path ahead of them. They used their flashlights to guide them.

Ellen had expected there to be a breeze this close to the river, but the air was hot, humid, and still.

"Is that the zoo over there?" Tanya asked, pointing her flashlight beyond the Tree of Life.

"Yep," Sue said. "Can't you smell it?"

"Is that what I smell?" Tanya asked. "At least it's not me this time."

"Not you," Ellen said. "Cornelius."

"Right," Tanya laughed.

"That's supposed to be the giraffe exhibit on the other side of that fence," Sue said. "The website said that if you climb up the tree, you can get a great view of it."

As they grew close to the old oak, Ellen stopped to shine her light on it. "Wow. Look at it."

The thick trunk and its mass of gnarly roots appeared to be at least thirty feet in diameter, and the twisting, knobby branches spread out more than a hundred and fifty feet, drooping all the way to the ground in places.

"What if the devil child is buried beneath those roots?" Tanya asked. "Oh, God. I think I'm going to be sick."

"Let's set up the séance," Sue said. "And try to have a positive attitude."

They unfolded their camping chairs and placed them in a circle. Sue made a line of salt around them and lit the candles at the four cardinal points, while Ellen put donuts and cola (offering for the spirits), along with Delphine's diary, on some paper towels in the circle's center. Tanya positioned the EMF detector, EVP recorder, motion sensors, and geophone vibration sensor around the perimeter of their circle. Ellen grabbed the video recorder, and Sue took a reading on the thermometer.

"Ready?" Ellen asked.

"Ready," Tanya said.

"Let me just finish this donut real quick," Sue said before stuffing the last bite into her mouth. Then she took a swig of her cherry coke. A few seconds later she nodded. "Okay. Ready."

"Recording," Ellen said.

"It's eighty-eight degrees," Sue said.

Ellen pointed the camera at Tanya. "Tanya, why don't you take the lead on this one?"

"What was that sound?" Tanya asked. "I heard something in the tree—like an animal or something."

"Probably a bird or a squirrel. Try to ignore it," Ellen said. "Go ahead and start."

Tanya nodded and took a deep breath. "Spirits of the other realm, we mean you no harm. We are looking for Delphine Lalaurie, who died around 1858. Delphine Lalaurie, we call upon you to help us find the devil child, which you buried beneath this tree in 1832. We have your diary, hoping you will sense it, along with our offering of food and drink. Follow the light of our candles and allow your diary to pull you to us. Madame Delphine Lalaurie, we call upon you for help and guidance."

"Delphine Lalaurie," Sue said. "Marie Laveau once threatened to curse you, and maybe she did curse you. She's also cursed my friend, sitting here with us. If you don't help us, she could die."

"Sue," Ellen interrupted, noticing Tanya's tears welling up again.

"It's okay," Tanya said. "I'm okay."

"Please help us save our friend from Marie Laveau's curse, as you once tried to save yourself and your children," Sue said. "Delphine Lalaurie, please show us where you buried the devil child."

"Delphine Lalaurie, are you here?" Tanya asked. "If so, please give us a sign."

After a minute passed and nothing happened, Tanya picked up the dousing rods. "Calling Madame Delphine Lalaurie. If you're here with us, please move the tips of these rods closer together."

They watched the rods in silence, but nothing happened.

Tanya shook her head and whispered, "I don't feel anything."

Many minutes passed as they sat in their camping chairs in the sticky night, calling out to the spirit of Delphine Lalaurie. The candles flickered a few times, but it seemed more likely to have been caused by a slight breeze than a ghost. Ellen was trying to stay optimistic, but she could sense that Tanya was feeling desperate.

"Guys, this isn't working," Tanya said when nearly an hour had passed, and it was approaching midnight. "What are we going to do?"

"We're not going to give up," Ellen said. "That's what we're going to do."

"Try speaking in French," Sue suggested.

Tanya held the rods parallel and repeated her speech in French. Still nothing happened.

The sound of approaching footsteps startled Ellen and her friends, and they all turned their flashlights in the direction they were coming from.

"What's going on here?"

It was a security guard. Ellen hadn't expected the park to be patrolled this late at night.

"We're having a séance," Sue said. "A paranormal investigation."

"Is there a problem officer?" Ellen asked, pointing her camera at him.

"You can't have those candles lit out here," he said. "You're going to have to put them out."

"Oh, no," Tanya said. "We need them to stay lit."

"It's okay, Tanya," Ellen said. "We can work without the candles."

Ellen and Tanya got up and blew the candles out.

"It's okay if we continue, isn't it?" Ellen asked the security guard. "As long as we keep the candles unlit?"

"Yes, ma'am," the officer said. "I hate to ruin your fun, but it's the law. You could start a fire out here, and then we'd all be in trouble, especially those animals on the other side of the fence."

"We didn't think about that," Sue said. "Please accept our apologies."

"No problem," the officer said. "But just know there's a $500 for anyone who lights a flame of any sort that's not in one of the grills in the picnic area."

"Yes, sir," Ellen said. "Thank you."

The officer bid them good night and then headed back toward the road, where his patrol vehicle was parked.

"Should I start digging?" Tanya asked. "I don't think we're going to get any spirits without the candles."

"That's not necessarily true," Sue said. "We can use our flashlights. Now, come on. Don't give up so easily. We can stay out here all night, if we need to."

Ellen pointed the camera at Tanya. "Begin again."

Tanya repeated the same speech, calling out to the spirit of Delphine Lalaurie. When she got tired of talking, Sue took over. Another hour past without any sign. Ellen was getting worried that they would have to start digging and keep digging all night.

"I don't think Delphine wants to help us," Tanya said. "Even if she can hear us, she doesn't want to help Marie Laveau."

"You could be right," Ellen admitted.

"Let's try calling the slave who dug the hole for her," Sue said. "What was his name? Bastien?"

"Good idea!" Ellen said.

"But we don't have anything of his," Tanya pointed out. "Do you think it would work?"

"We should try," Ellen said. "We may as well."

"I wish we knew his last name," Sue said. "Okay, here I go." She cleared her throat. "Spirits of the other realm, I'm looking for Bastien, a man who lived in this area and was the butler for Madam Delphine Lalaurie in the eighteen-hundreds. Bastien, if you can hear me, we mean you no harm. We're here to help bring peace to the devil child, named after Marie Laveau's father, Charles. According to Delphine's diary, you dug the hole the child was buried in. If you can hear me, please give us a sign."

A cry rang out in the dark night.

"What was that?" Ellen whispered.

"An animal, I think," Sue said.

"I don't think we can count that as a sign," Tanya said.

"Bastien," Sue said aloud. "Please give us a sign, something we'll know came from you."

One of the flashlights flickered and then went off.

"Was that a sign?" Tanya whispered. "Or did we buy bad batteries?"

Ellen moved the camera in the direction of the flashlight that had gone out. Through the lens of the camera, she saw a dark shadow standing there, outside of their circle.

"Guys, I think I see something," she said. "Bastien? Is that you?"

The silhouette of a person emerged from the shadow as one of the other flashlights flickered and went out.

All three of them gasped.

"They couldn't all be bad batteries," Sue whispered. Then, aloud, she said, "Bastien, if you can hear me, please show us where the devil child was buried."

"You can show me by moving the rod tips closer together as I move toward the spot," Tanya said.

Ellen saw the silhouette of a man step from the edge of their circle and leap to where a thick branch of the tree touched the ground. The shadowy figure pointed to the ground before it disappeared.

"Did you guys see that?" Ellen asked, trying to keep from shaking the camera with her trembling hands.

"See what?" Tanya asked.

"I felt something," Sue said. "What did you see?"

"He pointed to the ground over there, where that branch dips down," Ellen explained.

"Seriously?" Tanya asked.

"I promise that's what I saw," Ellen said, turning off the camera. "Let's start digging!"

They each took a sip of their drinks before grabbing their shovels and moving to the spot where Ellen had seen the ghost disappear.

"You do the honors, Tanya," Sue said. "You break ground."

They all laughed. Ellen felt both ridiculous and profoundly important. Once Tanya drove her shovel through the earth, the others got digging, too.

"This ground is much easier than the rock and clay we have in San Antonio," Ellen said.

"Thank God," Sue said. "Digging through rock would take all night."

"It still might take us all night," Tanya said. "Who knows how deeply Bastien buried the child, or how much the terrain has changed since 1832. They may have added layers of topsoil when they created the park."

"Not this close to the tree," Ellen pointed out. "It would have killed it."

"Or, there could be nothing left of the child's remains," Tanya said before she drove her shovel into the ground.

After she'd dug out two or three scoops of dirt, Sue dropped her shovel. "I'm getting my chair. I think I can do this better sitting down."

Ellen and Tanya rolled their eyes at each other as they kept digging. Sue took her time getting her chair. Then she plopped into it and used her feet to stick the shovel into the earth.

"Well, I guess this wasn't a good idea after all," Sue said. She climbed to her feet.

By that time, Tanya and Ellen had already made a hole about two feet deep. The deeper they went, the harder the ground seemed to get. Tanya stopped to catch her breath. Ellen returned to their circle to get their drinks. The hot and sticky air wasn't helping.

"I think I'm getting a blister," Sue said as she tossed a shovel of dirt behind her.

"Take a break," Tanya insisted. "I can do the digging."

Ellen handed them each a bottled water. She guzzled half of hers down before she dropped it on the ground and returned to her digging.

"I hope we're not just wasting our time and energy," Tanya said. "If y'all want to rest, I can keep going."

"You're the one who should rest," Sue said. "You don't look so good."

"I *am* feeling a little dizzy," Tanya admitted.

Ellen grabbed Tanya's shovel from her. "Sit down and take a break."

"Maybe for a few minutes." Tanya sat in the chair Sue had brought over from their circle. "Gosh, it's so hot."

Sue went and brought the other two camping chairs closer to their digging site. "Why don't we all take a breather."

"Thanks, Sue." Ellen sat down and finished her water.

"It's too bad Michael Rouchelle couldn't be here with us tonight," Sue said. "It might be more fun to watch him dig than to do it ourselves."

Ellen chuckled. "We wanted an adventure, didn't we?"

"Well, maybe not quite like this," Sue said. "I'd rather Tanya's life not be on the line."

"Sue!" Ellen chastised.

"It's okay," Tanya said, wiping her eyes. "Sue's right. This might have to be the last haunted house I flip with you guys. It's gotten to be too much, you know?"

"Don't say that!" Ellen said with wide eyes. "Seriously, Tanya. We'll get through this."

Tanya covered her face and sobbed.

Sue, who was closer to Tanya, reached over and patted her back. "Ellen's right. We'll get through this. But we'll understand, whatever you decide."

Tanya nodded, but kept her face covered.

Ellen climbed to her feet and grabbed her shovel. She understood how frightened Tanya was, but she hated the idea of her giving up on Ghost Healers, Inc. It had become the highlight of Ellen's life. Her children were busy with their own lives. Even Paul seemed to have moved on to his own things. Solving mysteries and bringing peace to ghosts, while returning historical buildings to their former glory, gave her a true sense of purpose.

She threw herself into the shovel and was surprised when she struck something solid in the earth.

Sue climbed to her feet. "What was that?"

"I don't know." Ellen dug around carefully. Then she crouched on the ground and used her hands to dig around the object. "It's a wooden crate!"

They all three crouched down and dug with their hands, revealing the top of a wooden box. Once they had cleared the top of it, Ellen used her shovel to crack open the lid.

Inside they found tattered pieces of fabric covered in meal worms and a small human skeleton.

"Oh my gosh!" Tanya cried. "We found the devil child!"

CHAPTER NINETEEN

The Fire of April 10, 1834

With the remains of the devil child in the trunk of their rental, Ellen drove Tanya and Sue back to the house on Chartres Street. It was after three in the morning by the time they reached the guesthouse and unloaded their gear. They each showered and, soon after, went to sleep, exhausted. In the morning, Ellen called Maria Nunnery to share the good news. Ellen asked Maria to arrange for the child's internment in the Laveau family tomb.

"Glapion," Maria corrected. "It's the Glapion family tomb. And, my goodness, I can't believe this! I will call the archdiocese as soon as we hang up. I can't thank you and your friends enough. I'm so relieved that Cornelius will finally find peace!"

"Please let us know where and when to deliver the remains," Ellen said.

"I will, Ellen. God bless you."

Tanya, who'd been making sausage and eggs in the kitchen, asked, "What do you guys want to do next? Finish reading Delphine's diary, or go over the recordings from our investigations?"

"Finish the diary," Sue said.

Ellen nodded. "I'm dying to know what really happened on the day of the fire and will throw that book across the room—I don't care how old it is—if Delphine doesn't tell us what the plan was and how it went wrong."

Once they had finished their breakfast, Tanya and Ellen curled up on opposite ends of the couch, and Sue took the chair, resting her stockinged feet on the coffee table. They sipped on their coffees as Tanya found where she had left off in the diary.

March 22, 1835

I met a handsome Frenchman at the parish carnival yesterday. He was a widower with three grown sons and a good deal of wealth. I permitted him to escort me around the grounds. He was a pleasant distraction from my pain and sorrow.

As much as I would like to believe that I might still find happiness, I know I am cursed for all eternity.

Marie Laveau made that very clear when she came to claim her devil child the day Bastien and I buried him. I told her she could go to hell. She told me that I would soon know hell on earth.

How I wish I would have heeded her warning, dug up the child, and returned him to her. Perhaps I would still be in my home on Royal Street today—not happy, but not miserable.

March 30, 1835

One year from today, Rachel said it was time for me to wake up and face facts.

She was the only slave, aside from Bastien, who could speak to me in such a manner.

"What do you mean?" I asked her.

She told me that the suffering in the attic had gone on for too long. The doctor's slaves needed to be put out of their misery. For months, one of the captives, Catherine, a cousin of Rachel's, had pleaded with Rachel to obtain some poison for her, so she could kill herself; however, the doctor controlled everything that went in and out of the room. He kept the garret locked and carefully guarded the key.

"There's only one way to free them," Rachel said. "We have to burn the house down."

I told her too many people might be injured or killed. She said we could start the fire on a Sunday, while the slaves were off, and the children were at their catechism. Only those locked in the attic would remain.

"You do not believe it too horrible a way to die?" I asked. "To be burned alive? Some of them are still conscious."

"The smoke would kill them before the flames," Rachel said.

"But what about my valuables?" I argued.

She said I could think of a reason to ask Borquita and Jeanne to store them for me.

"But what of the furniture?" I asked.

She said that some things were more important than furniture. Human suffering was one of those things.

I told her I would give it some thought.

Honestly, as poorly as I felt over the fates of those locked in the garret, I did not wish to give up my home and valuables. There was no method for relocating everything I wanted to save. And I could not try to do so without raising my husband's suspicion. I was not certain that I was prepared to make such sacrifices for the wellbeing of a handful of slaves.

I chained Rachel to the stove, explaining that I needed more time and feared she would not allow for it. I believed I was preventing her from carrying on without me—an assumption I will regret forever.

April 5, 1835

One year from this day, I told Rachel I would conspire with her to end the suffering of the doctor's slaves.

I came to this conclusion because of something I witnessed through the window of the garret door.

Seven of the doctor's slaves were chained and bolted to the floor. This much I already knew. Four of them—Lizzy, Tina, Carol, and Armand—lay on cots with tubes and bags attached to them, presumably for consuming and excreting fluids. They rarely moved anymore, though their moans and groans indicated that they were still alive and somewhat conscious. They had been operated on many times, and their bodies were covered in scars, where the doctor had taken flesh and grafted it onto the devil child.

The other three—Thomas, Catherine, and Lucas—sat or lay on the floor. They shared a common chamber pot that was rarely emptied, and they slept without bedding. They appeared emaciated and dehydrated. Catherine wore a spiked iron collar that prevented her from moving. She sat with her back against the wall with her eyes closed. Her breaths were rapid. I could not tell if she was conscious.

As I secretly peered through the iron bars of the tiny window in the door, I held my breath—to avoid the foul stench and to prevent myself from screaming.

The doctor bent over Catherine and peeled off a section of her scalp, exposing her skull! Then, before I could pull myself away, Catherine opened her eyes and glared at me!

I was nearly sick beside the door. I fought the urge to vomit and fled the attic before the doctor discovered me. I went directly to the kitchen, where I told Rachel I would agree to help her carry out her plan the next day.

I kept her chained to the stove, so she would not act before I was ready.

April 10, 1835

I dread the letters I shall receive in the coming months from my loved ones in New Orleans, because they will no doubt mention the papers' inevitable reminders of the catastrophe that took place this time last year. The papers will refer to me as the "monstrous Madame Delphine Lalaurie" and make no mention of Louis. I am sure of it. Marie Laveau has won.

But she shall never have her devil child.

On Sunday, April 6th, 1834, I called off Rachel's plan to start the fire. We had just celebrated Easter the previous Sunday, and because I had been busy preparing for it, I had not had adequate time to move my valuables to the houses of my daughters for safekeeping. I promised Rachel we would carry out our plan the following Sunday, April 13th.

Rachel did not object, so I was taken by surprise when smoke infiltrated my breakfast table on the morning of Thursday, April 10th. As I stood from my chair, the sound of a loud pop from the kitchen startled me. Although it was unexpected, the fire was less of a surprise to me than it was to Louis. He ran straight for his medical books and journals and ignored anyone who tried to stop him.

I stumbled to the kitchen to question Rachel only to find it engulfed in flames. As I stood there in shock, I heard Rachel's screams. I cried out to her, "Why? Why did you do this?" But it was too late. She was gone.

My next priority was the children. Once I saw to their safety, I endeavored to salvage as many of my jewels and other valuables as I could. A few of our neighbors came to help, and I gave them instructions on what to save and what to leave behind.

The fire brigade soon arrived and contained the fire, saving much of our home. The house might have survived, and my reputation along with it, had my ill-bred cousin Montreuil not asked about the slaves chained in the garret. Judge Canongo asked Louis and me if there were slaves upstairs. We both denied it but for different reasons. Montreuil insisted that he spoke the truth. The judge followed Montreuil and our other neighbor, Fernandez, upstairs. They quickly returned, hacking up smoke. Then another neighbor, Felix Lefebrve, came to them and said he had discovered the slaves behind a locked door in the attic. The men followed Lefebrve, as Louis and I continued to salvage all we could of our valuables. I prayed the seven captives were already dead, but when the men returned, I saw my husband's victims were still alive.

The seven slaves were taken away. It did not take long for word to spread about their horrific mistreatment. People also heard that both my husband and I had refused to help them or to admit that they had been chained, defenseless, upstairs during the conflagration. People were outraged, as they had every right to be. However, I was mortified when they turned their outrage on me and my home.

What the fire brigade had saved, the mob of outraged citizens destroyed. Realizing our lives were in danger, Louis instructed me to take the children in the carriage to Bayou St. John and to board a boat. He would meet us in Mandeville as soon as he could. Fearing for my children's lives, I did as he said. I waved at the angry people when we passed on the road, hoping they would see my innocence.

I soon discovered that Marie Laveau had succeeded in making my life into a living hell.

April 19, 1835

Without any notice, Louis came to Paris and attended Easter Mass with the children and me this morning. Out of obligation, I invited him to luncheon afterward. Even though his presence was confusing and upsetting to Jean Louis and to the other children, I am glad my husband came. I discovered the answer to something that has been weighing on my mind for over a year.

In a private interview with me before his departure this evening, he brought up the anniversary of the fire that had destroyed our Royal Street home. I asked him if he had ever learned any news about what might have caused it. He said that the fire marshal had concluded it had begun in the kitchen. Louis believed Rachel had started it intentionally. When I asked why he thought this to be true, he confided in me that his poor judgment had been the cause of it. He said that he had made the mistake of letting Bastien become aware the morning of the fire of the doctor's intention to begin practicing that evening on Rachel's grand-daughter, a slave Louis had purchased from my aunt. Louis speculated that Bastien must have told Rachel, and Rachel, wishing to spare her granddaughter, set the house ablaze, even though it meant her own certain death.

Louis apologized for that part he played in the catastrophe, having no knowledge of his greater role or of my plans with Rachel. Although he was acquainted with the rumors about me, he made no apology about them. He offered no words of comfort or regret. He made no acknowledgment of the fact that my life now lay in ruins.

Tanya looked up from the journal and muttered, "Wow. Should I keep going?"

"Why don't we take a moment to process what you've just read?" Ellen suggested.

Sue took a sip of her coffee. "I can't believe I feel sorry for Delphine."

"Me, too," Tanya admitted.

"I wonder if this diary will change anything," Ellen said. "Or if history will continue to paint her as a monster."

"That's a good question," Tanya said.

"Why don't we ponder it over lunch?" Sue said. "I made another reservation for us at Antoine's."

When the three friends returned from lunch, they hooked up the camcorder to Sue's laptop to review the footage they'd taken in both the main house with Priestess Isabel and at Audubon Park beneath the Tree of Life.

Sue sat between Tanya and Ellen on the couch with her laptop on her lap. Ellen kept notes in her journal as they watched.

"That curtain by the French doors keeps moving," Sue pointed out. "Did you see that?"

"There could be a draft coming through," Ellen said. "We should check that out."

Tanya pointed to the screen. "I keep seeing a shadow on me. Do you guys notice it?"

Ellen nodded. "I saw the same thing in the photo that was taken of us at Drummond Lodge."

"You think it's Cornelius?" Tanya asked.

"I think so," Sue said.

"Oh, look! Pause it!" Ellen said, excitedly. "Another shadow fell on Isabel, when she started speaking in tongues."

"Not in tongues," Tanya said. "It was French. Remember?"

"Oh, yeah." Ellen wrote in her journal: *ghost attachment or possession leaves shadow on victim.*

They continued watching the footage from the main house but didn't see anything more that was noteworthy. However, the audio picked up on something that did not seem like the other traffic noise they heard.

"Play that again," Ellen said.

Sue rewound the video. It sounded like a low human voice, possibly female: *ja MA NA na ee ee uh BYE.*

They played it a few more times.

"Let's see if the EVP recorder picked it up better." Ellen crossed the room and turned on the machine.

Playing back the audio on the EVP recorder allowed them to find a similar sound pattern throughout the investigation in the main house: *ja MA NA na ee ee uh BYE.*

Ellen slowed the recording down and turned the volume all the way up. "Here we go," she said before pressing *play*.

In a low, gravelly voice, the sounds manifested into words: "Jamar Nunnery is alive."

CHAPTER TWENTY

The Peace of Heaven

J amar Nunnery is alive?" Tanya repeated.

"Jamar is Cornelius's father, right?" Ellen asked, to be sure.

Sue nodded. "And Maria's husband. Oh, my God. Do you think it's true?"

"I don't know," Ellen said. "But why would a ghost say it, if it wasn't?"

"To mess with us, maybe?" Sue speculated. "Cause mischief?"

"Should we tell Maria?" Tanya wondered.

"Let's try to find some more answers first," Sue said. "We don't want to get her hopes up and then not be able to find him."

"Let's use the Ouija Board." Ellen found the board in the kitchen, where it was laying among their other gear. "Ready?"

"As ready as I'll ever be," Sue said.

Sue and Tanya stayed seated on the couch while Ellen sat on the floor opposite them with the board on the coffee table between them. They rested their fingers on the planchette.

"I'll start," Sue said. "Spirits of the other realm, we mean you no harm. We're looking for answers about Jamar Nunnery, who was a victim in Hurricane Katrina. Is anyone there?"

The planchette flew to "Yes."

"Who is this?" Sue asked.

"C-O-R-N-E-L-I-U-S."

"Cornelius," Sue said. "Is your father still alive?"

The planchette did not move.

"Cornelius, are you there?" Ellen asked.

The light overhead flickered as the planchette circled around the board and returned to "yes."

"Is your father, Jamar Nunnery, still alive?" Sue repeated.

"I-D-O-N-O-T-K-N-O-W."

"He doesn't know," Tanya said. "Now what?"

"Cornelius," Sue began again. "Is there anyone there with you? Anyone from the other side?"

The light overhead flickered again as the planchette flew to "yes."

"Do you know who?" Sue asked. "Can you tell us their name?"

"G-R-A-N-D-M-A-N-U-N-N-E-R-Y."

"Grandma Nunnery," Tanya said.

"Can we talk to Grandma Nunnery?" Ellen asked, noticing a drop in the temperature.

The planchette slowly moved to "yes."

"It's getting cold in here," Tanya whispered.

"Grandma Nunnery?" Sue asked. "Are we speaking with you now?"

The planchette circled around and returned to "yes."

"Is Jamar Nunnery your son?" Ellen asked.

The planchette circled around the board and returned to "yes."

"Is Jamar still alive?" Sue asked.

The planchette circled around and returned to "yes."

"Do you know where he is?" Tanya asked.

The planchette slowly moved to "no."

"How do you know he's alive?" Sue asked.

"H-E-I-S-N-O-T-H-E-R-E."

"He is no…" Ellen began.

"He is not here," Tanya said. "He must not be on the other side, with the dead. That's how she knows he's still alive."

The planchette flew to "yes."

"But she doesn't know where he is," Sue said. "So how do we find him?"

The planchette spelled out: "I-D-O-N-O-T-K-N-O-W."

Then it spelled, "H-E-L-P."

"We'll do our best," Ellen said. "We'll do everything we can to find him."

The planchette spelled, "T-H-A-N-K-Y-O-U."

Then the light overhead went out.

"Looks like we need a new bulb," Sue said.

"Do you have anything else to tell us, Grandma Nunnery?" Ellen asked.

The planchette didn't move.

"I think she's gone," Sue said.

"My phone's dead again." Tanya crossed the room and plugged the phone into her charger. "We should see if Jamar has a Facebook page."

"Found it," Sue said, using her phone. "Oh, it's so sad. It's become a memorial to him. Oh, my gosh. Maria posts to his page nearly every day."

"If he's still alive, why doesn't he answer?" Ellen wondered.

"He must have amnesia," Tanya said. "That's the only explanation for him not finding his wife and daughter."

"That means he could be anywhere," Ellen said.

"Chances are he isn't that far away," Sue said. "We should send his Facebook profile picture to all the hospitals in Louisiana."

"I can't believe he's never come across his old page," Ellen said. "I hope he's not a vegetable."

"Regardless, Maria should know," Sue said. "If we find him, that is."

"Do you think the police can help us?" Tanya asked.

"What would we say to them?" Sue lifted her palms. "That we spoke to his dead mother with the Ouija Board, and she says her son's still alive?"

"Good point," Tanya said. "I guess we're on our own."

Two days later, Ellen, Sue, and Tanya gathered beneath the hot, blistering son in the Saint Louis Cemetery #1 with Maria and Cecilia Nunnery, Beatrice Leland, Priestess Isabel, and Father Tony.

It was a Saturday afternoon, and tour groups were roaming the grounds. But no one bothered them as Father Tony, a tall, thin man with a gentle voice, prayed over the Glapion family tomb.

The previous day, Ellen and her friends had delivered the remains of the devil child to the cemetery, at Maria's request. The remains were placed in the chamber at the bottom of the Glapion family tomb, above ground. Ellen and her friends were told that in a matter of weeks, what was left of the remains would be essentially cremated, naturally, by the hot conditions of New Orleans. Those ashes would then be pushed to the back of the tomb the next time a family member needed to be interred there.

What mattered most to Ellen was that the devil child was now resting with Marie Laveau on consecrated ground. Marie, her devil child, and Cornelius would finally find peace, and Tanya's life would no longer be in jeopardy.

During the ceremony, Father Tony, who'd been told the entire story about Cornelius, Marie Laveau, and her devil child, said a few words about living in the eighteen-hundreds, about being born with disorders that were misunderstood, about the love and mercy of the almighty creator, and about life and love everlasting.

He said, "Lord our God, you are the source of life. In you we live and move and have our being. Keep us in life and death in your love, and, by your grace, lead us to your kingdom through your son, Jesus Christ, our lord, Amen."

Ellen kept her eye on Tanya, hoping for evidence that her spirit attachment had ended. Nothing seemed profoundly different about her today, however, and Ellen was worried.

After the priest finished his prayers, he asked if anyone else wanted to say a few words. Maria lifted her hand and stepped forward.

"I'd just like to say thank you to Sue, Tanya, and Ellen for finding my ancestor Marie Laveau's precious child, Charles. I thank Priestess Isabel, too, for the part she played. I thank Father Tony for his kind words, and I thank my good friend, Bea, for being there for me all these years. I thank my daughter, Cecilia, for helping me through it all. I also want to say a special thank you to my son, Cornelius…" Maria's eyes filled with tears.

Cecilia broke down, too, and took her mother's hand.

"Cornelius," Maria continued, "if you can hear me, I want you to know how much your sister and I love you and how badly we want you to join your father in heaven. It has been an unbearable burden, a terrible curse, knowing that you have been without peace, my son. Please fly into Jesus's arms and find comfort in our lord and savior."

Maria stepped back into line with the others as her daughter and friend comforted her. Ellen noticed tears in Sue and Tanya's eyes.

But it wasn't until Father Tony raised a palm over the tomb and said, "In the name of God, the merciful Father, we commit the body of Charles Laveau to the peace of the grave," that Ellen noticed a change in Tanya.

Father Tony stooped over and took a handful of dirt into his hand. As he let the dirt fall over the tomb, he said, "From dust you came, to dust you shall return." He poured two more handfuls of dirt onto the tomb as he said, "Heavenly Father, you gave him life. Receive him in your peace and give him, through Jesus Christ, a joyful resurrection. May your perpetual light shine upon the soul of Charles Laveau. Amen."

Tanya began to tremble.

"You okay?" Ellen whispered beside her.

Tanya did not reply. Her body shook more rigidly, as though she were having a *gran mal* seizure.

"Tanya?" Sue cried.

Both Sue and Ellen held the arms of their friend as her body suddenly relaxed and nearly fell to the ground.

"Heavenly Father!" Father Tony cried. "Please receive the soul of
your son, Cornelius Nunnery. Receive him in your peace and grant him,
through Jesus Christ, a joyful resurrection. May your perpetual light
shine upon his soul as he joins you in your heavenly kingdom."

Maria Nunnery fell to her knees and rasped, through heavy sobs,
"Amen."

After the graveside ceremony, Ellen and her friends invited the group
for sandwiches, tea, and cupcakes at the guesthouse on Chartres, where
Maria, Cecilia, and Beatrice shared stories about Cornelius and Jamar.
Ellen could tell how badly Sue and Tanya wanted to mention what
they'd heard on the EVP recorder, because she wanted to say something, too; however, they held back, not wanting to create false hope.

Later that evening, after everyone had gone, Ellen, Sue, and Tanya
sat together in the guesthouse with Delphine's diary. Tanya read Delphine's entries from 1835 through 1840, which focused mostly on a
growing concern for her youngest child's hearing. Jean Louis visited a
number of medical experts and began an experimental treatment in 1838
that seemed to work. Delphine wrote in an April 1840 entry that she
believed her son was cured.

Delphine also wrote about her daughter, Pauline, and the fear that
she would never marry. Although Pauline's hunch seems to have been
radically reduced by Dr. Lalaurie's treatments, it was never fully eradi-
cated, and, according to Delphine's letters, it continued to impact Pauline's confidence.

Delphine's daughter, Jeanne, came to Paris with her husband and
children for a visit in 1838 and again in 1840. The entries in the wakes of
those visits were full of longing.

In the fall of 1840, Delphine wrote about a love affair. She mentioned no names, only the initials G.B. But, by the end of 1841, the man

had broken her heart. In an entry dated August 1841, she swore off all men and became more determined than ever to return to New Orleans.

The entries throughout 1842 focused on the preparations Delphine made for the return to New Orleans and the arguments she had with Paulin and Pauline, who were not keen to move. By the end of the year, she, Pauline, and Jean Louis resided with Jeanne and her children in the house on Chartres Street now owned by Sue, Tanya, and Ellen.

"Why don't we stop there?" Sue said with a yawn. "I'm ready for bed."

"I didn't realize how late it was," Tanya said. "It's nearly midnight."

"We should review the recordings from our Audubon Park investigation tomorrow," Ellen said, "in case we received any other messages, especially regarding Jamar."

"Yes, we should," Tanya agreed.

"How do you feel, Tanya?" Sue asked. "Still good?"

"Great," Tanya said as tears formed in her eyes. "So relieved. I can't thank you guys enough for helping me."

"It was a team effort," Sue said.

Ellen nodded. "Absolutely, but our work isn't done yet."

"Oh, I know," Tanya said. "I'm anxious to see if we can find Jamar Nunnery. I'll draft an email tomorrow with his Facebook profile picture."

"We can start with hospitals within a hundred-mile radius of here," Sue said. "And we can work outward from there."

"We also need to return Marie Laveau's turban," Ellen pointed out. "I think I'll mail it anonymously to the museum tomorrow."

"Good idea," Tanya said as she pulled out the sofa sleeper and arranged her bedding. "Good night."

"Good night," Sue and Ellen said as they headed upstairs.

Once in her room, Ellen flipped on the lamp by her bed and changed into her pajamas. It felt colder upstairs, so she unfolded the blanket at the foot of her bed and spread it over the sheet before climbing beneath it.

Her lamp flickered twice, and the room dropped in temperature by several degrees Ellen sat up and held very still. Her breath condensed into a tiny cloud. Then suddenly the lamp went out and the bedroom door, which she'd left ajar, slammed shut. The hair on the back of Ellen's neck stood on end.

"Who's there?" she said through trembling lips.

When no answer came, she climbed from the bed and took her EMF reader from her purse. As soon as she turned it on, it showed high readings of electromagnetic activity. Using the flashlight on her phone, Ellen crossed the room to the door, but the bedroom door wouldn't budge.

Ellen pounded on the door. "Sue? Sue? Can you hear me? I need your help! I'm trapped!"

Ellen kept turning the doorknob and pounding on the door, but it wouldn't open, even though there was no lock.

"Sue? Tanya?"

Suddenly, the door opened. Sue stood on the stairwell landing. She was as white as a sheet as she pointed to writing on the wall. It hadn't been painted but scratched into the drywall. It read: *Get out.*

"Please tell me this is a joke," Ellen said to Sue.

Tanya reached the top of the stairs. "What's going on?" Then she saw the words scratched into the wall. "Oh, my God. Sue? Did you do that?"

"No, I swear," Sue said. "The light went off in my room, all on its own, and when I opened the door, I saw this."

Ellen recounted what had happened to her.

"I thought Cornelius moved on," Tanya said. "Why is this happening?"

"Tanya, you need to start wearing your gris-gris bag," Ellen said, as she fingered her own.

"I have a feeling it's Delphine," Sue said. "Think about it. We just gave Marie Laveau what she wanted, the thing Delphine vowed never to give her."

Ellen shuddered. "You think the ghost of Delphine is here? In this house?"

Sue nodded. "I bet she's mad at us."

"I don't want to stay here," Tanya said. "Let's go to a hotel."

"Or we could try to talk to her," Sue said.

"I don't know," Tanya said. "This act was really aggressive."

"We'll make a circle of protection," Ellen said. "Come on. Let's give it a shot."

"You two weren't almost possessed," Tanya said. "I never want that to happen again."

Ellen went downstairs in search of Tanya's gris-gris bag. The others followed.

Ellen handed the bag to Tanya. "This will protect you."

"Maybe we should do a smudge stick ritual to get rid of her," Tanya said.

"That will only make her angrier with us," Sue said. "She'll come back with a vengeance."

Ellen patted Tanya's hand. "And aren't we about *healing* the spirits? Maybe we can heal Delphine."

Tanya took a deep breath and let it out. Ellen could tell she was frightened. They all were, but Tanya had been in the most danger, and she'd finally been freed. Ellen understood her friend's reluctance.

"Okay," Tanya finally said.

"Are you sure?" Sue asked her. "We don't want to push you into something you're not comfortable doing."

"I'm sure."

"Then let's get started," Ellen said.

Sue drew a circle of salt around the perimeter of the room. Ellen lit a candle. Tanya set out a leftover sandwich and glass of punch. Then Tanya and Ellen sat on the end of the sleeper bed while Tanya took the chair. With the Ouija Board on Tanya's lap, they touched their fingers to the planchette. All of them were trembling.

"Spirits of the other realm, we mean you no harm," Sue began. "Is someone there?"

Before Sue had finished her question, the planchette spelled, "G-E-T-O-U-T."

The temperature had dropped significantly. This was confirmed when Ellen noticed their breath condensed into tiny clouds.

"Is this Delphine Lalaurie?" Ellen asked.

The planchette spelled, "G-E-T-O-U-T" a second time.

"We want to help," Tanya said. "We're reading your diary. We can use it to clear your name, so people know the truth."

"We can lift the curse," Ellen added. "People will no longer think of you as a monster."

The planchette spelled, "N-O-O-N-E-W-I-L-L-B-E-L-I-E-V-E-Y-O-U."

"Maybe not all," Tanya said. "But some."

Again, the planchette spelled, "G-E-T-O-U-T."

"We had no choice," Ellen said. "Marie Laveau threatened Tanya's life."

"Wait," Tanya said. "We have the doctor's medical journals. He admits to using the slaves."

"That's right!" Ellen said. "The medical journals, along with Delphine's diary, would certainly be more credible."

"We can have someone authenticate them," Sue said. "A historian."

"Give us a chance, Delphine," Ellen pleaded. "Please?"

The planchette didn't move, but the temperature returned to normal, which Ellen took as a good sign.

"Are you still there, Delphine?" Sue asked.

The planchette didn't move.

"We've got our work cut out for us," Sue said.

"You've got that right," Ellen said. "But I don't think I can sleep in my room."

"You can sleep down here with me, if you want," Tanya offered. "Both of you."

"I'll sleep in the chair," Sue said. "I'll go get my blanket from upstairs. Ellen, will you come with me?"

"Sure. I need to grab my blanket, too."

On the way back downstairs, Sue said, "Next time we go to the store, we need to stock up on light bulbs."

Once they were settled with the lights out, the circle of protection gave Ellen some comfort, but she continued to fear the ghost of Delphine Lalaurie. The legend surrounding Delphine and the fire of 1834 had been around for almost two hundred years. Was it possible to change it?

CHAPTER TWENTY-ONE

Reconstruction

A week after the devil child's funeral, Ellen and her friends met with Michael Rouchell in his office to go over the renovation plans.

Ellen was nervous and embarrassed about seeing him after what he'd overheard, but she was an adult, and it was time to act like one.

As handsome and charming as ever, he offered them each a chair before taking his own behind his desk.

"Did you ladies hear about Lalaurie Mansion?" he asked as he rolled out the plans and flattened them on his desk.

"No," Sue said. "What about it?"

"It's on the market again."

"Seriously?" Ellen asked. "That's so bizarre."

"Bizarre?" Michael repeated. "Why? That house has never remained with one owner for very long. They say it's cursed."

"I've heard that, too," Tanya said. "Nicolas Cage went bankrupt while he owned it."

"Apparently, that's what's happened to the Texas tycoon who owns it now," Michael said.

"Really? Bankruptcy?" Ellen asked.

"It was in the papers this morning."

"Are you thinking what I'm thinking?" Sue asked Ellen and Tanya.

"No," Tanya said. "Absolutely not."

"Well," Ellen smiled at Sue. "We should at least consider it."

Michael gawked. "Don't tell me you're thinking of buying Lalaurie Mansion."

"No," Tanya said flatly. "We're not."

"We sort of are," Ellen said.

"Think about it, Tanya," Sue said. "We could turn it into a museum devoted to the truth."

"It's the most famous haunted house in the world," Michael put in. "You'd certainly attract a lot of tourists if you opened it up to the public."

Tanya sighed. "I like the idea, but that's a lot of money to have tied up in two properties."

"Looks like she's thinking about it," Michael said with a laugh. "That didn't take long."

After their meeting with the architect, the three friends went to Coop's Place for lunch, where they discussed Lalaurie Mansion over jambalaya.

"What if we go bankrupt, too?" Tanya said. "We have a responsibility to Greenwood to be careful with how we spend the oil money."

"From what I've heard," Sue said, "the curse has only affected people who have tried to *live* in the mansion. If we turn it into a museum…"

"No one will live in it," Ellen finished. "And maybe we can lift the curse altogether. If we expose the truth about what was really going on…"

"Our husbands aren't going to like this," Tanya said. "Would we *sell* the museum? How will we get our investment back?"

"We sold Monroe Social Club," Sue pointed out. "And we make great money with the Gold House."

"It will be at least a year before we see any kind of return on the condos on Chartres," Tanya said. "If we move forward on Lalaurie Mansion, we could be strapped financially for who knows how long."

"Why don't we call Lionel and arrange for a viewing," Sue said. "We don't have to decide today."

Tanya agreed, so Ellen took out her phone and dialed the realtor.

"Only serious buyers are allowed viewings," Lionel said. "Are you ladies curious or serious?"

"Serious," Ellen said.

"Alrighty, then. I'll see what I can do and call you back."

From Coop's Place, Ellen drove her friends out of the French Quarter to the other side of town to shop for cabinets, countertops, tile, and other materials Michael had requested after they'd approved his plans that morning. Ellen loved looking at the slabs of marble and granite at the warehouse Michael had recommended. She'd convinced Tanya and Sue that they should choose the countertops first and build their design from there. They agreed that the two condos should not be identical but should complement one another, so they chose granite for one and marble for the other, both with a creamy base from which they would pull their paint colors.

Tanya found tile for the backsplash that had Ellen jumping up and down. It couldn't be more perfect for the condo with the granite. Together, they found a similar tile that worked perfectly with the marble. They recorded the product details to send to Michael later.

With granite and marble samples in hand, they then headed to a paint store and spent nearly an hour holding the paint cards against the stone. This was such an exciting part of the process for Ellen, and soon she'd forgotten all about the ghost of Delphine Lalaurie.

Next, they went to Lowe's and Home Depot to shop for appliances, sinks, faucets, and fixtures. From there, they visited antique shops. Sue found a chandelier that resembled the historical one in the Chartres house living room. Tanya found some incredible light fixtures. Ellen found corbels that they believed matched those on the fireplace mantel. The three friends couldn't be more excited about their finds.

They'd just returned to their favorite bakery in the French Quarter to pick up sandwiches and cupcakes to take home to the guesthouse when

Lionel Hurd called, saying he'd arranged for a viewing of Lalaurie mansion that evening.

Armed with their gris-gris bags hanging from their necks, Ellen, Sue, and Tanya waited for Lionel Hurd on the sidewalk in front of Lalaurie Mansion at eight thirty in the evening. Dusk had fallen, and the streets were busy with tour groups. One of the groups had stopped across the street as their guide talked about "Mad Madame Delphine Lalaurie," who had tortured her slaves behind closed doors for years until a fire in 1834 exposed her to the world.

"I want to say something," Ellen said to her friends.

"It won't do any good," Sue said. "You'll just cause a scene."

Two more tour groups walked by with guides telling the same story about "Mad Madame Delphine Lalaurie," the sadist who tortured her slaves. It made Ellen angry that Dr. Lalaurie was not mentioned and that Delphine had been forced to take the blame. Ellen was appalled by how exaggerated the tales had become—not seven slaves, but dozens, with their limbs resewn on at odd angles, like a crab, with sex change operations, with their intestines tied around their waists, with their skin peeled in a spiral. No wonder Delphine's ghost hadn't found peace. What a torment it must be for her to listen to the lies spread about her for nearly two hundred years.

Delphine had been wrong not to expose the doctor. She'd been wrong to chain Rachel to the stove. And she'd been wrong to keep the devil child from Marie Laveau. But how long must she be forced to pay for her sins?

Lionel's arrival brought Ellen from her reverie. She was surprised, as they walked through the beautifully updated and renovated mansion, by how similar it was in structure to their house on Chartres—except the courtyard was indoors. Ellen was convinced that this property must have been the inspiration for the Mikaelson mansion in *The Originals*.

"We wouldn't need to do a thing to it," Sue said, "aside from creating a photo gallery telling Delphine's story."

Lionel glanced back at Sue, his interest piqued, but he said nothing as he continued the tour.

"We could hang prints of key pages from both her diary and the doctor's medical journals," Ellen said.

"Maybe we could work with the historical society," Tanya said. "They could buy it instead. We could make a proposition."

Ellen stopped in her tracks. That was actually a good idea.

The following day, Ellen and her friends met with Nora Wetzel, the president of the Louisiana Historical Society, at a local diner. They showed her Delphine's diary, Jeanne Blanque De Lassus's letters, Louis's medical journals, and some of the other books from the house on Chartres. They offered to donate everything to the historical society, along with one million dollars, if the society would agree to purchase Lalaurie mansion and transform it into a museum dedicated to the truth about what had happened behind its walls. They repeated what Michael had said, about it being the most famous haunted house in the world. It would draw people from all over.

Nora seemed excited by both their discoveries and their proposal, agreeing to present them to the board at their next meeting, in two weeks. Ellen and her friends agreed to leave Jeanne's letters and one of Louis's medical journals with Nora, but they kept possession of everything else, not forgetting their promise to Isabel to let her read the diary once they were finished with it.

A few days later, Ellen and her friends were on a plane headed back to San Antonio. Tanya sat between them, reading the last pages of Delphine's diary. The subject of those last pages was Delphine's joy at being reunited with her older daughters and her grandchildren. She lived under a different name and continued to be troubled by the rumors circulating about her, but she took strength from her family and was relatively happy. She wrote of making every effort to avoid an encounter with Marie Laveau, fearing the Voodoo queen would want her devil child. Delphine's last entry was in January of 1858, in which she wrote that she had come down with pneumonia and would have to miss her grandson's birthday party.

Tanya and Sue were both worried that Delphine's ghost might have followed the diary back to San Antonio, so Ellen offered to hold onto the diary, even though she was a little afraid, too. In six weeks, they would loan it to Isabel, when they returned to New Orleans to check on Michael's progress on the Chartres house.

In the meantime, they searched for Jamar Nunnery.

The data collected from their investigation at Audubon Park had provided no further clues regarding Jamar or his whereabouts. Their emails and phone calls to hospitals in Louisiana also proved futile. One night, alone in Nolan's old bedroom, where Ellen went to escape her husband's cold shoulder, Ellen got on her phone and went to Jamar's Facebook page. On a whim, she sent a private message to the page: "Where are you, Jamar?"

Ellen was shocked when a reply came within seconds: "Who is this?"

Ellen gasped and sat up in the bed, bumping her head on the headboard.

She stared at the message for a full minute, wondering how to respond. Should she call Sue and Tanya first?

She glanced at the clock. It was after eleven. Sue would be up, but Tanya would be fast asleep.

"Hello?" came another reply through Facebook messenger.

"Hello," Ellen wrote. "I'm a paranormal investigator. Is this Jamar?"

"What's it to you?"

"I've been looking for him," she wrote. "The ghost of his mother told me that he's still alive."

Ellen waited for a reply, but none came.

"Hello?" she wrote. "Please talk to me and tell me what you know."

Ellen lay beneath the covers in Nolan's old bed staring at her phone, praying for a reply, until she couldn't keep her eyes open a moment longer.

"It's got to be Jamar," Sue said over lunch the next day. "Who else would it be?"

"But why wouldn't he have contacted Maria and Cecilia?" Tanya pointed out. "Could he have amnesia but still know his name?"

"I guess that's possible," Ellen said before taking a sip of her tea. "But surely, he would have reached out to Maria, out of curiosity, if that were the case. It's got to be something else."

"Maybe he feels responsible for Cornelius's death," Sue offered. "Maybe he was the one who discouraged them from evacuating."

Ellen raised her brows. "That could be it—though thirteen years is a long time to hold onto that guilt."

"We have to find out if it's him," Tanya said. "Let's draft a message to him and see if he responds."

Ellen found an old grocery list in her purse and turned it over and began putting into words what they wanted to say to Jamar—if he was the person to whom she'd been privately chatting through his profile page.

Once they agreed on a final draft, she typed the message to him:

Jamar, if this is you, please hear me out. I began this journey two months ago when I discovered one of my best friends had a spirit attached to her. Spirit attachments can be life-threatening, because they use up your life force. To save my friend, I took her to a Voodoo high priestess for help. We eventually discovered that your son, Cornelius, was attached to my friend, Tanya, because his ancestor, Voodoo queen Marie Laveau, wouldn't let him pass to the other side and find peace until her "devil child" was consecrated to her family tomb. For the past thirteen years, your son's spirit has been trying to find the remains of the devil child. We finally found them four weeks ago. Cornelius has found peace.

Your wife, Maria, and your daughter, Cecilia, were there to witness it at the funeral service for the devil child. When the priest prayed over the tomb and asked that the child be given a joyful resurrection, Tanya felt Cornelius pass on. We could see it happen in the way she was affected.

I don't know why you haven't reached out to your surviving family members, but I wish you would let us help you to reunite with them. If you check this page, you know what they've been doing: Cecilia recently graduated law school and works for a prestigious firm, and Maria is waiting for Cecilia to help her to rebuild your home.

Cornelius's death was not your fault, even if you discouraged the evacuation from your home. No one could have foreseen the failure of the levees that allowed the flood waters to destroy much of New Orleans.

If there is some other reason why you have not come forward, I'm sure we can work something out. My friends and I are in the business of bringing peace to both the living and the dead. We'd like nothing more than to see you reunited with your family in peace.

If this isn't Jamar, then please say so. It's not fair to give an old woman false hope.

Ellen was shocked when the messenger app on her phone began showing the ellipses symbol. indicating that the person was writing a response.

"Guys, he's writing something," she said.

They stared at her phone, waiting and waiting. A minute, two minutes, three minutes went by before the message finally appeared on the phone.

It sounds like you already have false hope. Jamar is dead. He died in Hurricane Katrina. There's no paranormal investigator alive who can resurrect him.

Tanya wrinkled her brow. "That last line…"

"I know," Sue said. "I might have believed him if it weren't for that last line."

"You think that's Jamar?" Ellen asked. "You think he's lying to us?"

"Not lying, exactly. I think he's speaking metaphorically." Sue took the last bite of her pie.

"Should I message him again?" Ellen asked. "I'm going to ask him if he'll meet with us to talk about Jamar."

She wrote her message and hit "send."

The reply soon followed: *For what purpose?*

Ellen wrote: *closure. I need closure.*

They waited for many minutes for a reply, but none came. Even after they'd finished their lunch and paid their tickets, a reply hadn't come.

"What now?" Ellen asked.

"Let's see who else posts to his page," Sue said, looking at her own phone.

Tanya took hers out, too. "Wow, Maria posts nearly every day. I see a few from Cecilia."

"What's this blog, *Voices from the Dead?*" Ellen wondered. "I see regular posts from it."

Ellen clicked on one of the links to the blog.

"It's a poetry blog," Sue said. "Written by Jeffrey Nicholson. Let me click on his avatar. Hmm. There's no photo."

"Do you think Jeffrey Nicholson is Jamar Nunnery?" Tanya asked.

"Listen to this," Ellen said. She read one of the poems from Jeffrey's blog:

I walk among the dead
The dead walk alongside me
Their faces, like mine,
Are twisted in agony.

The dead follow me to work

They see me on the street
They call me out by name
Every time we meet.

We are kindred souls
We know what hell's about
Just look me in the eye
If ever you're in doubt.

"Wow," Tanya said. "Here's another one."
Tanya read:

Death doesn't care about faith and prayer.
Death doesn't heed a man's good deed.
Death doesn't find, if a person is kind,
Or mean, or in between,
Relevant.

"Ooh, I like this one," Sue said, before reading:

My name is What-Will-Never-Be.
I live in No-Man's Land.
I pray to One-Who-Never-Was.
I live by No-Command.

I drink from an empty glass
I eat from an empty plate
I live in an empty home
And sit by an empty grate.

"Guys," Tanya said, her eyes filling with tears. "These poems are making me cry. Do you think Jamar wrote them?"

"I think there's a good chance," Sue said.

Ellen nodded. "It's worth investigating, and I have an idea."

CHAPTER TWENTY-TWO

Leads

Y ou're leaving again?" Paul asked Ellen in their bedroom, where she was packing her bags.

"We have to check on the progress of the Chartres house. The architect needs our approval for a few changes."

"Were you going to leave without saying anything?" he asked.

She looked at him for the first time in weeks. He looked hurt. Upset. She hadn't noticed before now.

"I didn't think you cared."

He mumbled, "Son of a bitch," and walked out of the room.

Ellen sighed, wondering whether she should follow him. Lately, she'd felt like giving up, like their marriage had become a sham. Maybe it had always been a sham.

She hadn't decided how best to respond when he returned, his face red, his eyes narrowed.

"For years, I was the primary breadwinner in this household," he said through gritted teeth. "You used your teaching income for extras, but I paid the bills."

"What's your point?"

"Did I ever make you feel like your opinion didn't count? Did I ever make a financial decision without consulting you? The answer is no, Ellen. I considered you my partner...in everything."

"Paul..."

"But you haven't showed me a fraction of that same respect since the oil money. You see that money as *yours*...not ours. And you're moving on to better things. You're moving on and leaving me behind, like an old rag you no longer need."

Ellen's eyes filled with tears, and her mouth fell open. She'd had no idea he was feeling that way. She thought he resented her, but she had no idea that he was feeling left behind. "Paul..."

"I don't need your pity. But I deserve your respect. I want you to consult with me before making important financial decisions. Will you do that, Ellen?"

"Paul, I'm so sorry. Of course. Yes. I will. I promise."

As she moved toward him, he left the room.

She didn't follow.

Tanya's son, Mike, and his partner, Seth, both in their mid-twenties, joined Tanya, Ellen, and Sue on a flight to New Orleans the week before Halloween. Mike and Seth had convinced them to attend the LGBT Halloween festivities that raised money for Project Lazarus, a home for men and women with AIDS. The festivities began on Thursday with a silent auction and dinner party.

Ellen was pleasantly surprised to see people there that she knew. Eduardo Mankiller from Tulsa was there with his partner, Felipe. Lionel Hurd was there with his wife, Tanisha. And Michael Rouchell was there without a date. When he asked if he could join them at their table, Ellen and Sue nearly fell out of their chairs.

They spent Friday afternoon with Michael going over the progress on the Chartres house. He'd had to alter his plans slightly, to accommodate the new stairwell, which Ellen and her friends approved. Overall, they were very pleased with how the work was coming along. The units had been divided, the drywall painted. The kitchen and dining room had been renovated into an open concept. Although the countertops had not been installed, the cabinets were in, and painted, and the floor refinished.

The library and office had been converted into the second unit's open-concept kitchen and dining area. The marble countertop had just been put in, and workers were installing the backsplash. Ellen and her friends were elated.

Michael was convinced that the condos would be ready to rent before Thanksgiving.

"Will you ladies be at the VIP Lounge tonight?" Michael asked as he was preparing to leave the Chartres house.

"Not tonight," Tanya replied when Sue and Ellen seemed incapable of speech. "But we'll be there tomorrow night for the costume contest and dance."

"Tanya's son and his partner are competing," Sue explained.

"I hope you'll save me a dance," Michael said as he waved goodbye.

Once the door was closed behind him, Ellen screamed. "What does he think he's doing?"

Sue laughed. "I think he's enjoying our attention."

"You guys," Tanya scoffed.

Not long after Michael had left, the three friends headed to the Voodoo Spiritual Temple to loan Priestess Isabel the diary of Delphine Lalaurie, as promised.

When they walked in, Isabel stood next to the counter with a can of Sprite in her hand. A boy in his late teens sat at the computer behind the counter.

"Well, hello again," Isabel said. "You have something for me?"

Ellen handed over Delphine's diary.

"Most of it's in French," Isabel said as she leafed through the pages. "I can't read French. Can you?"

"I can," Tanya said.

Isabel handed the diary to Tanya. "What did it say?"

"Um, a lot," Tanya said.

"Do you have dinner plans?" Sue asked. "We have a reservation at Antoine's at seven. I bet it's not too late to add one more to our table. We can tell you all about the diary then."

"Antoine's is my favorite," Isabel said.

"Can we pick you up at 6:45?" Ellen asked.

Isabel nodded. "I'll be here."

Six a.m. came way too early for Ellen Saturday morning as she reached for her phone and turned off the alarm. The dinner at Antoine's had kept her and her friends up late, as they'd conveyed to Isabel all they'd learned about Delphine and the fire of 1834.

But this morning, she and her friends had a three-hour road trip ahead of them. They were going to the Louisiana State Penitentiary, also known as Angola Prison, to visit inmate and poet, Jeffrey Nicholson.

At ten a.m., they arrived at the front gate, where a staff member checked to see if their names were on the guest list of Jeffrey Nicholson. Fortunately, they were. They'd been added two weeks ago, when Ellen had contacted him through his blog. She'd used her married name—Ellen Mohr—and had hoped he would not suspect that she was the same Ellen who had contacted him through Facebook messenger. When Ellen had set up her Facebook page years ago, she had followed her daughter Alison's advice and had used her maiden name, Ellen Porter.

Either the prisoner hadn't suspected she was the same woman who had privately messaged him on Facebook, or he knew and wanted to meet with her anyway.

After a brief search of their rental vehicle, they parked and entered the visitor's center. They underwent a metal detector and canine search before boarding a bus with nine other visitors—three young mothers and their small children. As the bus took them to the visiting room, one of the security guards reminded everyone that contact between visitors and inmates was limited to a hug and brief kiss at the beginning and end of the visit. No lingering kisses were allowed and would be grounds for removal of the inmate from the visiting room. While small children were permitted to sit on an inmate's lap, only handholding was permitted between adults.

"I'm 'a sit on Daddy's lap first," one boy said to his siblings.

The bus pulled up in front of the visiting room. All passengers were led inside the building, through two sets of bars, and into the main visitation area, which resembled a school cafeteria. There were televisions on the walls on low volume. One displayed a football game, another cartoons, and a third, HGTV. There was also a kid area in one corner with toys and coloring books, where the three young mothers and their children went to meet the fathers. Food and hand-crafted items were being sold along two back walls by a few inmates.

The first thing Ellen thought when she walked in was, "Where are all the white people?"

Only one table of the dozens in the room had a white family sitting at it. Everyone else was black. Shouldn't the population of a prison reflect the rest of the population? If blacks were a minority on the outside, why wouldn't they be a minority on the inside? Not for the first time, Ellen questioned the fairness of the justice system in America.

A security guard escorted Ellen, Sue, and Tanya across the room to a table where a man in his late forties was sitting alone. Even though he was aged, Ellen recognized him from his Facebook profile. The man sitting there was Jamar Nunnery!

Ellen tried not to show her surprise, so as not to alarm him. She and her friends didn't want him to know they were looking for him with the hope of reuniting him with his family. They wanted him to think they were there to publish his poetry.

He stood up and smiled at them as they each shook his hand before sitting down again at the table. Ellen, Sue, and Tanya each took a seat.

"You've written some impressive work," Sue began.

"Thank you," Jamar said. "I'm glad you like it."

"We'd like to include a brief biography with a few of your poems in the publication," Ellen said. "Can you tell us a little about yourself?"

"I was born and raised in Louisiana. I had a wife and kids, but they were taken by Hurricane Katrina."

"We're so sorry to hear that," Sue said, glancing at Tanya and Ellen. "How awful."

"I ain't never been the same since," he said, his smile gone.

"How did you end up in this high security prison?" Sue asked. "Can you tell us about that?"

"Sure. I knew you was gonna ask. You see, Katrina washed away my home and carried me and my family away with it. I was rescued and taken to the Superdome with thousands of other people. You heard about all that, I'm sure."

The three friends nodded.

"What happened while you were there?" Ellen asked.

"I was searching for my family," he said. "I was desperate, you hear me?"

"I can only imagine," Ellen said.

"They kept saying they was gonna send us some busses, to take us to better shelters, but every day, the busses never came. People was starvin', you hear me? And they was scared. Most of us were walkin' around in a fog. All I could think about was findin' my family. I had to know if they was dead or alive."

Ellen shuddered. She glanced at Tanya and noticed her eyes had welled with tears.

"When the busses finally came, we were all desperate to get out. Some wanted safety. Others wanted food. But most of us, we just wanted to find our family. And the Superdome, that was the worst. No organization. No control. Nothing. A mob of us stormed the busses, trying to be the first to get on."

Ellen noticed that Jamar's face was tautly drawn in a frown of grief and agony. His eyes were red and filled with tears.

"The police officers shot at us," Jamar continued. "The guy next to me, he had my back, you hear me? We watched out for each other during that whole mess. He fell to the ground. Shot straight to the heart. The police could have aimed for his foot, for his leg. No, man. He was shot in the heart. He was dead in a matter of minutes. I lost it man. I seen the guy who shot him. I rushed him with a mob of others and snapped his neck. That's how I ended up here. I didn't contest the charge. I was guilty, plain and simple."

"There's nothing plain and simple about it," Ellen said.

"Let's get back to your poetry," Sue said, trying to change the mood. "Tell us about your inspiration."

"Loss is my inspiration," Jamar said. "I lost everything. You the first visitors I've had since I been here."

"You have no other family or friends still living?" Ellen asked.

"None I care to talk to," he said.

Ellen cleared her throat, not sure where to go from there.

"Tell us which three are your favorite poems," Sue said. "You can help us decide which ones to feature."

On the shuttle from the visiting room, Ellen turned to Tanya and Sue. "How are we going to get Maria and Cecilia in to see him? They have to be on the visitor list, and there's no way he'll agree to put them on there."

"I don't think that's true of attorneys," Sue said. "Cecilia can request a visit as an attorney interested in appealing his case."

"You're so smart!" Ellen said, beaming. "I'm so glad you know things that most of us don't."

Sue laughed. "It sounds like you want to buy me lunch."

After a late lunch, Ellen and her friends left Angola and drove back to New Orleans to meet with board members of the Louisiana Historical

Society at 4 p.m. at the Round Table on St. Charles Avenue. They were surprised to learn the building was adjacent to Audubon Park.

"Boy, does that bring back memories," Sue said as they drove north on East Drive, past the Tree of Life.

Ellen had decided to take a longer path around the park, because she had wanted a glimpse of the tree during the daytime. Under the shining sun, it looked less ominous and foreboding than it had in the dark. In the daylight, it looked beautiful. Magnificent.

"To think that this land was once part of Delphine Lalaurie's family's sugar cane plantation," Tanya said.

Nora Wetzel greeted them in the lobby and led them to a meeting room where five others were already seated around a conference table. Nora introduced Ellen and her friends to Emily Ford, a New Orleans-based restoration mason, cemetery preservationist, and historian; Lydia Blackmore, Decorative Arts Curator, the Historic New Orleans Collection; James Mokhiber, an Associate Professor of African and World History at the University of New Orleans; Patricia Gay, Executive Director of the Preservation Resource Center; and Howard Margot, Archivist and Curator of the Historic New Orleans Collection.

"It's a pleasure to meet you," they each said as Ellen, Sue and Tanya, took their seats at the table.

"Did you bring the diary?" Howard Margot asked eagerly.

Ellen passed it over to him. He slipped on a pair of latex gloves before opening the book and leafing through the pages.

"It's incredible," he said. "I have every confidence that this book is authentic."

Howard Margot passed the book around the table, where each member did the same: latex gloves, glances through the pages, nodding heads, and smiles.

"Then, do we agree?" Nora asked the board.

"Unequivocally," the professor said. He turned to the other board members, who nodded in agreement.

"Is there a motion to move forward with the Lalaurie mansion project?" Nora asked.

"I motion that we move forward," Lydia said.

"I second," Patricia said.

"Motions accepted," Nora said. "I'll have our agent write up the offer and submit it immediately."

Ellen felt a rush of relief. She hoped the spirit of Delphine Lalaurie was aware that her legacy in American history was about to change forever.

That evening, Ellen and her friends fell asleep in the guesthouse living area and might have missed the LGBT Halloween costume competition and dance if Tanya's phone hadn't awakened them at nine-thirty. Mike was calling to ask where they were.

"Oh, my gosh!" Tanya cried. "Sue, Ellen, come on! We need to get ready! We're late!"

Half an hour later, Ellen drove them to the VIP Lounge, which, fortunately, was only seven minutes away near South Rampart Street.

When they entered the building, Ellen realized they stood out among the throng of partiers, all in elaborate costumes. Searching for a place to sit, they passed superheroes, Greek gods, the Village People, and characters from *Super Mario Kart*, *The Wizard of Oz*, *Sesame Street*, and *Alice in Wonderland*.

They eventually found Mike and Seth, who were dressed as Gryffindor wizards from *Harry Potter*.

"Where's your costumes?" Mike asked when they reached his table.

Tanya laughed. "Oh, silly. I told you we weren't wearing any."

"What about those witch costumes you guys wore a few years ago?" Mike said.

"You remember that?" Sue laughed. "You guys look great, though I see you have a lot of competition, don't you?"

"We don't care about winning," Seth said. "It's all for a good cause."

They squeezed together around the table, which was crammed between two other tables along the dance floor. Mike and Seth went to get them each a margarita. The couple hadn't been gone long when Michael Rouchell appeared at their table, dressed like the Wolverine.

Ellen felt her eyes nearly pop from their sockets. He was hot. She imagined the spirits agreeing with her as they used the planchette and the Ouija Board to spell, H-O-T.

"May I have this dance?" he asked her.

She pointed to her chest. "Me?"

He laughed and nodded his head, offering her is hand, which was strapped with Wolverine blades.

Awkwardly, she took his hand, laughing, and followed him to the dance floor. It was a fast beat, which she liked. Although out of shape, Ellen knew how to move and had been quite the clubber in her younger days, back when music was good, in the eighties.

When the song came to an end, it was replaced by a slow number.

"Shall we?" Michael asked, holding his arms open to her.

Did he expect her to walk into his arms? Ellen fanned her face as she stared back at him with indecision.

"Come on," he said. "One more."

She took a deep breath and allowed him to put his arms around her. She wrapped her arms around his neck. Their bodies touched. She was uncomfortably aware of every place they touched. Her sweat glands seemed to be working on overdrive.

"You smell nice," he said, close to her ear.

Was he kidding? She was covered in sweat.

"You must be picking up on my hormones," she said laughing. "They're way out of whack."

"You look nice, too," he said.

"It might be time for a visit to the optometrist," she said, still laughing.

She was so damned nervous.

"Why do you do that?" he asked.

"Do what?"

"Say such things. You're a beautiful woman, Ellen."

She didn't think it was possible to feel more uncomfortable, but she did. As attracted as she was to Michael Rouchell, as curious as she was to know how he kissed, as crazy as the fantasies of being with him had become, she was a married woman. It might be a sham marriage, but it was *her* sham marriage, and it was all she had.

Feeling slightly nauseous, she pulled away, thanking him for the dance. "I don't feel well. I need some air."

"Can I walk you outside?"

"No, thanks. I think I'm going to let my friends know that I'm ready to leave."

"I hope it's not because of me."

"No, of course not, Michael. You made my night. Really. But I'm married, you know."

"I wasn't sure."

"You see my ring, don't you?"

"People wear them even when their widowed or divorced."

Ellen wasn't sure what to say.

"I'm happy that I made your night. I'll walk you back to your table."

Once Ellen and her friends were back at the guesthouse on Chartres, Ellen sent a text to Paul: *I miss you, Honey. And I'm so very sorry. I want you to be my partner in everything.*

She was surprised when he replied, because it was after eleven o'clock—way past his bedtime.

I want that, too.

CHAPTER TWENTY-THREE

Reunions

S unday morning, Ellen called Maria Nunnery and asked if there was any way they could meet with her and Cecilia within the next couple of days. When Cecilia asked why, Ellen said that it was something she needed to tell them both in person. Cecilia wanted to know if it had something to do with Cornelius. Ellen told her that, in a way, it did. Ellen refused to say anything more about it over the phone.

Ellen hadn't expected Cecilia to drive from Houston right away, but she did, and later that evening, Ellen, Tanya, and Sue went to Maria's FEMA trailer to break the news about Jamar.

First, Ellen played back the sound they'd picked up with the EVP recorder during their investigation in the main house on Chartres.

"Jamar Nunnery is alive?" Cecilia repeated. "Did I hear that correctly?"

Ellen and her friends nodded.

"We used the Ouija Board to ask the spirits more questions," Sue explained, "and we spoke to your Grandma Nunnery."

Cecilia's face turned pale, and her eyes went wide. "I don't believe this. I mean, I believe you, but this is so…what did my grandma say?"

"She said your father must be alive because he wasn't on the other side," Tanya said.

"Could she be mistaken?" Cecilia asked. "Mama? You haven't said anything."

Maria's face was nearly as white as a sheet. "I, I don't know what to say. I don't know what to think, what to feel. I don't think I can handle this. Don't lead me on if this isn't true." Maria started crying.

"We did a little research online," Ellen continued. "And we found him."

"He's alive," Sue said.

Ellen and her friends were exhausted when their plane landed in San Antonio on Wednesday, Halloween day. Ellen was surprised to find Paul waiting for them at the gate. Tanya's husband, Dave, usually picked them up curbside after they'd picked up their bags.

"Is everything okay?" Ellen asked, as a knot formed in the pit of her stomach.

Paul nodded. "Dave's got a cold. He asked me to come."

"You didn't have to meet us at the gate, Honey."

"I know." He put an arm around her waist. "I missed you."

Ellen wrinkled her brow. Was Mercury in retrograde? Had the stars realigned? "Are you sure everything's okay?"

Paul had tears in his eyes. "Let's talk when we get home."

Ellen's stomach was in knots as they picked up their bags and walked to the car. Tanya and Sue tried to make small talk, but Paul's mood had affected everyone.

The drive to drop off Sue and Tanya was spent in awkward silence. Ellen worried about her children, wondering if something had happened to any of them. By the time they were alone in the car, Ellen couldn't take it any longer.

"Talk to me, Paul," she demanded.

He glanced over at her as he turned onto their street. "I thought I'd lost you."

"What are you talking about?"

"These last months that you've been gone," he said. "I felt like I'd lost you. Like you'd given up on us and had moved on. I even thought you might be having an affair."

Ellen took a deep breath, relieved that her children were okay.

"Paul, I…"

"When you sent that text the other night, I cried myself to sleep like a baby. The relief was real, Ellen." He sucked in his lips, fighting back tears and no longer able to speak.

She was at a loss for words as he pulled into the driveway, but as he helped her with her bags, she squeezed his hand. "Sometimes I did feel like giving up, Paul, but only because I felt so out of touch with you."

"I know," he said. "It's my fault."

"I'm not saying that."

"I am."

"But…"

"I worked so many hours, showing houses, even on weekends," he said. "Any free time, I spent on the golf course. I should have spent more of my time with you and the kids."

"You did spend time with us."

"Not a lot, Ellen. Not really. And then, when the kids left…well, I never spend time with you. It's my own damned fault."

"Let's go inside."

He helped her carry her bags into the house.

After they changed clothes, they went to the den to talk.

"I know this house flipping thing you got going is important to you," he said. "And I'm happy for you. But I think you and I need something to do together, too—something more than just watching television."

"I'm shocked to hear you say that. Count me in. What would you like to do?"

"Didn't we used to say that we wished we lived in a house on a lake?" he asked.

Ellen laughed. "That was a long time ago."

"Do you still wish it, even a little?"

"I would love it. We could have a little boat. You could fish. I could paint, maybe even do a little reading. It could be nice."

"Let's start looking," he said. "What do you say?"

Ellen smiled. "Let's do it."

Ellen sat in her art studio on All Saints' Day sitting before a large blank canvas. The night before, an idea had come to her, suddenly, like the strike of an unseen snake coiled in the grass. She'd had a vision of Delphine Lalaurie cradling the devil baby as she handed him over to Marie Laveau.

The image had been vivid, as if Ellen had been standing on the corner of Royal Street watching as Marie Laveau stood on the front stoop beneath the portico of Lalaurie Mansion. Ellen had watched as the voodoo queen rang the bell and waited. A slave opened the door, but it was Delphine who stepped from the house with the baby in her arms. The two women did not look at one another. Instead, they each gazed down at the child with loving smiles on their faces.

It was that one moment—the two formidable foes smiling at a common object of love—that Ellen meant to capture on canvas. She took up her brush, dabbed it in paint, and began.

A week later, Ellen was having lunch at Sue's favorite restaurant with her friends when her phone started ringing. By the time she'd unzipped her purse and found her phone, she'd missed the call.

"You should keep your phone on the table, like I do," Sue chastised.

"I think that's rude," Ellen said, half-teasing. "Oh, my gosh! It was from Cecilia Nunnery!"

"Do you think she finally got in to see her father?" Tanya asked before taking a sip of her water.

"Let's find out," Ellen said, pressing the call-back icon on her phone.

Within seconds, Cecilia answered.

"I just left Angola Prison," Cecilia said over the speaker.

Ellen, Sue, and Tanya leaned over the table, listening closely to Ellen's phone.

"And?" Sue asked. "How did it go? Was he angry?"

"Well," Cecilia began. "At first, he was confused. He didn't recognize me."

"I bet that wasn't very easy for you," Ellen said.

"It's been thirteen years," Cecilia began. "I've changed a lot in thirteen years."

"Of course, you have," Tanya said. "So, what happened then?"

"He started crying," Cecilia said. "He couldn't even speak for the longest time. I cried, too."

"I can only imagine," Sue said.

"So, while my daddy cried, I told him how happy I was to learn that he was still alive, and how sorry I was that he'd been stuck in prison. I told him that I had heard what had happened, and that I was going to do everything I could to get his sentence reduced. I told him, with good behavior, he could get out on parole in as few as five years. I said that my mama couldn't wait to see him. He stopped me right there and asked about her. I told him about the FEMA trailer and about how she's waiting for me to rebuild our house. And I told him how her face lit up when you told her he was alive. I told him she was waiting at the gate to see him, but he needed to add her to the list. I said, 'Daddy, please tell me you will let us back into your life. We love you and have missed you so much.' He couldn't answer. His whole body was shaking in a terrible, ugly cry. But then he nodded, and he waved the guard over. And when he could speak, he asked the guard to let my mama in. Oh, ladies, I wish you could have seen it. They weren't allowed but a brief hug and kiss, but the looks on their faces." Cecilia paused, and the sounds of sniffles came through the speaker.

"We're so happy for you," Tanya said through her own tears.

All three of them were crying. The people at the tables next to them, who could hear Cecilia over the speaker phone, were crying, too.

"We have something else we want to tell you," Ellen said. "Two things, really."

"Okay. I'm listening."

"We want to offer your mother a job managing the condos we're having redone on Chartres Street. There's a guesthouse she can stay in until…"

"Oh, really?" Cecilia asked. "Mama, they're offering you a job, until…until what?"

"We want to have your parents' house rebuilt," Sue said. "We've already contacted Brad Pitt's Make It Right Foundation, and they've agreed to use our donation to build your parents' house. It won't be like it was. They want to make it sustainable and stuff."

"Oh, my God!" Cecilia shouted.

Now the whole restaurant was smiling and in tears.

"Oh, my God!" Cecilia said again. "Mama, did you hear that? My mother is sitting next to me in the car. We're pulled over, outside of the gate. She's crying her eyes out again, but she's nodding her head, just like my daddy did. I hope she doesn't have a heart attack. Take a deep breath, Mama."

"We'll call your mom and let her know when the guesthouse is ready, okay?" Ellen asked.

"Thank you!" Maria cried into the phone.

"And please keep us posted on your father's case," Tanya added.

"I will!" Cecilia said. "I promise!"

The weekend before Thanksgiving, Ellen, Sue, and Tanya met with Michael Rouchell in the courtyard of their new condos on Chartres Street for a final walk-though. Maria and Cecilia Nunnery were there as well, with the good news that Jamar's court date had been set. As they stood together in the courtyard in the cool autumn air with the sound of water flowing in the fountain beside them, Ellen felt like she was in an episode of HGTV, just before the big reveal. The condos wouldn't be furnished; nevertheless, she couldn't wait to see how the floors, finishes, countertops, and fixtures looked together in the final product.

As they walked through the units, Ellen, Sue, and Tanya couldn't say enough good things. By the end of the tour, they were thanking Michael for his excellent work.

"I want to thank you again for recommending me to the Louisiana Historical Society for the work we've been doing on the Lalaurie Museum," he said, when they'd returned to the courtyard. "Will you come back next month for the grand opening?"

Ellen had brought her painting of Delphine Lalaurie, Marie Laveau, and the devil baby with her. Michael had promised to find the right place to mount it in the museum.

"Do you have to ask?" Sue said with a laugh.

"Well, ladies," Sue said as they were about to board their plane to New Orleans from San Antonio in early December, "mark this date down in history. Our husbands are actually going on a trip with us for once."

"Show us a good time, and we might go more often," Dave, Tanya's husband, said with a grin.

"His idea of a good time might be very different from ours," Tanya said as they entered the gate to board.

"As long as he likes good food, we'll get along just fine," Sue said.

"Hear, hear for good food," Paul said with a wink.

Ellen was pleased to be sitting beside her husband on a plane to anywhere. More than once, she caught him smiling at her. Their relationship had taken such an unexpected turn, almost as if it were brand new again.

"What are you grinning about?" she finally asked him.

"How nice it is to be sitting here with my pretty wife," he said.

Ellen's mouth dropped open. She couldn't recall the last time he'd called her pretty. She wasn't even sure that he ever had. He'd said she looked, "nice," but never "pretty."

"Keep that up, and you're not going to get any sleep on this trip," she whispered.

He laughed. "That's all right with me."

Once they had landed, they rented a van and drove straight to the condos on Chartres Street to introduce their husbands to Maria Nunnery and to show them the property. The units had already been rented out to two young families with children. Two boys were playing in the courtyard when Maria led Ellen and her friends and their husbands to the first unit and knocked on the door.

The men were impressed with the investment. After a celebratory dinner at Antoine's, they drove a few blocks to the new Lalaurie Museum's grand opening. It was a semi-formal affair, for which they had all six suffered traveling in their dressy clothes. It began with a self-guided tour, during which cocktails and hors d'oeuvre were served by waiters in tuxedoes. Elevator music played softly in the background. The exhibit began with Ellen's painting, along with this text:

The stories you may have heard about Madame Delphine Lalaurie, her husband, Dr. Louis Lalaurie, and the catastrophic fire that burned the original house in 1834, may or may not hold up to the facts presented to you today in historical documents recently unearthed.

The sconces on the walls lit the displays of copies made from the doctor's medical journals, Jeanne Blanque's letters, and Delphine's diary. Translations to English were printed in a symmetrical display beside each copy. They were arranged to tell a story, beginning with Delphine's first marriage to Don Ramon when she had just turned thirteen years of age.

When she reached the end, Ellen was pleased. The exhibit did a beautiful job of exonerating Delphine without making her into a martyr. The exhibit also treated the subject of Marie Laveau and the child she called the "devil child" with great respect.

"It's a work of art," Tanya said. "Just like your painting, Ellen."

"I'm really happy with the way it turned out," Sue said. "Aren't you, Ellen?"

Ellen glanced at Paul, who beamed down at her with pride.

"I'm very happy with the way it turned out," she said. "All of it."

THE END

Thank you for reading my story. I hope you enjoyed it! If you did, please consider leaving a review. Reviews help other readers to discover my books, which helps me.

Please enjoy the first chapter of the next book in the series, *The Hidden Tunnel*.

Saying Goodbye

Ellen sat between two of her children beneath the canopy in the cemetery on the warm spring afternoon in a folding metal chair across from the coffin holding Paul's body. The priest was talking about eternal life and God's heavenly kingdom, but Ellen wasn't listening. She was thinking about the last time Paul was alive and what he had said to her.

Although a large crowd of family and friends surrounded her, including her three kids, Sue and Tanya, Paul's family from New Braunfels, Ellen's brother and his family, and many of Paul's colleagues, Ellen kept forgetting about them. Each time she looked up from her thoughts during the priest's sermon, she glanced around at all the familiar faces, trying to hide the fact that she'd just remembered they were there.

Then she'd stare at the polished coffin until it disappeared again, and she was once again sitting beside Paul's hospital bed on the day he had died.

They'd been laughing. Ellen and Paul hadn't laughed together like that in a long time. During the months before he'd been admitted, they'd been looking at lakefront properties, hoping to find either a vacation home or a place close enough to their kids to move into permanently. They'd been especially fond of Marble Falls, which was only an hour away from Austin, where Lane and Alison attended college. It had been a happy time, full of dreams and expectations. Making plans had reinvigorated them, had brought them back to life. That's why, on the day Paul died, it hadn't occurred to either of them that he would.

He'd developed a cough that had held on for a few months. At one point, he'd been diagnosed with walking pneumonia but had seemed to be on the mend. Then, the night before he died, he asked her to take him to the emergency room because he couldn't breathe properly and was experiencing chest pains. They'd both assumed the pneumonia was back.

That's why, as they waited for test results, Ellen and Paul had been laughing their heads off. The nurse had just walked out, after Paul had farted eight times in a row during a coughing fit. It had sounded like a marching band—the coughing, wheezing, and blasts of gas. What had made them both break out into laughter was the look the nurse had given Paul just before she'd left the room.

As their laughter had finally subsided, they smiled at each other, eyes full of tears from laughing so damn hard. Paul had taken her hand and had squeezed it. Then he had said, "I'm so glad it's you and me, kid."

She'd been surprised. Paul had never been one to use words to convey his feelings.

Ellen had laughed and had said, "I think your gas fumes are getting to my head. It almost sounded like you gave me a compliment."

Paul had busted out laughing, forcing out another fart, which had made Ellen laugh, too.

"I'm getting out of here," she'd said. "It stinks to high heaven. I'm going to shower and change. I'll be right back."

She'd pecked him on the head, and that was the last time she'd seen him alive.

The doctor had called it a pulmonary embolism. A blood clot, that had likely formed in Paul's leg, had traveled to his lung. Ellen had just gotten dressed at home when she received the call that Paul had been taken into emergency surgery. She had rushed like a mad woman, but by the time she'd arrived, Paul was gone.

As she sat between her children, she still couldn't believe Paul's body was lying in the polished coffin across from her. It seemed more likely that he was on a golf course. It had been an inexplicable whirlwind, and she was still caught up in it. Nothing seemed real.

Her son Nolan was suddenly speaking in place of the priest. Ellen snapped to attention to hear what he had to say.

Tears flowed freely from his green eyes down his cheeks. He didn't try to stop the tears or wipe them from his face. He stood beside the priest, trembling, looking like a boy, not a man, even though his large stature overpowered the small man beside him.

"I can't believe my dad is gone. He was a good father." Nolan ran a hand through his curly brown hair. "He tried for years to get me into sports, especially golf, but he eventually realized that was a waste. I was no athlete." Nolan chuckled. "And he supported me when I became interested in other things. He once learned how to play Magic the Gathering—a fantasy card game—just so he could play it with me. We had some good times fishing together, too. He worked hard—he and my mom—to give our family a good life. I wish…" Nolan couldn't speak for several seconds, which broke Ellen's heart. She jumped up and went to his side and squeezed his hand. Nolan smiled at Ellen and turned back to the crowd. "I wish he hadn't left us so soon. He was loved dearly and will be dearly missed."

Ellen hugged her son. He hugged her back. She held his shaking, trembling, sobbing form in her arms like she had when he was a boy and had gotten hurt. It was at that moment that Ellen finally realized Paul was gone, and she, too, began to weep.

After the funeral, family and friends gathered at Ellen's house, and for a while, she escaped her grief to play hostess. People had brought so much food. Ellen arranged the containers of sandwiches, pasta, casseroles, and other dishes along her kitchen bar and invited everyone to make a plate, buffet style. Tanya and Sue were at her side in the kitchen, brewing tea and filling paper cups with ice.

Once everyone had gone, except for Ellen's children and Sue and Tanya, the six of them sat together in the den. Alison was cuddled against Ellen on the loveseat, like she used to do when she was a girl. Her long brown hair hung in her face, as if she was hiding behind a curtain, not wanting to be seen. Nolan and Lane sat beside one another on the sofa, each clutching a decorative pillow in his lap. Two boys could never be so different. Nolan had dark hair, was a doctor and scientist, and was interested in superheroes, anime, and video games; whereas Lane had lighter hair, like Ellen's, and was a musician and artist whose paintings were every bit as good as Ellen's, if not better. Sue sat in Paul's recliner eating a piece of chocolate pie. Her dark bangs needed a trim, for they nearly covered her round, dark eyes. Tanya, her blonde hair pulled back into a ponytail, sipped a warm mug of tea in a chair beside Sue.

"You should get a dog," Alison said to Ellen. "Maybe a miniature poodle, to keep you company."

Ellen patted her daughter's knee. "I'll be alright." The thought of a dog was comforting, but she traveled too often.

"A dog is the last thing she needs," Sue said, as she lifted a piece of chocolate pie with her fork. "What she really needs is a cruise."

Ellen rolled her eyes. "I'm not ready for that. Not yet."

"What about a trip to Portland?" Tanya asked.

"Portland, Texas or Portland, Oregon?" Lane asked.

"Oregon," Tanya clarified.

"Why *there*, of all places?" Nolan asked.

Tanya glanced at Sue.

Then Sue said, "I was going to hold off talking to you about this, Ellen, but Tanya's jumped the gun."

"Jumped the gun about what?" Ellen straightened her back. "Might as well tell me now."

"I was contacted through my blog by a billionaire from Portland," Sue explained.

"Wait a minute," Ellen said. "You have a blog?"

"How was *blog* the word in that sentence that caught your attention?" Tanya asked.

"I told you about it," Sue said. "I blog about our projects, about Ghost Healer's, Inc." Sue took another bite of her pie.

"She has quite a following," Tanya added.

"Why do you think I'm always taking so many pictures?" Sue asked.

"To document the before and after," Ellen said.

"Exactly," Sue said. "For my blog. And I write about the ghost mysteries we solve."

Tanya took a sip of her tea. "She gets requests from people almost every day asking for our help."

"That's really cool," Lane said.

"So, who's the billionaire?" Alison asked.

"His name is Brian McManius," Sue said. "He's one of two wealthy brothers from Portland who own a huge chain."

"What kind of chain?" Nolan asked.

"A brewery," Tanya said.

"It's much more than that," Sue explained. "They own hotels, bed and breakfasts, pubs, restaurants, meeting facilities—over fifty establishments. They like to restore historic places."

"Like we do," Tanya said before taking another sip of her tea.

"And they've seen a lot of paranormal activity, too," Sue said.

"Is that why he contacted you?" Ellen asked.

"No." Sue sat her empty plate on the end table beside her. "His brother's missing."

"But why would he contact *you* about that?" Nolan asked. "Shouldn't he go to the police?"

"He did," Sue said. "Weeks ago. They haven't turned up any leads."

"His brother went missing while working on their most recent project," Tanya said. "A carriage house in downtown Portland."

"Chances are, he's already dead," Nolan said. "I hate to say it."

"Does the brother want you to do a séance or something?" Alison asked.

"He does," Sue said. "He wants us to conduct a full paranormal investigation. And to make it worth our while, he says if we *do* find his brother, he'll give us their current restoration project."

"The one where he went missing?" Alison asked.

Tanya nodded. "It's worth 3.2 million."

Ellen's mouth fell open. "He must be desperate."

"He is," Sue said. "He said he's tried everything—local law enforcement, private detectives, state troopers, local paranormal teams. He said he's putting his last hope in us."

"What did you tell him?" Ellen asked.

"Nothing yet," Sue said. "I told him I'd get back with him. I wanted to wait and talk to you about it, in a few days." Sue gave Tanya a look of reproach.

"Sorry," Tanya said. "I just thought it might help take her mind off …of things."

"Tell him we'll do it," Ellen said. "Tanya's right. I need this. I can't sit around in this big empty house all day. I want to go to Portland."

"Mom, are you sure?" Alison asked.

"Unless you kids need me." Ellen squeezed Alison's hand. "If you want me to stay close by for a while…"

"No, it's okay," Lane said. "We'll be fine."

"We don't have to go right away," Tanya said. "Take as much time as you need, Ellen."

"I don't want time," Ellen said. "I need to keep busy."

Sue shifted in the recliner. "Should I tell Brian McManius to expect us next Saturday?"

Ellen put an arm around Alison. "Is that okay with you, sweet girl?"

"I've got to get back to school anyway," she said. "I only planned to stay a couple of days."

"Nolan?" Ellen asked.

"I think it's a good idea," he said. "I think Dad would want you to go."

On Saturday morning, with her rolling suitcase waiting by the door, Ellen walked around the house, turning off lights, and caught herself as she was about to call out to Paul. She stopped short and put her face in her hands, fighting tears. She'd been crying all week, and her eyes, as swollen as golf balls, hurt. She'd gotten into the sick habit of pretending Paul was there in the other room watching television in his recliner while she read or watched her shows in the front room. It had been comforting, this pretending. She'd even talked to him out loud, as if he were there, listening. At night, she convinced herself that his ghost visited her. She even thought she'd felt his presence.

Talking to his ghost had to be healthier than pretending like he'd never died, but she'd continue to do both. Now she walked into the den, looked at his recliner, and said, "I'll be back soon, Paul. I love you."

As she turned to leave, she could have sworn she saw the recliner move. She turned back and stared at it. It wasn't moving now, but in her peripheral vision, it had seemed to. Had she imagined it?

Her phone vibrated, bringing her from her ponderings. It was Sue, waiting out front with Tanya in a cab. Ellen grabbed her suitcase, locked up the front door, and headed toward her next adventure. It would be good for her, she reminded herself. It would be good to keep busy and focus on other things.

The cabby put her suitcase in the trunk while she climbed in the backseat beside Tanya, who was sitting in the middle with Sue on the opposite side.

Sue leaned forward and smiled at Ellen. "Ready?"

Ellen buckled her seatbelt. "Let's do this. Let's find the missing brother."

"Look at you, sounding like a bad-ass," Tanya said with a laugh.

"That's exactly what we are, Tanya," Ellen said.

Sue leaned back in her seat. "And don't y'all forget it."

Eva Pohler is a *USA Today* bestselling author of over thirty novels in multiple genres, including mysteries, thrillers, and young adult paranormal romance based on Greek mythology. Her books have been described as "addictive" and "sure to thrill"—*Kirkus Reviews*.

To learn more about Eva and her books, and to sign up to hear about new releases, and sales, please visit her website at www.evapohler.com.

Printed in the USA
CPSIA information can be obtained
at www.ICGtesting.com
LVHW050341020524
778994LV00011B/299